THE ALTAR GIRL

ALSO BY OREST STELMACH

The Boy from Reactor 4

The Boy Who Stole from the Dead

The Boy Who Glowed in the Dark

THE ALTAR GIRL

OREST STELMACH

This is a work of fiction. Names, characters, organizations, places, events, and incidents are either products of the author's imagination or are used fictitiously.

Published by Thomas & Mercer, Seattle

www.apub.com

ISBN-13: 9781477827970
ISBN-10: 1477827978

Cover design by David Drummond

Library of Congress Control Number: 2014953211

Printed in the United States of America

For my parents, Eudokia and Bohdan Stelmach.
Child refugees, proud Americans, devoted parents.
Мамі і Татові—Вічная Пам'ямь!

CHAPTER 1

HE SNATCHED ME A BLOCK AWAY FROM MY APARTMENT.

I'd just driven back to New York after attending my godfather's funeral in Hartford. A drive to Connecticut usually unwinds me. I crack open the moonroof and the wind sucks out my stress like God's vacuum cleaner. Beauty surrounds me, along country roads, on rolling hills, and in the sound of silence. Once I reenter New York, however, the parkway twists and turns my insides. Gridlock awaits, at the toll bridge, on the sidewalks, and on the rungs of the corporate ladder. At least that's how it always was for me.

Until tonight.

I'd sped toward the border of New York as though the Red Army were pursuing me in a fleet of Audis. I couldn't wait to get out of Connecticut and leave my suspicions behind me. I didn't really think anyone was following me, but I feared my godfather's death might not have been an accident. That deduction didn't bother me when I was among people, at the wake and the reception. Once I'd climbed into my car, however, the silence was too loud, the hills too desolate. I wondered if I'd asked too many questions and who'd heard me. Suddenly, I'd longed for the familiarity of the gridlock.

After leaving my car at the garage at midnight, I walked along 1st Avenue savoring the smells of my neighborhood. The smell of pups from the doggie day care center, the aroma of rising crust from the pizzeria. I spied my apartment building up ahead. A hot shower awaited, the pizza was next door, and if I could have uncorked the Chianti telepathically, I would have. I was safe at home. No one would touch me here.

I stopped at the corner of 82nd Street to let a car go by.

A glove covered my mouth. A second set of hands lifted me off the pavement.

A shiny black van screeched to a halt. The back doors opened.

They hurled me inside.

I landed on my elbow and hip. Pain ripped through me.

The doors slammed shut. Darkness enveloped me.

"Don't scream," a man said. "And don't move."

I froze.

It all happened so fast I had no time to fight, no time to resist, no time to even think. One minute I was a random carbohydrate addict dreaming of medicating with food and wine, and the next minute I was some stranger's prisoner.

"We go way back, Nadia. Be good. Don't make me hurt you even more than I got to."

Except he wasn't a stranger. I recognized the voice as soon as I heard it, but I couldn't place it. It boasted a mellifluous tone that contrasted with coarse enunciation and gutter grammar. He knew me. We knew each other. According to him, we went way back. But I didn't frequent the gutter, so who was he? I could see him sitting in a chair at the far end of the van, but I couldn't make out his face or any of the objects around him. My eyes hadn't adjusted to the darkness.

The van started moving.

A sense of helplessness gripped me. First, I'd lost my freedom. Now I was being taken somewhere against my will. I was an average woman. I wasn't trained in self-defense. I wasn't a cop, spy, or martial artist. I was a financial analyst. I was good with numbers, but math skills weren't going to get me out of this situation.

These men could do anything they wanted to me, and I would be helpless to stop them.

The thump of my heartbeat echoed in my ears.

He lit a match. Long, elegant fingers cupped the flame to a face. Dirt clung to the skin beneath one of his nails. The flame illuminated a pair of lush lips, the kind that could suck a grapefruit dry from across the room. I caught a glimpse of his face. It belonged to a man who'd grown up with me in the Ukrainian-American community in Hartford. I hadn't seen him since graduating high school, but I'd heard stories about him. Everyone in the community had heard the stories.

The bad seed. The most handsome first-generation Ukrainian-American boy, the one mothers and their daughters had dreamed about until he revealed himself to be a true sociopath. This one didn't hide his tendencies. There'd been arrests for a string of burglaries, illegal weapons possession, even rumors he was the lead suspect in two drug-related murders in Hartford. People spoke in whispers about him at church, that he'd gotten involved with the wrong crowd, lived on the edge of society. Outwardly, the community distanced itself from him. Secretly, however, many of the seniors enjoyed some *Schadenfreude* at the expense of his parents, for he created the illusion that their own dysfunctional first-generation kids were normal.

Dim lights came to life in the ceiling. Recessed lights. Bright, brighter, full power.

Donnie Angel sat facing me in one of two captain's chairs.

In full light, he still resembled the boy I'd grown up with, but time had been unkind to him. His lush cheeks had turned hollow. His jacket hung loosely on his formerly broad shoulders while a slight paunch pressed against his belt. As his midsection had thickened, his hair had thinned. Gone was most of the rock-star mane so many girls had dreamed of running their hands through.

Someone once told me that spouses begin to look like each other over time. I'd never believed it but now I wasn't so sure. Donnie Angel was evidence the theory might be true, if a man was married to his job and his job was crime.

He wore a blue blazer with gold buttons, natty gray slacks, and black track shoes with white stripes. His eyes lit up when he saw that I recognized him. His lips stretched wide. It was a smile as spontaneous and genuine as the pile of shit I'd stepped in was deep. His teeth were still white and perfect. He could still smile. My God could he smile.

"You look great, Nadia," he said. "Just great. Someone told me they seen you at the funeral. Said you lost weight. Not that it didn't look good on you. You always had a cute face, for a smart girl. You know what I mean. So how you been?"

I could tell he was serious. He meant what he said—that I looked good, for a smart girl—and what he didn't say. That in some sick way he was happy to see me even though he'd kidnapped me and made it perfectly clear that he was going to hurt me. That he was compelled to hurt me, presumably for something I'd done. I wasn't particularly happy to see him, which meant I had to lie. I had to pretend to be cool even if I was petrified on the inside.

"I've been good, Donnie. Real good." My voice sounded unsteady. I prayed he couldn't tell. I nodded at his blazer, its gold buttons to be specific. "Nice jacket. You look like you just got off the yacht in Newport. Free enterprise agrees with you." I gave him a once-over and forced a smile of my own. "How've you been?"

"Oh, I think you're looking at it." He gestured toward an assortment of decanters partially filled with liquor. "How about a drink?"

"A drink?"

"I got some Champagne in the fridge. French stuff in a bottle with flowers on it. Got a case of it from a guy who got it from a guy. Been saving this bottle for a special occasion."

I couldn't believe he was acting as though we'd stumbled into each other at the Ukrainian National Home's bar. There had been a time when the thought of Donnie Angel pulling out a bottle of champagne for me would have been the highlight of my life. Now, given the circumstances, it terrified me.

"Donnie," I said. "Why am I here?"

He stood up and walked over to a small refrigerator in the corner of the van. Beside it, a side table was covered with a white sheet. A glint at his feet caught my eye. I glanced at the floor and realized his athletic shoes had metal spikes attached to the bottom, the kind worn by golfers, and track and field athletes. I tried to conjure various reasons why a sane man would wear spikes but couldn't think of one. Then I tried to think of some reasons why an insane one would wear them during an interrogation and could think of only one.

Bile rose up my throat.

He twisted his body to reach into the corner and opened the fridge. He didn't raise his voice or bother to look at me. He spoke matter-of-factly. "You know why you're here."

"No I don't. There must be some misunderstanding—"

"Don't do that." He stood up from the fridge, *Perrier Jouët* in hand, his knuckles white. "Don't patronage me. My mother used to patronage me. My mother's dead now."

"Donnie, I'm not patronizing you."

"You were asking questions you shouldn't have been asking. At the *panakhyda* and the reception after the funeral." The *panakhyda* was a Ukrainian Catholic memorial service held the night before the funeral. "You know better. We're gonna have to . . . we're gonna have to talk about that."

"Talk about it?" I glanced at his cleats again.

He looked me over and licked his lips. It was the look of an addict delaying gratification for a few minutes, or kidding himself that this time it would be different. This time he wouldn't smoke, drink, or do whatever it was he meant when he said he had to hurt me. He smiled quickly as though that would erase the gesture from my memory.

It didn't.

"Let's don't worry about that now. Let's have a drink and catch up. You work in New York, right? Investments or some shit, isn't it? I bet all the Ukes are really proud of you. They should be. You were a classy girl. I always thought the world of you." He glanced at the Champagne, turned back to me and raised his eyebrows. Tilted the bottle in my direction so I could see the label. "Money, right?"

I vaguely heard myself answering him because I was too busy searching for a means of escape. But there was none. A wall prevented access to the front of the van. The windows were blacked out and covered with shades. The only exit was through the rear door, and Donnie would have had his hands on me before I could raise the latch. The problem was that I was certain he was going to put his hands on me even if I didn't try to escape. And he wasn't going to use them to give me a warm embrace.

Despite the adrenaline, the all-consuming nature of my body's fight-or-flight response, I was still lucid enough to reason. I understood that there was a decent probability he might do serious bodily harm to me, or even kill me. It was this ability to reason that gave me hope.

A crinkling sound snapped me from my stupor. Donnie peeled aluminum foil from around the cork.

"This is just like a date," he said, cheerily. "Did you ever think you'd go on another date with me?"

"No, Donnie." The operative word in his question was "another." I'd done my best to forget the first one, and was hoping that after all his probable substance abuse, he might have forgotten about it, too.

Instead, he popped the cork. Champagne burst out of the bottle and poured down its sides, covering his hand and the carpet. He licked two fingers and gave me a rakish grin.

"You do remember our first date?" he said.

I looked away from him. Tried not to blush, urged the blood out of my face so as not to give him any satisfaction. It did the opposite of what I requested, of course, and flooded my cheeks so badly my entire face stung.

"Yeah, Donnie," I said. "Of course I remember."

Although I wished I could forget my date with Donnie, there were other childhood memories I'd worked even harder to forget.

CHAPTER 2

After studying his compass and map carefully, Nadia's father hacked off a dead limb from one of the trees. The morning sun poured through the gaps between the branches and made a circle of light atop a bed of pine needles. He told Nadia to sit down precisely in that spot, and she obeyed. Nadia's brother, Marko, stood off to the side sipping water from his canteen.

Beads of sweat covered her arms as though her skin was a pancake in the making. Her body pulsated from the two-mile hike. She was warmed up. Ready for the survival test. The details were a closely guarded secret, but she figured she'd have to build a camp and survive a night alone.

Nadia took three deep breaths. She could do it. Whatever it took, she could do it. She wouldn't let her father and her brother down. Heck, the forest wasn't the worst place in the world. Not even close. In a month, she'd turn twelve and school would start again. Sixth grade. The day before summer vacation, Rachel Backus and her friends had promised to flush her "disgusting Russian head down the toilet" in September. She'd told them her parents were Ukrainian, not Russian, and that there was a big difference. They'd disagreed, and promised her head was going down the toilet no matter where it came from.

Nadia looked around. Recognized the dip in the path ahead that lead down to the river. Diamondback Pass, they called it, because you could hear the rattlers hiss if you stepped in the wrong place. She spent her summers twenty miles away on a five-hundred-acre lot of land in northwestern Connecticut that Ukrainian immigrants had bought on the cheap in the 1950s. They used it as the setting for their PLAST scout camps. Plastun *was the historical Ukrainian name for a Cossack scout or sentry. Sometimes the counselors bussed the* plastuny *and* plastunky *north to the Appalachian Trail to hike for the day. Nadia remembered the spot by its pine groves.*

Her father walked up to her. He reminded her of an old lion, with sandy hair combed straight back and blown thick by the wind.

"Nadia, you live in America," he said in Ukrainian. "The greatest country in the world. This makes you a lucky girl. You understand that, don't you, my kitten?"

"Yes, father."

"And you're sitting at the exact point," he said, tapping his right index finger on the map in his left hand, "where Connecticut, Massachusetts, and New York meet. This makes you an even luckier girl. How many girls can say they've been in three states at the same time?"

Nadia glanced at the ground beside her. "Really?" A smile spread on her already-chapped lips. "That is so cool."

"And now you're going to become the youngest girl ever to pass the PLAST survival test. Are you ready?"

"Yes, father."

"Good.

"Here is your knapsack. Inside you'll find a compass and map, food and water for one day, three matches, a knife, a poncho, a plastic bag, some twine, a flashlight, and a mess kit. Attached to the bottom of the knapsack is your sleeping bag. You must survive three nights on your own with just these things. Do you understand?"

What? Three nights? Nadia nodded her head mechanically and managed a "Yes, father." He couldn't possibly mean it. He and Marko would probably be close by. Yeah, that was it. They'd be close by.

"Your brother and I will be far away," he said. He glared at Marko the way he did when he was ready to ream one of them out, which was pretty much all the time. "Neither of us will be holding your hand."

Marko gave their father a blank stare in return, but Nadia knew Marko was probably fantasizing about drop-kicking him from here to Niagara Falls.

Her father knelt before her so they were face-to-face. Nadia bit her tongue to try to look strong.

"Your parents are immigrants," he said. "You have a strange name. You speak a strange language. And you are not a Barbie doll. That is the cruel truth. You aren't going to get by in this world with your looks alone.

"To succeed in this country, you're going to have to compete with men. Men are selfish, petty, and cruel. The world where this behavior is rewarded is called business. To beat men in business you will have to be smarter and tougher than them. We know you're smart. We know you're very, very smart. But are you tough?"

Nadia tried to sniff in the tears before they rolled out. She bit down harder on her tongue. "Yes, father."

He smiled for a beat, and turned his face into granite. "We'll see. You're on your own for three days." He handed Nadia a whistle attached to a long pink chain she could wear around her neck. "For emergency purposes. If all else fails, get to high ground, and blow." He turned to Marko. "Let's go, slacker."

Marko walked over to Nadia. She spied the concern and affection in his eyes that always perked her up. As soon as Marko caught her glance, though, he put on his easygoing smile, the one that wanted to make light of any situation.

"It's just three days, Nancy Drew," he said. "Three days is nothing. You and me, we can take three days of anything, right?"

Nadia stood up and looked her brother in the eyes. "Right."

She tried to muster her inner strength, but her lips trembled and her eyes watered. She was about to look like a pathetic little girl, the same weakling she'd been before Marko had made her strong. The thought of him seeing her cry was unbearable, so she jumped up, grabbed her knapsack, and ran farther into the forest. She knew how to appear cool even if she was nervous. It was part of daily living because her father made her nervous all the time.

"I'll be okay," she said over her shoulder. "I can do this. If a boy can do it, I can do it."

"That's right, Nancy Drew. If a boy can do it, you can do it." A few seconds passed and then she heard Marko's voice again. Louder now, to make sure she heard him. "Hey little sister. What's your name?"

"Nadia," she said.

"What does it mean?"

This time she turned her face to the side so her voice would carry in his direction and shouted, "Hope."

She walked aimlessly for a minute, wishing she'd never agreed to take the stupid test. The merit badge wouldn't make a difference. All the kids would still pick on her. Compete with men? What the heck was her father talking about? This whole thing was wacko. She didn't want to compete with anybody. She wanted to be left alone.

Eventually the walking calmed her down, and her training kicked in. Her PLAST troop master was Mrs. Chimchak, a woman who'd fought for a free Ukraine against the Nazis and the communists in World War II. She thought American kids were spoiled, so her purpose in life was to make her scouts miserable. She'd taught them survival skills, how to build a shelter and an eternal fire, even how to gather water from dew with nothing more than a bowl, a plastic bag, and a pebble.

Nadia headed down the path in the opposite direction from where her father and brother had disappeared. The first thing she had to do was find the right place to build her camp. It had to be near water so she could boil it and drink it, but on higher ground so if it rained the water would flow away from her. As a plan for a campsite began to take shape, the tears stopped flowing and she started to believe she could do this. In fact, it might not be so bad. Maybe she'd want to stay a fourth and fifth day for fun.

But as she descended toward the river, the sun vanished behind a patch of clouds and the darkness of the forest enveloped her. A light wind shook the pine trees to either side of her and they began to whisper and move as though they were human, capable of pulling her to their trunks with their branches and devouring her with hidden mouths, and deep down, Nadia knew she was mistaken.

CHAPTER 3

He'd picked me up in a black Camaro IROC with tinted windows and an exhaust note so loud my father started swearing as soon as he heard it. He thought it was the neighbor next door, a truck driver who liked to rev his motorcycle as loud as possible to piss off the low-rent boat people from Eastern Europe. At least that's what he called us. But when my father saw it was Donnie he became all smiles. Sure the kid neglected his schoolwork and didn't know Ukrainian from uranium, but this was America and he was only a freshman in high school. Our Uke parents were prepared to overlook all sorts of questionable character traits if it meant their sons and daughters might marry a purebred.

I was thirteen at the time. Most parents wouldn't have allowed their thirteen-year-old daughter to go out on a date with a sixteen-year-old boy, including mine. But in this case they were willing to make an exception because he was Ukrainian. My father had a private chat with Donnie before we went out. I'm sure Donnie fed him a well-rehearsed series of lies about his intentions, and my father happily digested them. My mother seemed less sanguine about the matter, but she told me that I was a lucky girl to be going out with such a handsome young man.

Donnie said he was going to take me to the McDonald's on the Silas Deane Highway in Newington—I liked it because it was the only one around with the old-fashioned arches. But instead of pulling in, he drove straight past it to the parking lot of the Grantmoor, a motel known for hourly room rates used by married couples, the kind who weren't wed to each other. Donnie said we were going to work up an appetite first. Who was I to say no? I was a mere mortal. The thought of being kissed by an angel terrified and enthralled me at the same time.

In fact, I'd never been kissed before he leaned over and pressed his lips to mine. Soon he was working his fingers expertly and turning me into his personal puddle of mush. The sensations racked me with such fury I was prepared to marry him on the spot. Then he pulled away and said, "Do you fuck?" I shrank back in the seat with horror and embarrassment and shook my head no.

He tried to force himself on me but I had to give him credit. As soon as he felt my flesh turn cold and heard the word "No," he stopped. I didn't get a burger, fries, or a milkshake, and within a week the story went around that he'd gone out with me because he'd never fucked a fat girl, and he wanted to see if they were really as grateful as all the guys said they were.

Now, here he was, pouring me a flute of Champagne.

"C'mon," he said. "It wasn't that bad. I never forget it when a girl's hips buckle, especially for the first time. We had a moment. You felt it. Big time. I know you did."

I suppressed my revulsion. "Yeah, but you never bought me that cheeseburger."

He chuckled in a patronizing way. "That's why I'm giving you the bubbly now."

He offered me a flute.

I shook my head. "I can't, Donnie."

His face dropped. Something between disappointment and anger. "Are you saying no to my generosity?"

If corporate America had taught me one thing, it was that strength respects strength. My goal was to be agreeable but not arrogant, and to use my intelligence to weaken his resolve. That's the only weapon I had with which to defend myself. My brain.

"No, Donnie. I'm not saying no to you. I'm saying yes to my policy."

"Policy? What policy?"

"Never drink with your kidnappers."

He lifted his eyebrows, tilted his head, thought about it for a few seconds, and nodded. "Can't say that I blame you." He drained one of the flutes. "You want something else? I got birch beer. It's white on account of the particular birch sap they used. You know what they call chocolate ice cream with birch beer in Pennsylvania?"

"Birch beer float?"

"No. A black cow. Love me a black cow now and then. What do you know about your godfather's business?"

Donnie asked the question as though it were a natural extension of the black cow discussion.

"He sold antiques," I said. "He loved old things. Loved their smell, the stories behind them. Almost as much as he loved Ukraine. He liked you, too, Donnie."

Donnie blinked three times quickly, as though I'd interrupted his train of thought. His lips parted in surprise. "He did?"

"Absolutely. You had a Tryzub sticker in the rear windshield of your Camaro." The *Tryzub* was the national symbol of Ukraine, a yellow trident atop a blue shield. "I remember my godfather saying, 'He's a good boy.'"

"He said that?"

"He did."

"About me?"

"He said you have a Ukrainian soul."

A faint smile spread across Donnie's lips.

"And that meant you'd be strong and compassionate. You'd be a survivor. We Ukes, we're survivors above all else. The Turks, the Austrians and Hungarians, the Poles, the Russians, the Nazis and the communists. They all ruled Ukraine at one time or another.

Stalin tried to starve the country. Millions upon millions dead in 1933. But still, our ancestors survived, didn't they?"

A mist covered Donnie's eyes. He was looking in my direction but appeared lost in reflection.

"Your godfather always nodded at me when he saw me," he said. "From a distance, I thought it was a nasty look. A 'you're a piece of shit and we both know it' kind of look. Like all the old-timers gave me."

Donnie was right, of course. My godfather hadn't liked him. He'd told my father to make sure he kept me away from him. And once Donnie proved himself to be an unrepentant criminal, my godfather had hated him like everyone else. By choosing to ignore the law of the land, he'd abused the second greatest gift after life itself. His American citizenship. And for people who'd suffered through World War II, that was a hard sin to forgive.

"You were so wrong," I said. "It's funny how we can think one thing for years, and then discover that the truth was the complete opposite."

"Ain't that so."

The police thought my godfather had fallen down the cellar stairs and died from a blow to the head. But I knew better without knowing much more. He never went down those stairs at night. *Never.* In fact, he was mentally incapable of making the descent once the sun came down.

I considered the possibility that Donnie had killed my godfather. But regret and self-loathing shone in his eyes, not guilt. I felt confident in my conclusion because I knew the look well. I'd seen it in the mirror many times. I reminded myself that didn't mean Donnie hadn't killed him anyways.

"I never got a chance to say good-bye to him," I said. "Not only that, I hadn't spoken to him in three years. Did I talk to people about him at the *panakhyda* and the reception? Of course I did. Did I make chitchat about his business? Sure. That's what people do. That's why we have these ceremonies, to help us move on."

Donnie's eyes scrunched together. He nodded solemnly. "That's all it was?"

"That's all it was."

"Swear to God on the Holy Bible? Now you were an altar girl—you can't lie to me."

"No, Donnie. I can't lie to you. And even if I wanted to, I'm no good at it."

He stared at me for a moment. I was certain he could see straight into my Ukrainian-American soul. He could tell I was a liar, manipulator, and a fraud. But instead of protesting, he shrugged his shoulders.

"Okay, then. Let's call the whole thing a mistake. The boys have been circling the Upper East Side. I'll tell them to go back to your apartment. No harm, no foul. That's what they say, isn't it? We'll pretend we were two friends getting caught up. How does that sound?"

I tempered a sense of euphoria. I wasn't quite home yet, though I could smell the pizza again and picture the cork coming out of the bottle.

"Sounds like what it really was," I said.

He smiled the Donnie Angel smile. "Okay, babe. Give us a hug."

He opened his arms and beckoned me to come. I would have rather embraced some poison oak, but I had to continue my performance to the bitter end. I walked into his open arms. He smelled of nicotine and musk. When he stepped forward to pull me closer, the spike beneath his shoe slid atop mine. He pulled it away quickly before he could hurt me.

"Oops. Sorry about my shoes. I was playing soccer when I got the call to follow you and pick you up. I had some clothes in the van but I have no idea what I did with my shoes, and I can't walk around in socks. Only a heathen walks around in socks."

A few million Japanese might have disagreed. "Soccer. Of course. I figured it was something like that."

He leaned in and whispered in my ear. "You miss your father, Nadia?"

It was a strange question to ask and it caught me off guard, but given the previous conversation it sounded heartfelt and genuine, so I responded in kind.

"In some ways I do, but in other ways—much as I hate to say it—I don't."

"You're lucky then. I don't miss my old man in any way at all. I'm glad the bastard's dead." Donnie pulled back and looked me in the eyes. "He only taught me one thing that ever made any sense. Know what that was?"

I shook my head.

He leaned in to my ear again.

"My old man used to say, 'If the devil's powerless, send him a woman.'"

He grabbed me by the neck and dragged me across the floor. Ripped the white sheet away to reveal the piece of furniture beneath it. I'd thought it was a side table. I was wrong. It didn't look like any table I'd ever seen. A wooden arm connected two half-circle metal supports at each end of the contraption, the kind that would allow for the display of a cylindrical item, like an antique rifle or sword. But the unibody design included a stool at one end, too.

Donnie pushed me down onto that stool.

The entire exercise took three seconds. Three seconds ago I could taste the wine. Now I was gasping for breath, my neck fairly wrenched, staring at those metal supports.

Then it hit me. I realized their function and why I was sitting on the stool in front of them. An overwhelming sense of terror gripped me, the kind I hadn't felt since I was twelve years old, alone on the Appalachian Trail.

"Tell me again," Donnie said, without a trace of emotion, as he measured the length of my leg with his eyes. "What do you know about your godfather's business?"

CHAPTER 4

As soon as her father and brother disappeared, Nadia did what she'd been dying to do for the last hour. She ate.

She needed to ration her food because there was no way she was going to hunt small game. No rabbits or snakes were going to find their way into her mess kit. She was fully prepared to boil water but that was it. A human being could survive for a long time without food as long as she had water. Three days wasn't going to be a problem, especially if she worked her way through her rations slowly.

Her knapsack contained a slice of buckwheat bread, a breakfast-sized jar of honey, and a bag with about twenty almonds and raisins. Nadia ate five almonds and raisins each and washed them down with some water. The water tasted like warm metal, but she savored the salt and sugar. They tasted so good together, like Doritos and M&M's. Sometimes she ate a handful of each when she got home after school. There was nothing like it. The thought of chips and candy made her even hungrier, so she ate five more of each. Then she decided she needed her strength now because she would only be building her shelter once, so she ate the rest of the almonds and raisins. A pang of guilt gnawed at her when she was done, but she still had the bread and honey, and half the canteen of water. She vowed not to eat until tomorrow.

Nadia used the map and her compass to find a stream three-quarters of a mile away. She'd studied cartography during summer camps and was an expert with a compass. Once she found the stream, she continued toward high ground to find a campsite.

Finding a source of water quickly cheered her up. She was able to look around and enjoy the sights. She loved the Appalachian Trail and the surrounding forest. Loved everything about it. Plants and animals were nice. People weren't. Out here, no one threw dodgeballs at her head at recess when she wasn't looking.

Danger also lurked on the AT, sometimes disguised as beauty. She picked her way through a giant ravine filled with storm-tossed birch trees: severed branches, strips of white bark, and tree rot scattered as if aliens had nuked the place. Amidst the rubble, moisture had given birth to a supersized colony of spectacular white mushrooms.

Nadia sidestepped the fungi, miniature flying saucers docked on rippling stalks, a preview of life on Mars. To the inexperienced hiker, they might have looked like tasty appetizers for the grill. Nadia knew better. Mrs. Chimchak had taught that certain fungi were lethal. Best not to mess with Martian spaceships when you're living off the AT.

Nadia paused at the top of a hill and looked around. The terrain had flattened out. Water would flow down from here. A small gap amidst a grove of spruce trees would allow the flames of her fire to rise without burning down the entire East Coast. And a pair of young trees were set wide enough apart for her to build a lean-to.

This was the spot.

Nadia dropped her knapsack and turned around to memorize the path she'd taken.

Mrs. Chimchak stood before her with a blank expression.

Nadia jumped and shrieked. She covered her mouth with her hand. Cursed at herself for having shown weakness. But how could she not have been surprised?

There'd been no noise. No sign of a human being approaching.

Of course there hadn't been. Kids called Mrs. Chimchak the Razor Blade for a reason. If she stood sideways, sometimes you couldn't even see she was there. In the forest, she moved like a fern with invisible legs. She stood relaxed but poised, the way she always did, in a navy blue work shirt and pants. Never had such a tiny person looked so big and scary.

"Hotujsh," *Mrs. Chimchak said in Ukrainian, the traditional greeting among young scouts.*

Nadia snapped her feet to attention, returned the greeting, and saluted her elder. The salute consisted of a V formed with the second and third fingers of her right hand. The odd thing was that in the English-speaking world it was the peace sign. But the greeting that went along with it in Ukrainian had more to do with war than peace.

Hotujsh. *Prepare yourself.*

"What are you doing here?" Nadia said.

Mrs. Chimchak studied the terrain. "This is good," she said, ignoring Nadia's question. "Good spot for a fire. No branches overhead. You won't burn down the entire forest, will you?"

"Uh-uh," Nadia said. "Why are you here? I mean, it's an unexpected surprise."

"I wanted to make sure you put the right stakes in the fire. You must use live trees. You must cut down two saplings to stack the logs that will roll into the fire and feed it when you sleep. If you use dead trees, they will burn, your fire will die, and you will be at risk."

"I know."

"And be careful not to suffocate the fire with too much brush. Let it breathe when you light it."

"A-huh."

"And your mess kit. When you boil water from the stream, don't touch it with your hands until it's cooled down. Use a stick to lift it off the fire. Young people get all excited, sometimes they forget and they make mistakes. I've seen burns on hands like a roasted pig's behind."

"Uh-uh."

"You have your poncho? Packed at the top in your knapsack?"

"A-huh."

"Good. Good."

What was up with Mrs. Chimchak? This was basic camping stuff. Nadia knew it cold, forward and backward, like the number pi rounded to eight decimals.

"PLAST was abolished in 1922 when the communists took Ukraine. It survived in secrecy until we brought it to America. You're the best girl scout we have in this troop. You and others like you are the only hope for a free Ukraine someday."

Nadia cringed. Why was someone always telling her she was the future? She wished she had a Mounds bar. She wanted to run away but nodded instead.

Mrs. Chimchak's eyes grew larger as though they were tearing up. Nadia couldn't believe what she was seeing. Everyone knew that Mrs. Chimchak didn't have tear ducts.

"I want you to know how proud I am of you," she said. "If I had a daughter, I'd want her to be just like you. Will you remember that?"

"Yes," Nadia said. She had no choice but to be polite, but the comment weirded her out. It was hard enough having two parents. She didn't need to worry about pleasing someone else, too.

Mrs. Chimchak pulled a small tin box out of her pocket. "Here. Take these mints. Keep them close to you. When a person doesn't feel well, a mint will always improve her spirits."

Nadia wanted to roll her eyes but didn't. Stupid Altoids. What she needed was an industrial-sized Hershey's Mr. Goodbar, not a box of mints.

Nadia thanked her.

"Now, my young and fearless warrior, would you share a sip of water from your canteen with an old woman before she sets off on her journey home?"

"Of course."

Nadia hustled over to her knapsack and grabbed her canteen. When she turned around, Mrs. Chimchak was gone.

No noise. No sign that another human being had been there.

Nadia stored the Altoids in her knapsack and went in search of two saplings to act as the feeding mechanism for her fire. Mrs. Chimchak's words rang in her ears: Nadia was the only hope for a free Ukraine. Great. And she was her father's only hope, too, given he considered Marko to be a hopeless delinquent. Her father worked on the assembly line in a gun factory. His daughter had to do better. Terrific. Oh, and let's not forget her mother, who had told her she regretted ever marrying her father. Nadia was the only hope for her mother, too.

Couldn't all these people get a life? It was hard enough to survive a school year or a summer camp. How could she make everyone happy at the same time? Did they have no clue that she was a person, too?

She cut down two saplings with her knife, stripped them of leaves and branches, and sharpened them to a point. Once the stakes were ready, she began to build a textbook campfire. Nadia loved building fires. So much attention to detail was needed to make it come out right.

The sun slid behind the peaks of the giant oaks. The forest darkened. She picked a flat spot in a clearing away from trees where sparks and flames were less likely to ignite a tree branch. She fell to her hands and knees and cleared the area of leaves and brush until the ground was bare. When she stood up, she was caked in sweat and dirt, but she didn't care.

She built a mound of dry twigs and created a long fuse of white birch bark. She lined strip after strip in an overlapping fashion so that once she lit it, the flame would zip toward its target the way it did in the last scene in The Bridge on the River Kwai. *Marko loved that movie, and she watched it with him whenever it was on TV. In three days, she'd be able to tell him she'd been thinking about it when she'd built her fuse. He'd love it. That would be so cool.*

Nadia gathered wood into piles based on thickness. She crafted a wooden square around the kindling, using small branches from the second pile. Afterward, she erected a tepee around the square. She moved on to each successive pile of thicker wood, alternately building squares and tepees. When she was finished, Nadia admired her quadruple-layered bonfire with its long, white fuse snaking out on one side.

The final step was to take the two live stakes and nail them into the ground at a forty-five-degree angle to the center of the fire. She'd stack logs from the sixth pile against the stakes. A fresh log would roll into the fire before it died. That way, if she fell asleep, her fire would keep burning. When she was done, she treated herself to another swig of warm water from her canteen.

Dusk had arrived. A pileated woodpecker hammered at a tree in search of ants. Its drumming reminded Nadia that the seconds were ticking away. A cool wind blew through her sweaty clothes and body. She shivered. She needed fire. She needed fire now.

Nadia pulled a baggie from her pocket. It contained her life-blood: three matches. They were the strike-anywhere kind that could be lit by scratching against any hard surface. At summer camp, Roxanne Stashinski could hold one in her right hand and strike it off the nail of her thumb without using her left hand. Nadia wished she could do something that neat, but those types of things didn't come naturally to her.

Although the matches could be struck anywhere, she grabbed the same clean gray stone she'd used to bang the stakes into the ground to make sure it lit. As she swiped the match against the rock, a mosquito flew right into her ear. The matchstick snapped in her hand before it lit. She quickly reached down to get it, but the stick had broken so close to the head that it was useless.

One down, two to go. If tonight's fire went out, she'd have only one more chance to relight it during her three-day test.

She took a second match and struck it on the same stone. Nothing happened. She tried again. Nothing. She tried again, and again, and again, but it wouldn't light.

She stared at the head. Most of the red lighting compound was gone. There was a tiny spot left. Nadia aimed it at the stone, and with a shaky right hand, snapped her wrist one more time. Nothing. The second match was dead, too.

She was staring at three nights alone with one match left. That reality shook her to the bone. She took two long sips of water from her canteen to try to calm herself, and realized there were only four ounces left. Not enough for one day, let alone for two.

One match, no fire, and soon, no water.

Nadia pulled the last match out of her bag and took aim at the stone.

The match lit on the first try. Nadia cupped her palm around the flame to keep it alive and lit the fuse. The birch bark sizzled. A flame rolled forward like it did when they blew up the bridge on the River Kwai.

Awesome. Nadia wished Marko were here to see it.

She dropped down on all fours and crawled up to the fire. She didn't care if she bruised her knees. This was survival of the fittest, not the prettiest. She waited for the kindling to light, and fanned the flame with her breath to keep it from dying.

A flame rose from the smoke. The kindling crackled and spit.

Nadia sat up and watched as the fire came alive. It was glorious, maybe the best feeling she'd ever had in her life, except that time she'd scored the winning goal in a soccer game at PLAST summer camp. All her teammates had cheered for her. Daria Hryn, the most popular girl, had actually hugged her. Even now, alone in the wilderness in the middle of nowhere, the memory brought tears to her eyes.

With the fire blazing, Nadia built her shelter. She took three long branches and placed them beside a pair of sturdy young saplings that were growing parallel to each other. She tied one branch perpendicular to the two saplings, making sure it was at neck height.

She secured the other two branches at the same height, one to each sapling, letting them fall to the ground at forty-five-degree angles. A lattice of smaller branches created a nice roof for her home. Nadia also stuck a few sticks in the ground on the sides of the lean-to so she could seal those holes up, too.

When she was finished with the skeleton of her shelter, she spread her poncho on top and connected it to the branches with twine. The poncho had holes in each corner for exactly that purpose. She wove ferns into a roof over the poncho, and did the same along the sides where she'd put the sticks. She also spread ferns on the floor of the lean-to, creating a mattress for her sleeping bag.

Her shelter built, Nadia sat down by the fire's edge. The heat from the flames penetrated her clothes and dried her uniform and her body.

She ate a small piece of the buckwheat bread and went to sleep. She was so exhausted she packed it in after dinner and slept through the night. When she awoke the next morning, the sun's rays poked into the entrance to her lean-to. Nadia stuck her head out and saw that her feeding mechanism was working well. A total of three logs had rolled successively into the fire. Its yellow flames still reached two feet high.

Awesome. She and her fire had both survived. That was key because they were both dependent on each other.

The sound of human feet bounding through the brush toward her broke her concentration. They didn't sound like her brother's and father's long strides. They were short, crisp, and purposeful. They echoed through the forest.

Mrs. Chimchak.

Nadia pushed herself up and burst out of her lean-to, a smile already etched on her face. It would be good to see a familiar face, even if that person was there to remind her she was the only hope for one person or another, or some such painful thing.

She saw the strangers and realized there had been no echo of footsteps. She'd assumed one person was approaching, but there were actually two of them. A man and a woman.

They were both young. The woman reminded Nadia of a giraffe, a towering beauty with outrageously long legs, an elongated neck, and golden hair with streaks of caramel halfway down her back. She'd probably been popular in school, like the girls that terrorized Nadia on a daily basis. The man looked more like a kangaroo, much shorter with smaller features than the woman. He fidgeted beside the woman, wired with nervous energy. Both of them wore knapsacks on their backs and frowns on their faces.

Nadia's survival instincts sent a wave of fear through her body. There was something wrong about these two. They looked scared and out of place. More than that, they looked desperate.

Either something bad had happened, or was about to happen. And Nadia didn't come to this conclusion based on the strangers' faces.

It was the gun the man pulled from behind his back that told her this.

CHAPTER 5

BLOOD DRAINED FROM MY FACE. I REALIZED MY BREATHING had turned shallow.

I focused on extending my exhalations. Cursed at my self-delusion. I'd fooled myself into thinking I was managing a man who could not be managed. Then I cursed at myself for cursing at myself. I needed to relax. There was still a way out of this van with my life and body intact.

There is almost always a way out of trouble. The woman who keeps her emotions at bay can find the way.

Donnie looked down at me with a concerned look. I had no idea if it was mock or real. It was time to give up trying to read him, and buy time until a means of escape occurred to me.

"You okay?" he said.

"Yeah, I'm all right," I said.

I closed my eyes and pictured myself walking through the local park, my brother at my side, both of us in our teens. Nothing could touch us. We were young, resilient, and most of all, a pair. We could rely on each other.

"You want a glass of water?" Donnie said.

"No. I don't want any water. I don't need anything. You want to ask me more questions? Let's get on with it."

He pointed a finger at me. "Hey. You don't know how lucky you are. Be nice. I'll get you some water."

The biggest joke of all was that his first name wasn't Donnie. It was Bohdan. Most Ukrainian-American kids were tolerant of their given Ukrainian names. Most grew to be proud of them over time. But those who couldn't handle childhood abuse often adopted other English translations to assimilate into American society more easily. For instance, a Pavlo might become a Paul. But how a Bohdan became a Donnie was beyond my comprehension.

His last name wasn't Angel, either. It was Angelovich. I liked shortening it. For obvious reasons.

"I don't want any water, Donnie."

He stopped near the refrigerator. Sighed as though I were being an uncooperative guest.

"Suit yourself." He returned to the contraption. The stool was two feet off the ground. He towered over me. "So answer the question. What do you know about your godfather's business?"

"He was known for his expertise in antiques all over the East Coast and beyond. Everyone in the Uke community knew who he was. And he had a good reputation. So whenever a Uke had an antique for sale, he got the call. Death in the family, house full of furniture for sale, he got the call. A farmer with a barn full of old stuff, he got the call."

"What else?"

"Nothing."

"Nothing?"

I looked up into Donnie's eyes to make sure he could see mine. "Nothing."

It was the truth. I didn't know anything else about my godfather's business, though now I knew there was something else to know. Which struck me as a potential problem, because it made me a liability to Donnie and his organization. *Didn't it?*

"You're lying to me again," he said.

"I am not . . ." I infused some ferocity into my voice. It came easily under the circumstances. "I am not lying to you. Do you think I'm that careless? Am I in any position to be playing games with you? You ask the questions, I give you the truth. The truth. I don't know anything else about my godfather's business."

He started nodding before I finished talking, in a mechanical way that suggested he didn't believe a word I was saying. "The truth . . . right? You're giving me the truth?" He grabbed me by the collar of my shirt and lifted me off the chair. "Then why were you asking people if his business was doing okay? If he'd had any disagreements with people at work?"

"Let go of me," I said.

He didn't.

"I'll answer the question, if you let go of me and act like the boy my godfather said was good."

My words might have sounded preposterous if it hadn't been for the emotion that had flashed on his face when I made up the story about my godfather liking him. I knew it had left a mark. At least in this regard, Donnie was no different from any other person. No matter what our paths in life, we still remember moments from our childhood when we longed for a single word of praise.

His lips quivered, his eyes softened, and he lowered me gently back to the stool. Started fixing my collar but pulled his hands away before he could finish, as though he realized his touch was toxic.

I continued with my current strategy, telling him the absolute truth and looking him in the eyes as I did so. "I was asking if his business was okay because at the time I wasn't certain his death was an accident."

"Why not?"

"Because the story I heard at the wake was that it was raining hard and his cellar leaks. He went down to the cellar to check the flooding, slipped on the stairs, and hit his head."

"What's wrong with that story?"

"Nothing is wrong with it. Did you notice I used the past tense? I said 'at the time I wasn't certain his death was an accident.' I'm certain now. I buy it. I'm a believer."

"Why the change of heart?"

I glanced from Donnie to the machine and back to him again. "Because I understand the situation better now."

"What situation?"

"My situation. I'm still thinking there's a way for you to let me walk out of here in one piece."

"You're saying you asked questions then that you wouldn't ask now."

"Obviously."

One of those questions was, what happened to you, Donnie Angel? Except that was a lie. I didn't need to ask the question. Nothing Marko or I did was ever good enough for our parents, in school, at home, or in the community. I was sure Donnie had experienced the same single-minded pressure to excel. Only the exact details of what he had suffered were a mystery.

Donnie narrowed his eyes at me and then nodded. This time it was a slow nod, the kind that said he believed. He really believed. At least for the moment.

"You are going to walk out of here in one piece," he said. "Answer me one more question, and you got my word on that."

"Name it."

"I get that you had a change of heart. Nothing will change a man's mind faster than the sight of this here machine. But before you changed your mind, back at the wake, the funeral, the reception . . . why did you think the story of how your godfather died was bullshit? Didn't his cellar flood when it rained?"

"Yeah."

"Didn't he drink?"

"Nightly."

"So why don't you believe it happened that way?"

"He was too careful."

Donnie laughed. It sounded more like a condescending and derisive sneer. "What?"

"He was too careful to ever go down to his cellar once he started drinking."

"That's all? That's the reason you were suspicious?"

"That's all."

Donnie screwed his face tight. "That can't be all. What are you not telling me?"

"He suffered from bathmophobia."

"Bathmo what? He was scared of bathrooms? What the hell does that have to do with anything?"

"Bathmophobia isn't a fear of bathrooms. It's fear of steep slopes. For people who suffer from it, it's very, very serious. It's fear of stairs."

"You're saying your godfather was afraid to climb stairs? That's the biggest bunch of bullshit I ever heard."

"Not to him it wasn't. No one outside the family knew about it. It wasn't the sort of thing you want to get out in a community. You know how people are, Donnie. People are always looking to feel better about themselves by seeing weakness in others."

"So he didn't climb stairs?"

"No, of course he climbed stairs. But it made him nervous. Even during the day. When there was plenty of light."

"And at night?"

"He lived in a ranch-style house for a reason. All his rooms were on one floor for a reason. Walk down the stairs to the cellar? At night? No way, especially if he'd been drinking, and it was raining and he had to worry about water at the base of the stairs. But hey, what do I know? People do stupid things all the time. Maybe he got so drunk it loosened him up and he forgot about his phobia. Like I said, I wanted to know before. But that was then, and this is now."

Donnie stared at me with a blank expression. There were two possibilities. First, he'd killed my godfather, and he was disappointed to hear there was a case to be made that his death was not accidental. Second, he wasn't involved in my godfather's killing, but he'd been in business with him. Perhaps there was an unresolved element to their arrangement. Maybe Donnie was owed money. If he'd heard me asking questions about my godfather's death, he might have assumed my godfather and I had been close, wondered what else I knew. But now that he realized I didn't know anything, he might consider me dispensable. Had I been a fool by speaking honestly? Had I written my own death certificate?

"You were honest," he said. "I can tell. I appreciate that." He patted my shoulder. "You were a woman of your word, and I'm going to be a man of my word."

Donnie wasn't reacting like a man who'd committed a murder and was worried about someone outing him. A man like that wouldn't take any chances, I thought. He'd have killed me by now.

"I'm free to go?"

"Almost." He moved next to the adjustable brackets. "Give me your left leg."

"Why?" I choked on the word.

Donnie looked incredulous. "Because you're right-handed, which means you favor your right leg, too. It's not like I don't care about you, you know."

"No. I mean, why do you need either of my legs?"

"Because you've got to give me something."

"What do you mean, give you something?"

"You've got to give me something to prove to me that you're going to keep your mouth shut and not interfere with my business."

I knew what he meant even before he pulled a rubber mallet from beneath the contraption. He was going to break my leg. My left one, that was, because he was a nice guy and he cared about me. And there was nothing I could do about it.

I had no hope of overpowering him physically. If I made a run for the rear exit he'd wring my neck before I got one foot out the door. Even worse, if I tried to escape, I knew he might hurt me in a way that time and a cast might not heal.

"Don't worry," he said, as he handed me a mouth guard. "I've done this before. It'll be a clean break."

I barely heard his words. I was too busy repeating the ones I'd spoken to myself less than five minutes ago.

The woman who keeps her emotions at bay can find the way out.

Black splotches dotted my vision. Bolts of panic paralyzed me. All I could imagine was the sound of a bone breaking, an excruciating pain unlike any I'd felt before.

But I didn't fight the panic. I let my vision right itself. Surrendered to my wandering mind and let the visions slide. The experiences of my childhood had brought me face-to-face with fear before. I still had time. I still had a few seconds left.

I can find the way out.

I will find the way out.

CHAPTER 6

NADIA STOOD IN FRONT OF HER LEAN-TO STARING DOWN THE barrel of the gun fearing her heart might stop beating any second. She hadn't been this scared since she forgot the Ukrainian words to Hail Mary while saying morning prayers in her parents' bedroom. Her father had been shaving at the time, and when her voice stopped he bounded out of the bathroom, face foaming with lather, and slapped her in the head so hard she fell over and broke her nose.

She'd seen guns before. Some of the counselors for the boys—ROTC types that didn't party with the girl counselors—brought their hunting rifles with them to summer camp. But this gun was different. It was shiny and beautiful. This one looked more like something a private eye on TV would carry to look cool. Whatever it was, it sure didn't belong in the forest. Neither did its owner or his girlfriend.

"Sorry, kid," the Kangaroo said, as he lowered the barrel of the gun toward the ground. "I have a bad back. This thing weighs so much I took it out of the knapsack and stuck it in my belt. But that's no good either. I didn't mean to pull it out and scare you."

Nadia breathed easier. Only then did she realize her teeth were chattering.

"I told you not to bring it," the Giraffe said. "But you had to be such a man, didn't you? As if the entire camping thing wasn't stupid

enough, you had to go bring that gun with you. What you should have brought was something for all these damn mosquitoes." She slapped her neck. "I hate insects. I hate the outdoors. I hate this place, and I fucking hate you."

Nadia's mouth fell open. A woman giving her man the f-word? That was unbelievable. If her mother had ever said that to her father? Oh, man. That would have been ugly.

"Let's make the best of it," the Kangaroo said, "and focus on the task at hand."

The Giraffe swatted at her ears again. "This is ridiculous. They're eating me alive here. You're a banker," she said, spitting the words at her boyfriend. "You belong in the city. I'm a law student. I belong in the city. What possessed you to drag me out here to this godforsaken, living hell? And what possessed me to say yes? This is the stupidest decision I've ever made in my life."

The Kangaroo shook his head in frustration. He knelt down by the fire so he was eye to eye with Nadia and smiled.

"Honey, is there an adult with you nearby?"

His choice of words dropped him a notch right away. Nadia hated to be called "honey." It was thick, sweet, and came in a jar. None of those descriptions applied to her.

"Nope," Nadia said. "I'm alone."

The Kangaroo laughed in disbelief. "No way. You're alone? You can't be alone."

Nadia explained that she was alone on a Ukrainian girl scout survival test, and that her father or brother were camping somewhere on the trail, probably half a mile or so away. At least that was her best guess.

The Giraffe was smiling at her now, too. It was a heckuva smile. Nadia imagined being half as pretty as this woman. She'd have friends and no one would pick on her. What a life that would have been.

The Giraffe said, "Do you have a walkie-talkie from RadioShack or something like that, to talk to your father or brother? If there's an emergency?"

"Nope," Nadia said. "All I have is a whistle. I'm only supposed to use it if I'm in serious trouble. Like, really serious. But I do know the way back to the trail if you're lost."

"It's a bit more complicated," the Kangaroo said. "We're with another couple. My brother and his wife. And my brother's hurt. He tripped and rolled down a hill. His forehead is bleeding and we think he broke his leg. We need to get him some help."

"Do you have a first aid kit?" Nadia said.

"Yeah," the Giraffe said. "We put a bandage on his forehead, but there's nothing we can do for his leg. There's no way he can walk."

"Was there an Ace bandage in the first aid kit?"

"I think I remember seeing one," the Giraffe said.

Nadia knew what needed to be done. She was trained in first aid. She could help these people and it was her duty to do so.

Nadia said, "Do either of you have a poncho in your knapsack?"

"No," the Kangaroo said. "But I have an umbrella."

"Yeah," the Giraffe said, rolling her eyes. "A Burberry umbrella. Number one on the list of essential camping equipment. No, I don't have a poncho either. It wasn't supposed to rain. We're hiking for the day. We got lost because Magellan here forgot the compass in the car. He couldn't read the map when we took a detour off the trail."

"It's hard to read a map without a compass," Nadia said.

The Kangaroo sighed as though he'd had enough of people making fun of him, but the Giraffe rewarded Nadia with a belly laugh and a smile. Nadia savored an adrenaline rush. They were pals, she and the beautiful Giraffe. This made her a cool girl for the day, didn't it?

Now that they were buddies, Nadia would do anything for the Giraffe. Even sacrifice her poncho, which truly was essential survival equipment.

Nadia removed the poncho from her lean-to and folded it into a square. Threaded her belt through the sheath of her Bowie knife so that the giant blade hung down her left leg, and attached her canteen along her left side. Then she stood before the strangers with her hands at her sides, like a gunfighter from her brother's favorite spaghetti westerns.

"We're good to go," Nadia said. "I know first aid. Lead the way."

They laughed at her. At first Nadia felt her face start to burn. But then she realized they weren't making fun of her. They were laughing in a nice way. They appreciated that she was trying to help, but they doubted she could help the Kangaroo's injured brother. Nadia understood that they probably thought she was too young to know what she was doing.

To ease their minds, she told them exactly what she was going to do, step-by-step. When Nadia was done, the couple glanced at each other with shocked expressions and didn't say another word.

Nadia added two logs to her fire to make sure it had plenty of fuel and followed the couple deep into the woods, leaving the knapsack and camp behind her.

CHAPTER 7

Donnie lifted my hand, the one that held the mouth guard, and guided it toward my face. I opened my mouth and he stuffed it inside. I could have resisted, but there was no upside to that. Only downside. He pressed my nose and my chin together with his right hand to make sure my jaw was shut. Then he lifted my leg and placed it on the support brackets. His motions were firm but gentle, like those of a doctor. He touched my cheek with an open palm once the mouth guard was secure between my teeth. He held my leg with two hands and lifted it slowly so as not to strain any muscles before placing it onto the support.

All the while he kept babbling, also like a doctor, presumably to distract me from the sight of the mallet at his feet, and my immediate fate.

"You should be on your knees thanking me," he said. He pursed his lips and shook his head. "Okay, obviously you can't be on your knees right now, but you know what I mean. That is how grateful you should be to me. I was told to handle this. Any way I sees fit. Anyone else, you would be dead. But not me. Why? Because that's not how I want to live my life. And you and me, we understand each other. We're both old-school. Our parents kept their mouths shut about all the shit that went down in World War

II, all the shit they suffered, some of the lies some of them had to tell to get in this country. We know how to keep our mouths ziplocked. It's in our genes, and because I'm a good guy and you're a respectable woman—have I told you I have the highest respect for you?—I'm playing it this way. Giving you a chance to live. Yeah, you should be grateful. Just plain grateful."

He finished adjusting the brackets. One held my ankle; the other gripped my leg below the knee. He was going to strike between the knee and the ankle. I could tell by the structure of the machine. My upper leg was supported, my lower leg wasn't. The bone would cave right in.

I knew I had only seconds left. I could sense my panic. It was like an amorphous cloud hovering over me, waiting to wrap me up and render me incapable of thought. But it wasn't upon me yet, and I knew to keep it at bay by insisting I didn't care if it seized me, and focusing on a specific thing. In this case it was a specific task. The task was to buy some more time.

Donnie reached down for the mallet.

I pulled the mouth guard from between my teeth. He snapped to attention, mallet in hand, as soon as he saw what I'd done. The veins in his hand protruded as he tightened his grip on the hammer. He looked angry. Really angry.

"I changed my mind," I said.

His eyes narrowed. "About what?"

"The Champagne. It might help me with my nerves. If not right now, then in a few minutes when I'm going to need the help. At least the alcohol will be in my bloodstream, you know what I mean?"

His expression turned stern and he shook his head.

My pulse quickened. The amorphous cloud of panic moved in and engulfed me like fog.

You're a fraud, I thought. *You've been lying to yourself to make the time pass. To keep from passing out from sheer fear, like the pathetic little girl you are and always have been. This is going to happen. A man is going to break your leg and there is nothing, absolutely nothing, you can do about it because you're not that tough, and not as smart as you like to think you are.*

There is no hope. There is no hope. There is no hope.

And then Donnie stopped shaking his head. Maybe he saw the terror in my eyes at that very moment. Maybe he just liked the idea of me having a glass of his Champagne before he clubbed me.

Whatever the reason, he loosened my brackets and told me to sit up. Then he walked over to the refrigerator and started babbling again. I didn't pay any attention to what he was saying because by this time I'd remembered my brother telling me that he and I could put up with anything for three days. I recalled him asking what my name was on the Appalachian Trail, moments before leaving me to fend for myself.

As Donnie poured me a flute of bubbly, my mind unlocked the box where I kept the memory of that survival test stowed away to prevent myself from thinking about it. The locks were many and intricate, for this was not a memory that I wanted floating around my head. It loved to torture me so I'd had to design my own personal Fort Knox. Keys clicked in place and turned. Bolts slid open.

The memory escaped.

It overwhelmed my thoughts. Scene after scene flashed vividly before me.

One scene in particular resonated. A bolt of adrenaline rushed through me.

Donnie handed me the glass. He was still yapping about something.

I knocked back the entire flute. Exhaled loudly and with satisfaction.

"That's what I'm talking about," I said.

My lips and chin were dripping with liquid. I wiped them with the back of my hand, trying to make it look like as carnal an act as possible. I made my eyes go wild as though I was preparing myself for something that was going to hurt but feel good. I let out a guttural laugh to go with it.

"Do me again, Donnie," I said, pushing the glass toward him. "One more glass and I'm ready for this."

He took my glass, his expression a mix of shock and curiosity, and turned back to the refrigerator.

I took a deep breath and prepared myself for the brutality I was about to endure. The difference between my thoughts now and before was that this time I wasn't preparing to suffer the pain.

I was preparing to inflict it.

CHAPTER 8

The Kangaroo and the Giraffe led the way. Nadia followed. She hadn't eaten since yesterday afternoon so she tired quickly.

They found the second couple at the bottom of a small ravine, twenty minutes away from Nadia's camp. The other woman was the opposite of the Giraffe, with short brown hair and the face of a ferret. The injured guy had curly black hair and resembled an angry rodent. He didn't look very tough. He moaned and complained as soon as they arrived.

The Kangaroo and the two women stood in front of the Rodent and blocked Nadia's way so she couldn't see his lower body. Nadia was curious to study the man's injury. She'd never seen a broken leg. When she'd learned how to make a splint, someone pretended to be the patient. Now she would get to work with a real, live, injured person. She was psyched.

When the Rodent saw whom they'd brought with them to help, he went ballistic and called the Kangaroo his "moron brother from hell." The Ferret yelled at the Giraffe for coming back with some "pathetic little girl scout," and for a moment Nadia considered not helping the Rodent after all.

But she was an altar girl who took her Ukrainian Catholic

religion seriously, so she forgave the stranger and stepped closer to take a look.

The Giraffe touched her shoulder. "Just to warn you. It's a bit gruesome."

Nadia felt an injection of willpower from the Giraffe's touch. It was as though beautiful people had a special power, and with their mere touch could turn a social castoff into a more confident person.

Duly emboldened, Nadia peeked around the Giraffe's waist. The Rodent lay with his arms and legs at odd angles, like the outline of a dead person on the floor on a TV show. It was the left leg. The skin was turning black and blue around the front shin, and the tip of the bone was protruding.

Nadia looked away. Stifled a desire to puke. It wasn't neat at all. It was disgusting and scary. If the man weren't such a rodent, she would have felt sorry for him. Nadia closed her eyes and replayed scenes from Mrs. Chimchak's lectures on lower-body anatomy and first aid.

She could do this. Yeah, she could.

She was a soldier.

Nadia walked up to the Rodent, knelt down, and put her hand on his shoulder. It was a calming thing Mrs. Chimchak had taught her. This man needed the comfort of the human touch, but his wife the Ferret was too busy bitching at the Giraffe, probably because she was jealous of her, and the brother probably didn't want to touch him because they were always fighting. Not like her and Marko. They never fought.

Everyone stopped talking the second her hand touched his shoulder. The Rodent stopped moaning, too.

Nadia looked into the Rodent's beady eyes as his mouth dropped open in surprise. His forehead dripped with sweat. The man was hurting bad. Nadia could tell. She knew pain from breaking her nose and this was worse.

"How are you feeling?" Nadia said.

The Rodent exploded with mean laughter, the kind that's usually a prelude to swears and insults, but Nadia smiled and stopped him cold. Actually made him smile.

"I'm doing great, kid. A-plus, mother. Best day of my life. Who are you?"

"My name is Nadia. In five hours or less, you're going to be in a hospital, and they're going to take good care of you. I'm going to help you get there. Rehab is going to be like . . . like no fun at all, but that's not something you need to worry about now. Right? Positive thinking, positive thinking. It's so important. So tell me, before I start, how did this happen?"

The other three exchanged quiet looks of amazement. The Rodent's jaw hung open for an extra second.

"We were fooling around," he said. "I was chasing my wife downhill. I had to turn to avoid a rock and my foot just got stuck. The rest of my body moved but it didn't. I fell over. And then this."

A spasm of pain hit him so badly he screamed loud enough for anyone within a mile radius to hear. Problem was, the only people within a mile radius were probably at his feet. Unless her father and Marko were nearby. But if they were close, Nadia was surprised one of them hadn't helped the strangers. Maybe they were far away, just as her father had told her. It didn't matter now, she thought. She had the situation under control.

Nadia squeezed his shoulder the way Mrs. Chimchak had taught her. The squeeze provided extra comfort, reassurance that the original touch had true feeling behind it.

"You're going to be okay," Nadia said.

The Rodent gritted his teeth as a spasm of pain racked him. "You think so, kid?"

"I know so. There's a name for what happened to you. It's a common break for athletes and hikers and people like that. People like you."

That made him chuckle through the pain. He probably wasn't much of an athlete or hiker but Nadia thought it might cheer him up to hear her say it.

"Oh, yeah?" he said. "What's it called, kid?"

"Spiral tibial fracture. It happens when you plant one leg, twist it, and then fall. Yup. It's called a spiral tibial fracture."

CHAPTER 9

LIFE WAS MOVING IN SLOW MOTION NOW . . .

Donnie put my glass on the table. He didn't reach for the refrigerator door. Instead he paused to listen to himself. He grinned. I had no idea what he was talking about because I was focused on what I was about to do. Which was unthinkable. The conviction with which I needed to act, the suffering I was going to inflict, the repercussions to my face, body, and life if I messed it up . . .

"You still go to the blessing of the Easter baskets?"

I sharpened my focus. Heard Donnie. He'd just asked a question. I realized I'd better answer.

"Sure," I said. "I go every year." In fact, I couldn't remember when I'd last gone. Maybe fifteen years ago.

"I used to go with my mother. Everyone getting together in the school gym for the priest to go around and sprinkle holy water on their *babkas* and tacky colored eggs. It's all bullshit but I liked it. I liked it because it was the one day a year where no one gave a shit who you were. Your family welcomed you back. The community welcomed you back. It's just a great tradition. Wayward boys like me can come home for one day. No matter what you've done, everyone is happy to see you. Happy to see children with their mothers."

Donnie Angel extended his arm and grasped the fridge door. He had to twist a little bit to the right because of the refrigerator's location in the corner. He opened the door and reached inside to grab the bottle.

I jumped to my feet, stepped forward and curled my right leg up to my waist. This time I was the one with the element of surprise. His face registered shock but there was no time for him to react. His legs remained twisted, still facing the fridge. I snapped my heel against his lower left leg with all my might. The meat of my shoe connected with the bone.

I heard the crack. It was a sick, gut-wrenching noise. I must have closed my eyes before impact because the image of a paint stick breaking in half flashed in my mind. By the time I opened them, Donnie was lying on the floor wailing. He brought his hands to his leg and touched it, but that only made him scream even more.

My plan at this point was to get out of the van as quickly as possible. Much to my shock, however, I stood there staring down at the man who'd taken me against my will, who had a machine to break legs and was about to use it on me. The truth was I felt compassion for him. He was a human being. I'd hurt him. To make things worse, I truly believed that he liked me. In his own demented way, he believed he'd done me a favor by not killing me, and by planning to break my left instead of my right leg. And, as he'd said at the beginning, we went back. We went way back, all the way to the Grantmoor on the Berlin Turnpike.

Also, I'd been a devout Ukrainian Catholic growing up, and I took this cheek-turning business very seriously. I believed in the life-affirming power of unequivocal forgiveness. Based on my life until this moment, I would have expected to have been consumed with empathy for the man I'd hurt even though it was an act of self-defense. That's the way I was wired.

But now, compassion wasn't the only emotion that gripped me. Instead, a quiet rage had gathered inside me. It was accompanied by a giddy sense of satisfaction. It coursed through my veins, drowned my Catholic tendencies, and left me liberated. Perhaps I'd overdosed on humility, which was a way of saying I was sick of being pushed around. By my parents, my ex-husband, my bosses in New York, and now Donnie Angel. Whatever the reasons, I felt more empowered than I had since childhood as I gazed at the agony I'd inflicted.

"Bitch . . . Are you fucking crazy?" Donnie clenched his teeth as though gathering some more willpower to fight the pain. A deep breath. Eyes looking as though they might pop out of his sockets. "Do you have any idea what you've done?"

"Yeah," I said, nodding. "I know what I've done." The words rolled off my tongue one at a time. "Spiral . . . tibial . . . fracture."

I assumed the van was soundproofed for obvious reasons. The driver and the other man who'd lifted me off the street hadn't heard Donnie any more than they would have heard me if my leg were the one that had been broken. I found the phone beside the liquor decanters and lifted the receiver.

A man's voice. "Yeah?"

"Pull over," I said, sounding as agitated as I could. "I think he's having a heart attack."

The van swerved right and slowed down. I jumped out the back door before it came to a complete stop, leaving Donnie shouting obscenities in my wake. What impressed the hell out of me was that he'd switched to Ukrainian swear words. Maybe that line I'd made up about my godfather saying Donnie had a Ukrainian soul wasn't completely fiction after all.

I recognized my location as soon as my feet kissed the pavement. The grand stairs leading to the Metropolitan Museum of Art on the right. The former Stanhope Hotel on the left. Fifth Avenue and 81st Street. Six blocks from my apartment. They really had been circling my neighborhood.

I ran north along 5th past the museum. The van wouldn't be able to make a U-turn. Traffic flowed only one way and that was south. I didn't bother looking behind me. I kept my eyes focused on the lights atop the yellow cabs.

A vacant taxi appeared within four blocks. I jumped inside and told the driver to take an immediate left on 84th Street. The van was still parked to the side. I'd left the door open behind me but it was shut now. I suspected the men were tending to Donnie.

I told the cabbie to drive straight across 83rd and drop me off on 1st Avenue. I ran the final block to my apartment and locked myself inside. Logic dictated Donnie would expect me to go home, but I wasn't worried about him. I lived in a protected building with seasoned doormen. No thug was going to get past them. To make sure, I called downstairs and told them a blind date had gone bad and to keep me informed if any strangers asked about me. The doorman who picked up promised to keep me safe, and I was glad I'd been a generous tipper at the end of the year, back when I had the money to be one.

I trembled as I peeled my clothes off. Didn't leave the steaming shower for twenty minutes until I'd managed to calm down.

Then I did what I'd been planning to do all night.

I uncorked that bottle of wine and tried to figure out what I was going to do next.

CHAPTER 10

Nadia cut two small branches off a young oak tree and trimmed them to arm's length. Using some twine, she secured the sticks to each side of the Rodent's ankle with the Ace bandage to form a splint. That locked the ankle in place so that it wouldn't be hurt any worse when they moved him. He winced from the pain as she put it on, and Nadia did her best to keep him calm by talking to him as she worked.

Afterward, Nadia cut down two saplings with her knife. The whacking tired her out even more, and for a second she was afraid she might faint. Only adrenaline kept her going. The Giraffe noticed this and came rushing to her side with genuine concern, but Nadia waved her off and kept working. She asked the Giraffe to help her spread out the poncho.

After they did so, Nadia fixed a sapling to each side of her poncho and made a stretcher out of it. Together, the four of them lifted the Rodent onto the stretcher. The nearest ranger station was three miles away. Nadia drew a map for them and directed them toward the trail.

The Rodent thanked her profusely. He reached out with his hand, grasped her shoulder, and squeezed it the way she had done to his. The Kangaroo offered Nadia money, but she refused. She was almost insulted but realized they were city folk and they wouldn't understand the PLAST code, that it was her duty to help anyone who needed it. They offered to take her address and send her the poncho, but she refused that, too. She was worried her father would get mad at her for giving out their address to strangers.

The Giraffe came over and gave her a hug. Nadia recoiled at first because she wasn't used to anyone touching her, but she knew the Giraffe meant well so she decided it was okay.

Afterward, the Kangaroo and the Ferret lifted the stretcher and followed the Giraffe toward the trail.

Nadia made her way back toward camp. She'd given away her poncho, so if it rained she'd probably get soaked. It was a bad thing to be in the forest without a poncho. There was a reason Mrs. Chimchak had taught her to keep it at the top of her knapsack. Still, giving away the poncho was a matter of honor. She had to put the well-being of a sick individual above her own.

As soon as she returned to camp, though, Nadia realized she had an even bigger problem than life without a poncho.

Her fire had died. Partially burned wood and ashes were scattered all over the place. Some animal had ransacked her camp. There were no glowing embers, no sign of life for her to work with whatsoever.

She'd drunk all her water. She'd planned to boil some from the stream when she returned.

Now she had no poncho, no water, no fire, and no matches with which to light a new one.

And she had two days and two nights to go.

CHAPTER 11

I SLEPT FITFULLY AND WOKE UP THE NEXT MORNING WITH that dread in the pit of my stomach, the one that reminds you something horrible is going on in your life even before you're alert. Then I remembered my abduction, Donnie Angel's champagne wishes and caviar dreams, and breaking his leg like a paint stick. My hunger pains vanished in a blink, and I found a moment of joy amidst the misery. If nothing else good came out of it, my current predicament was going to help me lose those last seven and a half pounds.

Even before downing the second of three glasses of wine the night before, I knew exactly what I was going to do next. I'd become a competent financial analyst because of my detailed approach to understanding a business and its financial statements. One of the ways I dissected a complex holding company with a myriad of subsidiaries was to draw a picture. It helped me visualize what was going on among the individual entities, if money was being borrowed or lent to support one at the cost of another, or if funds were being siphoned off at the top to pay the owners. I spent the morning visualizing my godfather's life the same way, and plotting the course of my investigation. Then I placed a phone call to an old friend.

After lunch, I arranged for one of the doormen to walk me to my parking garage. His shift ended at 3:00 p.m., which worked out perfectly. I drove my usual route along the Hutchinson River Parkway, keeping a sharp eye on the rearview mirror, but darted onto I-684 at the last second. The entrance ramp twisted and turned onto a straightaway. I gunned the engine on my vintage Porsche 911 through the curve and then ducked into the right-hand lane and slowed down to fifty-five. Every single car passed me for the next ten miles. I didn't recognize any of them, and I didn't see anyone following me either.

Not that it mattered. By now it was early rush hour. Cars hugged each other's bumpers while cruising at the speed limit. Donnie may have gotten away with lifting me off a dimly lit New York street at midnight, but he wasn't going to be able to pull it off on the highway. The streets of Hartford would be an altogether different matter. It was going to be up to me to be prudent and cautious.

I knew he would be informed of my arrival because he somehow knew the details of the questions I'd asked Roxanne Stashinski at my godfather's funeral reception. Word would get around that I was back. It was a small community, and people talked. There was always the possibility that Roxy herself had betrayed me to Donnie Angel, or gossiped innocently to someone about the questions I'd asked her. But I doubted it. She had no motive, and I'd known her my entire life. I trusted her as much as anyone outside my family, though that wasn't saying all that much.

Roxy was my godfather's niece. She was also my best friend growing up. We'd gone to summer PLAST camps together, and attended Ukrainian School at night until she quit after the seventh grade. Her mother had studied ballet and she'd inherited her long, lithe frame and feline features. As a kid, I'd wished I looked more like her, but mostly I wished I'd fit in as well. Everyone thought Roxy was cool, at Uke camps and at American school. It helped that she was thin and did the kinds of things cool girls did, like smoke cigarettes and experiment with drugs.

Her popularity with boys, in fact, was the beginning of the end of our childhood friendship. During our last PLAST camp together, she turned cold and stopped being friends with me. Something had changed but I didn't know what, until I caught her giving a blow job to a sixteen-year-old boy from Brooklyn in the tall grass behind the propane tank. We were fourteen at the time.

Twenty years later she had the life every immigrant coveted for his child. She was married to a full-blooded Ukrainian and had two kids. He was a contractor, she was a homemaker, and when they went to church on Sunday, they were the envy of every parent whose children had either left or married outside the culture.

We'd rekindled our friendship five years ago when I'd married her brother.

I picked her up at a car wash two blocks away from the Ukrainian National Home, where she'd been cooking with the other Uke ladies in preparation for bingo night. She was frowning even before she pulled the passenger door open. She still sported killer legs in tight jeans but her face resembled a shrunken raisin. It reminded me of what some famous actress had once said: that as she aged, a woman had to decide whether to preserve her ass or her face. She couldn't keep both. I guess that's one of the things I'd always liked about Roxy. We were both flawed. Neither of us was pedestal material.

"The car wash? Really?" Roxy said.

"I'm sorry. I'll explain. Get in. Quick."

I looked around to see if my favorite van had arrived, or if a crazed man in cleats was running toward me with a mallet in his hands. Such was my state of mind since last night.

Roxy threw her bag in behind her and climbed in the car. She held what looked like a plate covered by a paper bag in her hands. The delicious smell of fried potatoes and onions hit me. I didn't wait for her to put her seat belt on. Instead I slammed the car into first and took off.

"Hey," Roxy said, her head snapping back from the torque. "What the . . ." She whipped her seat belt across her shoulder and snapped it in place. "I need to be back in an hour but you're taking that way too seriously."

I took off down Wethersfield Avenue and veered right onto Brown Street. The tires screeched. Roxy gripped the overhead handle. "What's going on? Am I missing something?"

"Yeah." I hammered the throttle. The engine sang and the car flew. "This morning when I called you. I didn't tell you everything."

I had told Roxy I was coming back to Hartford and that I needed to meet her. I hadn't given her any details because I didn't want to listen to her try to stop me. I also didn't like the idea of speaking to anyone on the phone about what had happened to me or about my godfather's death. If I were asking any questions about either subject, I wanted to be able to shine a flashlight in the other person's eyes so I could see what was going on behind them.

I gave her an abbreviated version of the previous night's events. She interrupted with a series of mild exclamations but otherwise listened until I was done.

"And that's it?" Roxy said. "That's everything?"

She asked the question in a tone that suggested I'd failed to mention something obvious. I quickly replayed what I'd told her in my mind.

"Yeah," I said. "That's everything."

"No. It's not everything. What you haven't told me yet is that you called the cops. If not last night then this morning. Tell me you called the cops, Diana."

Diana was an anagram for Nadia. Roxy had figured it out during PLAST camp and decided it would be my nickname. I secretly loved it at the time. It made me feel popular and glamorous. It made me feel that I was more assimilated and American, which I wanted above everything else.

Now I had mixed feelings about it. On the one hand, it was a sweet reminder of the times Roxy had been nice to me when we were kids. On the other hand, I felt hopelessly unworthy of sharing the name of an immortal princess. The thing with nicknames, though, is that once they stick, there's nothing you can do about them.

"No," I said. "I did not go to the cops."

"Why not?'

"That would be the wrong thing to do. Come on, Rox. You know that."

"If you report it, they'll arrest Donnie. They'll get him off the street. Otherwise, that sick bastard is coming after you. You know that."

"Yeah, I know that. I also know that it's not only Donnie I need to worry about. I doubt he's in this alone."

"Have you talked to your mother or brother about this?"

"No."

"Did you at least call them?"

I tried to look cool, but I swallowed before I could form a single word. "Of course I called. The question isn't whether I called them, the question is whether they picked up or called back."

"And did they?"

It was my turn to fire Roxy a disapproving glare for even asking. Of course they hadn't called back. They both hated me.

Roxy shook her head. "You've got to go to the police. You've got to go now."

"The number one rule is to stay inside the community," I said. "You know that. The minute I go outside the community for help all bets are off."

"But what if all bets are off already?"

"If Donnie wanted to kill me, he would have done it in the van. All he was doing was scaring me."

"Yeah. By breaking your leg. Except now you broke his. And what exactly do you think he's going to do next time?"

"It doesn't matter."

"What do you mean it doesn't matter? Do you want to die?"

"I didn't mean it doesn't matter in the sense that I don't care if I get hurt. I meant it doesn't matter what Donnie's planning. It's better than if I go to the cops. Then I'm threatening his entire organization. Then there's not even a debate my life is in danger."

Roxy stared out the windshield and took a few audible breaths. I waited for her to calm herself down before lobbing the questions I'd been waiting to ask.

"Did you see Donnie at the memorial service or the funeral?"

"God no," Roxy said. "Why would he be there?" Roxy was implying that he wasn't a relative or a close friend of the family.

"Exactly. That means someone must have told him I was asking questions. That I may have appeared suspicious about the circumstances of my godfather's death."

"Yeah. Obviously. I did."

I assumed she was joking until I glanced in her direction and saw her striking a defiant pose, looking straight ahead at the windshield, lips pressed tight, jaw elevated a few haughty inches. Then all my insides seemed to slide up into my throat. "You did what?"

Roxy turned toward me, tilted her head and widened her eyes. "You're kidding me, right?"

I took a deep breath and exhaled. I felt horrible for even contemplating my best friend had ratted me out. I waved my hand as though surrendering. "I wasn't suggesting that you talked to him—"

"Yeah you were. But that's okay. I understand. You've always been a cold psycho-bitch. I still love you. In fact, that's probably the reason I love you . . ."

"I'm just asking. How did he know what I was thinking? Did you mention our discussion to anyone?"

Roxy laughed. "You're officially on the verge of pissing me off. Yes. After you left the memorial service, I walked to the front, stood by the casket, and made an announcement to the general public. 'My psycho-bitch former sister-in-law thinks my uncle was murdered!'"

I shook my head and muttered a few Ukrainian obscenities under my breath, the kind that used to sneak past my father's gritted teeth whenever his family disappointed him, which was pretty much all the time. Roxy knew the same obscenities, I was sure. It was the order and cadence of delivery that distinguished one frustrated parent from another.

"There had to be two hundred people at the memorial service," Roxy said.

I nodded. "Anyone could have overheard me."

"Just because Donnie wasn't there, doesn't mean he didn't know half the people who were."

"True that," I said.

"Why are you doing this, Diana?"

"Because I loved my godfather and someone killed him. I want to find out who and why."

"Oh yeah? Diana the noble warrior, since when?"

I shrugged. "Since now."

"Come on. What's this really all about?"

I saw the logic in her question, but I didn't have the time or desire to contemplate it. "This is just something I have to do. That's all I know."

Roxy sat quietly for a moment. "So what's the plan?" She infused her voice with a note of determination.

"There's obviously a link between my godfather's business and Donnie Angel. I'm going to start there and see what I can figure out."

An incredulous laugh burst from Roxy's mouth. It sounded more like a bark. "Sure. Of course you are. Piece of cake. And you're going to do this all alone?"

"That's right. I do all my best work alone."

"It's good you're driving around in an old Porsche. You'll blend right in wherever you go."

"It is what it is." The truth was I had no choice. I couldn't afford a rental.

"Don't you think he might be waiting for you? At my uncle's house? Right now?"

"Highly unlikely. He expects me to stay in New York or go somewhere else to hide. The last place he expects me to go is to his turf in the Hartford area. And the absolute last place he expects me to go is the scene of the crime. That's why, for now, this is as safe a place as any for me to be."

"Yeah. For now."

"And by the way . . . After tonight, I don't want you involved. I don't want you in harm's way."

I needed Roxy tonight to get access to my godfather's house. As his niece, she had been his emergency contact and had a copy of the front door key.

"Yeah, yeah. Poor Diana. Doesn't want to be beholden to no one. Always the loner. Didn't have any friends growing up. Doesn't have any friends now. Blah, blah, blah, blah, blah. Spare me your martyr complex. I brought you potato pancakes, you know."

She lifted the paper from the plate. I caught another whiff of fried potatoes and onions. Under less urgent circumstances, it would have dissolved my morning willpower.

"Smells like heaven. You didn't tell me you were moonlighting at the Uke National Home."

"Money's getting tight. Our savings are tied up in a condo complex and my husband the real estate mogul can't move the units. He built them high-end in a middle-class neighborhood in New Britain, genius that he is. But that's not what irks me. One day he tells me to stop spending, and the next day he comes home with four hundred dollars worth of parts for his vintage Mustang."

"Ouch."

"You make your own money. You don't have to depend on a man. Don't ever give that up."

I thanked God it was dark in the car so Roxy couldn't see me blushing. This was a perfect moment for me to tell her I'd been fired six months ago during the latest round of job eliminations and that I was unemployed, but I nodded instead. I told myself I didn't want to distract her from the topic at hand but in truth I was too embarrassed to be honest with her. Roxy looked up to me because I had a career. Other than my job, I had nothing else. I knew it, and she knew it, too. I couldn't stand the thought of her thinking I was a failure.

We enjoyed some silence until we got to East Hartford. My godfather's house was an old multifamily home off Burnside Avenue. When he'd bought it in the seventies, it was probably a purely residential neighborhood. Now it was a mishmash of body shops, ethnic restaurants, and housing projects. I circled around the block and passed two tricked-out Honda Civics idling by the curb. The windows were tinted, but I could see smoke pouring out the driver's side of one car and the passenger side of the other.

"We were so worried about Donnie's crew," Roxy said, "we forgot about the natives. Not the best time to come here, when the sun goes down."

A flash of indecision washed over me, and I wondered if I was an idiot for being here. I took a deep breath and waited for the sensation to pass. "Look at the bright side."

"What's that?"

"It's dark out. It's an iffy neighborhood. Skulking around, we'll fit right in."

Roxy chuckled. "True that, Diana." She took a deep breath, fixed her jaw, and set her eyes on the house. "True that."

CHAPTER 12

We parked along the side of the road and walked up the steps. I hadn't been in my godfather's home since my early teens, when my father would come over occasionally to visit and bring me along. My godfather would mix me a non-alcoholic drink with a coconut flavor, and I'd sit in his parlor drinking it, thinking I'd died and gone to heaven.

There were two front doors, one for each of the attached houses. I waited beside Roxy on the stoop as she fished a key from her bag. There were no lights on in either house. Roxy gave me a penlight and asked me to shine it in her purse.

"Who are the tenants next door?" I said.

"There are none. He was using it as storage for the furniture he bought up."

"You're kidding me. Since when?"

"About six months ago."

That surprised me because my godfather had relied on the rental income to help pay his bills. His earnings from his antique business were modest and unreliable, or so I had always been told. This news suggested his profits had grown recently. I could hear Donnie Angel's voice in my ears.

Tell me what you know about your godfather's business.

The house was a hoarder's dream. Stacks of magazines and newspapers were piled four feet high on the floor, and on every seat in the living room. I saw an old copy of *Look* magazine from 1961 with a picture of an African-American girl walking among four uniformed white men. He appeared to have kept every issue ever printed of the Ukrainian-language newspaper *Svoboda*.

The kitchen resembled a storage closet for tableware and cutlery. Boxes upon boxes occupied every nook and cranny. Dirty dishes and glasses filled the sink. The two bedrooms on the second floor were no different. Every horizontal surface was covered with pottery or knickknacks. Dust clung to everything but the most frequently used surfaces.

I had no idea if any of the items I was looking at were valuable, but the state-of-the-art televisions in the kitchen, sitting room, and bedroom appeared expensive, as did the big daddy Cadillac in the garage.

After touring the house, we returned to the kitchen. I stood staring at the door to the basement.

"It's creepy," Roxy said. "I keep thinking, this man is gone forever. I'll never see him again and that's so sad. He was a good guy. A good uncle. He never preached or asked me for anything. He was just nice. And then you walk around looking at the stuff wondering what it's all worth. Makes you feel cheap. You think somebody would actually pay for these old cutlery sets?"

"Yeah," I said, eyes still glued to the basement entrance, wondering how my godfather had died, whether someone had pushed him down the stairs or walked him to the bottom and smashed his head in there.

"Really? You really think they're worth something?"

"Yeah." I was barely listening to Roxy's questions. "It is creepy." I took a deep breath. "Let's go downstairs."

A steep descent of narrow steps greeted us. To make matters worse, the center of the steps was covered with carpet so worn and weathered it had turned slippery. I found myself grasping the side railing out of fear I would slip and tumble.

"I can't believe he didn't replace these stupid steps given he was afraid of stairs," I said.

Roxy slid effortlessly down the stairs like a ninja, unperturbed by their slope or width. "Tell me about it. He used to send me to get a bottle of wine when I visited. Said it saved him the risk of falling and breaking his neck. Drove me nuts. But he refused to fix them. That would have cost money, and he said he didn't need luxuries at this point in his life."

The new televisions and car suggested otherwise, but I kept my deductions to myself. I held my breath as I got to the bottom of the stairs, fearful I'd see visible signs of how my godfather had died, but there weren't any. No chalk outline or tape, no garish bloodstain on the gray concrete floor or the strip of blue carpet at the bottom.

"The cops don't outline bodies anymore," Roxy said, after I told her of my surprise. "Our neighbor is a state trooper. He said they rely on digital photography. There was a small bloodstain on the floor. I got most of it out with grout cleaner. I couldn't leave it there. It felt disrespectful. You can still see where his head landed if you look close."

I saw what she was talking about. It looked like a coffee stain that had been washed a hundred times and had almost come out. The rest of the basement contained shelving with twenty or so cases of wine, a work area with tools, and a mountain of giant plastic containers filled with expensive-looking Christmas decorations, all in original boxes. The presence of plastic and absence of larger antiques made sense given the basement flooded during heavy rains.

We found his inventory of furniture next door in his former rental home. I'm not knowledgeable on the subject, but there was a ton of old and simple-looking stuff. Tables, cabinets, and chests. The utilitarian style of most of the pieces made me think it was early American. That made more sense than people might have guessed. Ukrainian immigrants owed their lives to America, and I could see my godfather specializing in its vintage furniture. I also remembered reading somewhere that prices had gone through the roof, and given my godfather had possessed a savvy eye, that also made sense.

I didn't see anything in either house that suggested my godfather had been anyone other than a retired antique dealer who didn't like to part with his acquisitions, not even an old newspaper. After we finished looking through the second house, we returned to the main house to turn off the lights.

"I knew you wouldn't find anything," Roxy said.

"Give me a minute to go through his study one more time," I said.

Leather-bound books, Dutch-looking paintings, and old maps in equally ancient frames packed my godfather's office. I had to walk sideways to get behind his desk. I sat down in a high-backed green leather chair. A banker's lamp with ornate gold hardware occupied one corner. Across from it stood two pictures in elegant black lacquer frames with Asian lettering on the side. Roxy and her family posed in one picture. The other one was a photograph of my godfather and me when I was still a child.

The sight of myself knocked the wind right out of me and brought memories flooding back. He was holding me over his head in the picture. I remembered my father screaming at him to put me down, and my brother snapping the picture with my father's old box camera. To those who didn't know me, my expression would have conveyed giddy joy. After all, what kid wouldn't have enjoyed getting twirled around in the air? I wouldn't have. To those who knew me, they would have spied the lie in my eyes and realized I was putting on the face that was expected of me, all the while praying I would wake up the next day an adult and on my own.

But as Roxy said, my godfather meant well, and overhead twirling aside, his arrival had always been a welcome sight. My father and he were friends in Ukraine, and he was one of the few people with whom my father socialized. Once I got my job and moved to New York, I'd let our relationship drift. I hadn't even sent him a Christmas card in as long as I could remember. I was always too busy. I never made the time to tell him that I appreciated his kindness and that he was an important person to me. Now I had all the time in the world, but he was gone. There was nothing I could do to bring him back, but perhaps I could find out exactly how and why he'd left this world.

I forced myself to lift my eyes off the picture, and they fell upon another striking image hanging on the wall directly in front of me. It was a framed poster depicting two exhausted prisoners in gray uniforms wearing a yoke made out of an enormous block of lumber. One held a hammer in his hand, the other a sickle. A uniformed guard brandished a gun behind them, the Cyrillic version of USSR splattered on the concrete floor beneath their feet. The caption read *This Was Soviet Freedom*!

The poster reminded me of the ordeal my godfather had doubtlessly suffered to escape the Nazis and the Soviets and start a new life in America. I didn't know the details, but I was sure his early life had been harrowing, and now it appeared his end had been the same. He deserved better.

Roxy's voice carried from the kitchen. "You find anything in there?"

"No," I said, and began opening the drawers to his desk.

"I told you there was nothing there. You almost done? I'm going to call home and tell my kids I'm on the way."

"Yup."

The drawers contained the usual office supplies, a slide rule and a calculator, a flashlight and three vintage copies of *Playboy* that appeared to have been perused three or four million times each. My godfather didn't have a computer, which didn't surprise me. My mother didn't have one either, and many of the older generation wanted no part of the latest technology. What did surprise me was the complete absence of business records of any kind. I was about to ask Roxy if she knew who kept his books when I noticed a small pad of paper was elevated an inch off the desk.

I lifted the pad and found a small notebook bound with burgundy leather. The first few pages contained phone numbers. I scanned the names. They featured the requisite servicers any homeowner would need, such as plumber, electrician, and duct cleaner. *Duct cleaner?* The others were either friends or business associates, I guessed. Some of the names were in English, but most were in Ukrainian. I recognized some of the latter.

I heard the toilet flush so I stood up to leave. The rest of the notebook turned out to be a calendar. Various appointments appeared on the pages, most of them self-explanatory. Out of sheer logic, I turned to the date he'd died. While all the other entries in the calendar had been written in a normal font size, this one had been scrawled in blue ink with enormous letters that took up the entire page.

The entry consisted of two letters: "DP." The "P" had a little curl at the top. It was impossible to tell which language my godfather had been using because the letters were written in cursive. In printed form, the English letter "D" corresponds to the Ukrainian "Д." But in cursive form, the "D" looked the same in both languages. The letter "P" was the Ukrainian version of an "R." Hence, if the note was in English, it was DP. If it was written in Ukrainian, it was DR.

People maintained calendars to keep track of meetings, which consisted of people and places. Hence, DP was most likely a person or a place. I skimmed through the calendar. Appointments pertaining to the Ukrainian community were noted in Ukrainian, details pertaining to those outside the community were written in English. They appeared evenly split with an average of one or two per week. Each entry contained a person's name, and some contained a reference to a place, as well.

An eye doctor's appointment was noted in English with the

address and phone number beside it. As with other appointments in English, the doctor's name and location were spelled out in English. In cases where the entry had been written in Ukrainian, he wrote the destinations out in longhand—"National Home, Credit Union, Church Hall"—but abbreviated the names of the people with their initials. There were sufficient Ukrainian entries containing Cyrillic letters for me to deduce that he used initials when he had appointments with Ukrainains: "lunch with БШ," "bingo with ЮТ," "fix gutter for ЄЖ." That meant the letters DP were probably someone's Ukrainian initials, which corresponded to DR in English.

The rest of the notebook provided no insight into his business. In fact, the calendar appeared to consist of his personal appointments, as though he kept his professional ones somewhere else, if not entirely in his mind.

I heard Roxy's footsteps and slipped the notebook into my bag. I'm not one hundred percent sure why I didn't want to share my discovery with her. Perhaps I wanted to trust her, but couldn't afford to put my faith in anyone for the time being.

"You find anything?" she said.

"Nope," I said, brushing aside my pangs of guilt. "Do you know who did your uncle's books?"

"Some Uke accountant. I'll get you the name."

We walked outside. I shined the light and Roxy closed the door. As I drove away, I noticed that one of the Hondas was still there but the other one was gone. The ignition wasn't on, however, and there didn't appear to be anyone inside.

Roxy tried to talk me into staying the night with her but I refused. I told her I was going straight to a motel but it was a lie. I knew only one man in the Ukrainian community with the Ukrainian initials DP. His name was Danilo Rus and I'd been in his home before.

He was my former father-in-law.

He was Roxy's father.

CHAPTER 13

THE HOUSE SMELLED OF MOTHBALLS AND ECHOED WITH THE sound of a tragic Ukrainian ballad, a powerful soprano wailing with unrelenting misery about her son's death in an ancient war with the Tatars. Darwin's law had prevailed after centuries of battles for the breadbasket of Europe: no one could cry like a Uke. We were the world heavyweight champions of mourning.

When I knocked, my former father-in-law opened the door and stood there mute, glaring at me, cane in hand. I refused to go away, so he moved aside to let me in. He stayed mum and kept his eyes on me as I passed him.

A solitary Tiffany desk lamp with an amber stained glass shade provided barely enough light in the living room to conduct a séance. A portrait of a baby-faced JFK hung on the center of the main wall, draped in black velvet. A framed picture of a battle-worn JFK rested on a dusty old piano, with the proclamation of a day of mourning from the Connecticut Legislature framed beside it. Both pictures looked as though they hadn't been touched for fifty years. The piano contained a collection of family photos. Conspicuous in its absence was any sign of me in any of the pictures. Also conspicuous was the second swath of black velvet resting atop a picture of Rus's son—my former husband. The photo showed him at his most professorial and dapper, speaking from a lectern with passion etched in his face. It had been taken the day he'd died fifteen months ago.

Parkinson's had gripped Rus since I'd last seen him. His tottering and twitching would have elicited nothing but empathy had he been someone else. But he wasn't someone else. He was the father-in-law who'd advised his son not to marry an unremarkable-looking girl who wasn't interested in homemaking. That only idiots and men who'd impregnated their girlfriends compromised at the altar.

We spoke Ukrainian. First-generation kids with any sliver of language skills spoke Ukrainian with their elders. It was better to mix in an English word when one's vocabulary fell short than to avoid Ukrainian altogether. The latter was an exercise in humiliation and embarrassment, and an admission that one had drifted so far from home that she couldn't remember the language of her youth.

"I thought we'd had our final words at his funeral," he said, after turning down the stereo. "When I told you I never wanted to see you again for the rest of my life. Why are you here? Why are you tempting me?"

I wasn't sure exactly what he meant when he said I was tempting him, but I knew he blamed me for his son's death. After all, my former husband had crashed his car while doing a special favor for me. Rus had blamed me for every moment of unhappiness in his son's life. There was no reason for his death to have been any different. We'd never talked about it, primarily because we'd never had a private conversation about anything.

"This will be quick," I said. "Trust me. I don't want to be here any more than you want me here. But I need to ask you a few questions."

"Questions?" He tried to laugh as though it were an absurd proposition but burst into a fit of coughing instead.

I waited for him to regain his breath.

"Questions about my godfather," I said. "About your brother."

"I just buried him. And now you're coming around asking questions? Who are you to ask any questions about him? Do you hear what I'm asking you? Who are *you*?"

"Did you have an appointment to meet with him on the day he died?"

Rus didn't answer. Instead, he locked eyes with me and ground his lips in a circle as though he was cranking up his hatred for me to a higher level.

"My son was a good boy," he said.

Normally I would have let the remark slide, waited a moment, and repeated my question. After all, my one and only goal was to get the answers I needed and leave. *Wasn't it?*

"No, he was not a good boy. Your son was a brilliant man. A brilliant professor of religion at Yale University. But everything had to be his way, and when that became impossible, he became impossible. No. He most definitely was not a good boy."

Rus's right palm crushed my cheek.

I could have stopped him. I could have blocked it with my arm. But I didn't. There's an unwritten rule in Ukrainian society that you never, ever, under any circumstances raise your hand to an elder. Even if you want to shake hands with someone to say hello, you wait for the older person to extend his hand first.

Had I reverted to the instincts my parents had honed, or did I actually want to get hit? Had I wanted to become a victim so I could prove to myself that I was a better person than my father-in-law? Whatever my reason for standing there and taking his blow, I couldn't have hated myself any more at that moment. I could feel myself shaking, my thoughts running away from me, as happened in those rare instances when I lost control.

My eyes watered and my nose stung. An acrid taste of blood and onions filled my mouth.

I inhaled my tears. "Like son, like father," I said.

I curled my hands into fists. No, I wasn't a cop, a former soldier, or a trained fighter, but I didn't care. Nor did it matter to me that he was an ailing old man, my elder, and my former father-in-law. If he raised his hand to me again I was going to hit him. The only question was whether I would have enough self-control to stop pummeling him once I started. I honestly wasn't sure.

Disdain shone in his face. His hand shook. He started to raise it again.

"Good," I said, barely recognizing my voice, which made me sound like someone who needed an exorcism. "Do it."

I must have looked the part, too, because he hesitated. His eyes fell to my fists. After a few more seconds of teeth grinding, he returned his hands to his side.

"He was a terrible husband but I stayed with him. I never threatened to leave. I never uttered the word 'divorce.' And I was prepared to stay with him the rest of my life no matter what it cost me. *Because I'm Ukrainian Catholic.* Because that's what I said I'd do when we took our vows."

"He'd be alive if he hadn't married you."

"Don't be so sure. Another woman in my shoes . . . Like one of those graduate students he slept with. I don't know what one of them would have done. He's gone and I'm sorry. I cried at his funeral. But it's not my fault. You want to think otherwise? That's your business. But don't put your own guilt on me. I'm not interested."

My former father-in-law had dropped his cane before hitting me. I picked it up and gave it back to him. He shuffled toward his recliner and sat down. Reached over and drained the rest of the amber liquid in his tumbler.

"Maybe if you'd stood up to him like that, things would have been better," he said, staring into space.

That was a new one. Now I could add timidity to my list of spousal flaws. It was the perfect counterpart to one of my other deficiencies, namely my stubborn insistence on having a career. They pretty much covered the gamut of personalities. On the surface, this latest remark left no doubt that I was and always would be a loser in his eyes. And yet, there was something forgiving in his tone. At a minimum, he was implying his son had issues. Otherwise, he wouldn't have suggested his wife should have stood up to him.

I decided to seize the moment and return to my original agenda. I sat down on the couch across from him. When interviewing company executives, it's sometimes useful to test their mettle with a shocking question, rather than slowly leading into it. The current conditions were ripe for such a strategy.

"Do you think your brother's death was an accident?"

Rus's head snapped upward. His eyes stretched wide momentarily before he could control his expression. "The police said it was an accident. Did they say they were wrong?"

"He was afraid of stairs. He never went down to the basement at night, did he?"

"Do you know something I don't?"

"If it was raining, and he knew the basement floor and the last couple of stairs would be wet, why would he have gone down there?"

Rus slammed his fist on his armrest. "Have the police told you something? Why would they tell you and not me?"

"You're acting as though you wouldn't be surprised if they had told me they'd made a mistake."

"Did they? Did they admit they were wrong? Do they know who killed him?"

"Then you admit you think it wasn't an accident, and that he was murdered."

"Of course he was murdered! He never went down the stairs at night. Never!"

"Hallelujah. We agree on something."

"How do you know this? Did the police—"

I stood up. "No. I haven't talked to the police. It's just my theory, and I'm pleased you agree. No one knew him better than you. And in answer to your next question, I have my own reasons for caring, not the least of which is that I loved my godfather, and I'm angry someone took him away before I could tell him that. Now, my last question is my first question, and it's very important. Did you have an appointment to see him on the day he died?"

He threw his hands up in the air. "Appointment? What appointment? He was my brother. We didn't make appointments. If I needed to see him, I picked up the phone and called. If he needed to see me, he showed up at my doorstep. He didn't need to call ahead, like some other people would, if they had manners."

"How can you possibly expect me to have manners when I'm such a hideous person to start with? So you didn't have an appointment."

He answered me with such venom I was afraid he might try to bury his cane in my eye. "No. I had no appointment."

"That's strange because I found the initials DP in his calendar for that day. In big letters. I don't know of any other Ukrainians in the community with those initials, do you?"

He sneered as he sat thinking about it. He confirmed my suspicions by saying nothing. Then his eyes brightened as though something had occurred to him. "How do you know it wasn't written in English? How do you know the appointment wasn't with an American?"

"I don't know. There was no one with the initials DP in his address book—"

"For that matter," Rus said, "how do you know it was a person at all?"

"Are you saying it's something else?"

Rus seemed to enjoy my uncertainty. He elevated his chin and chuckled. Curled his lips into a quizzical expression and shrugged. "Who knows? Maybe it was a pet. A dog. Or maybe a cat. Or maybe it was a ghost. A ghost from the past."

When I frowned, he laughed even harder. I stood there for a few seconds and waited for his laughter to subside. "Are you going to tell me what you mean by that?"

"I thought you were a mathematician. I thought you were ingenious. You can't figure this out on your own?"

I pressed him to reveal what he thought he knew but he wouldn't say anything more. I tried a soft tone, and then a harsher one. Nothing worked. I tried not to lead him with my suspicion about his deduction but when I failed with my general queries I gave it a try.

"You think DP is a place, not a person?" I said.

He smirked with the kind of intellectual arrogance befitting his deceased son. The way he arched his neck and wrinkled his nose left no doubt that he was certain he understood the meaning of DP.

"It's a person and a place," he said. "You can't figure it out on your own, go ask your mother. Maybe she can help you."

I marched toward the door and opened it to leave. Then I heard Rus's voice behind me.

"When was the last time you went to see him? Have you even been there once during the last year?"

I didn't answer. Instead I continued on my way out.

He hurled a few obscenities at my back. This was becoming a habit, I realized, people swearing at me as I left their homes. *On the surface, a potential cause for concern, but wasn't therapy supposed to be this way? Didn't pain precede healing?*

I slammed the door shut behind me. More therapy. A wave of relief washed over me as soon as it clicked shut. I'd survived and hadn't killed him, either. I wasn't sure if I'd made any progress but the latter two achievements were minor causes for celebration.

I drove eight miles to the bedroom community of Rocky Hill and checked into a Super 8 motel. It was cheap, well-lit, close to the highway, and had a good rating online.

The next morning I ate a short stack of pancakes at the Town Line Diner for breakfast. Then I made a trip across the Connecticut River to the suburb of Hebron to visit my deceased husband's grave. Rus was right. His son had been my husband. He may have been a terrible one but I'd promised before God to honor him for the rest of my life, and this former altar girl took her vows seriously. Afterward, I drove back to Rocky Hill to visit the person who'd killed him.

I drove to see my mother.

CHAPTER 14

I don't have many vivid memories from childhood. At least not many pleasant ones. That's not to say I was beaten constantly or struggled to survive. No. My parents made sure there was food on the table and clothes in our closet. My brother and I never suffered for anything other than calm. We were nervous all the time. In fact, our nerves remained on alert for the first eighteen years of our lives until each of us left for college. We simply never knew when our father would explode.

I do recall, however, one particular moment of joy. It was a moment of unconditional release and surrender. Fear and anxiety left me. Perhaps the constant trauma magnified its emotional resonance. Maybe that was a common experience for most kids. But to me it was anything but normal.

I was probably five or six years old and I hadn't learned to swim yet. My father ordered me to take my inflated swimming ring and follow him into deep water, where he would take it away from me and force me to swim back alone. I was so afraid I would drown, I looked at my mother and begged her to let me stay ashore with her. She scolded my father and told him to leave me alone. Then she picked me up at the ocean's edge and held me close to her breast. I could still feel her salty kiss on my forehead and the moisture of her bathing suit as she told me I didn't have to go, that she would take care of me. And as the waves crashed ashore and spilled water onto my legs, I hung onto her and believed that at least one person on Earth loved me and would protect me until the day that I died.

Now I stood at the door to her corner condominium unit in Rocky Hill, pulse racing, wondering if she would even let me in her house. The thought of her slamming the door in my face made my stomach turn, even more so than the thought of having to talk to her at all. There are few things worse in life than holding hate in one's heart for a parent, except the knowledge that the feeling is mutual.

The curtain in the front window moved. I couldn't see anything through the tinted glass. Then I heard the sound of the chain sliding open and the door swung open.

She was a shockingly fit woman with striking gray hair, so streamlined from head to toe that she wouldn't have needed the proverbial broom to take flight. The skin on her face glistened and belied her age. She didn't say anything. She simply stared at me with her cold, disapproving eyes. Someone needed to say something. I decided I was the visitor, so the obligation fell to me.

I nodded at the beaten and worn hiking boots standing at attention beside the door.

"What's with Marko's shoes?"

She frowned as though I were an idiot for having to ask. "When you're a woman living alone you can't take any chances. If a burglar sees those shoes, he'll assume there's a man inside and he'll go away. Unless the burglar knows my son and daughter. Then he'll waltz right in, rob me, and kill me because he'll know that neither of them stuck around to take care of me."

She stepped aside to let me in. My spirits soared. If I was entering her house, there was a chance for reconciliation. This was familial hate as I knew it. Beneath it lay a desperate desire for healing and the inner peace that had evaded me my entire life, which made the heartbreak all the more excruciating.

I followed her through the house. As we passed the dining room, I glanced at the corner étagère that contained my mother's prize possession, a jewelry box inlaid with rubies and emeralds. Her grandfather had been a craftsman commissioned by Czar Alexander III to produce such treasures. It was the only masterpiece that had stayed in the family and made it to America.

We entered the kitchen. The sweet smell of black cherries wafted into my nostrils. A rolling pin and cookie cutter rested on a cutting board covered with flour. Steam billowed from a huge silver pot on her stove. I knew by the smell and the utensils that my mother was making Ukrainian dumplings called *varenyky*. This particular batch would be stuffed with black cherries and served with melted cane sugar and sour cream. One of my childhood favorites. Mercy.

A mother never forgets her child's weakness. I spied her checking out my figure.

"You hungry?" she said.

Another mother might have meant it in a caring way. But I knew that cajoling me into leaving a pound heavier would provide her with a sick form of satisfaction. Some mothers try to help their daughters become as beautiful as possible, while others reach a point where they prefer to compete with them.

Another daughter might have cared, but she would have never tried my mother's black cherry *varenyky*. This is one of the benefits of aging. One can humble oneself when necessary to get the best out of life.

"Yes," I said. "I'd love a couple. So thoughtful of you to make these for me." Of course she hadn't made them for me. Even if she'd known I was visiting, she wouldn't have cooked for me.

My mother chuckled. "You're so lucky I'm your mother. How many girls have such a good sense of humor? Obviously you got it from me. Your father's idea of a joke was staring at the balance in his savings account. Sit down and let me fatten you up. You're too thin."

Her true motive, as suspected. What a surprise. "I did get my sense of humor from you, didn't I?"

I sat down at the square kitchen table. My knees shook. So far so good but how would we get through the visit without one of us offending the other? She spooned four *varenyky* onto a plate and added sugar and sour cream. Poured two cups of tea and took the seat beside me.

"I left you a voice mail," I said. "You didn't return my phone call."

"Why should I? You didn't talk to me at your godfather's funeral, or at the reception."

"I walked up to you but you turned your back on me."

"That's a lie."

"Oh, please, Mama." I wasn't making it up. She was always trying to pull my chain to make me feel miserable. In her world, guilt inspired remorse. Contrition was measured in dollars.

She stared ahead. "All those people watching and you didn't even sit with your mother. You should be ashamed of yourself."

"We should all be ashamed of ourselves."

"So what's changed to make you call and show up at my house unannounced? Are you making so much money the bottom of your mattress is stuffed full? I have room under mine, you know."

Love had been conditional in our house. Growing up it was based on scholastic achievement. Ever since I got a job, it was based on money.

"Really?" I said. "I would have guessed it would be stuffed by now with gifts from your many suitors."

My mother was the black widow in the Uke community. Every widower and lifelong bachelor wanted to taste her cooking. I knew she'd made the *varenyky* for one of them. Easter Sunday was in two days. No self-respecting Ukrainian woman made *varenyky* during Lent, which meant the man in question had to be rich.

"There's money and there's New York money," she said. "You'd think if my daughter had left me for a fancy job she would have bought me a Lexus by now. Especially given she's driving a Porsche."

It was a twelve-year-old car I'd bought six years ago with my first bonus. Other than my rapidly depleting savings and my paltry retirement account, it was the only hard asset I owned. A salary and bonus of a hundred thousand dollars doesn't amount to much in New York City, where the marginal tax rate is north of fifty percent and rents are stratospheric. But there was no telling my mother any of that. The fact I'd given her the down payment on her condo didn't matter, either. Her philosophy revolved around a single question: What have you done for me lately?

"As soon as I can afford to buy you a car, Mama, you'll be the first to know."

"I won't hold my breath."

I dug into the *varenyky* and momentarily forgot my agenda. Black cherries spilled open in my mouth. The juice blended with sugar while the tender dough melted with sour cream. The flavors exploded on my tongue. A moan escaped my lips. I brought my hand up quickly to cover it, but I was too late. When I glanced at my mother, I noted a curl of satisfaction on her lips. Whether she was happy I was consuming calories or deriving a cook's pleasure, I wasn't sure.

"Tell me why you're here," my mother said. "Something's happened. You need something from me. I only hear from my children when something terrible has happened. What is it?"

I explained my suspicions about my godfather's death and my visit to his house with Roxy. I had no choice. The minute I asked her for help with the initials, she would ask why. I decided I was better off being up-front and honest. I didn't mention my incident with Donnie Angel at all. If I had, she would have spent the next ten minutes screaming at me for being a fool and blamed my kidnapping on my carelessness.

Her expression changed from one of surprise to disgust as I told her my story.

"Did you just make all this garbage up to irritate me," she said, "or are you serious?"

I felt the heat rise to my face. "I'm serious. Of course I'm serious. When have you known me not to be serious?"

"Who do you think you are? Angie Dickinson?"

"Who?"

"Angie Dickinson. The actress. She was *Police Woman*. Did you go to police school or did you go to business school?"

"Neither, actually—"

"Don't get wise with me, child. This is the stupidest thing I've ever heard. My daughter, a financial executive in New York City, wasting her vacation time solving a crime that doesn't even exist."

"You think he fell down the stairs?"

"You are doing this on your vacation, right?"

"Of course. Answer my question."

"The police said he fell down the stairs. What could you possibly know that they don't know?"

"The same thing you do. That my godfather had a fear of stairs and never, ever would have gone down to the basement on a rainy night."

"Let me tell you something about men, child. You give a man enough wine and he'll climb the roof of his house and dance naked under the antennas during a thunderstorm. Especially that homemade wine your godfather used to make. Why are you doing this? Do you still feel guilty about your husband's death? Are you trying to punish yourself for some reason?"

In fact, she should have felt guilty about his death. She was the one who'd called me in Manhattan the day of his death sounding frantic. One of her suitors had gotten drunk and was about to rape her. Help me, she pleaded. Don't call the police, I don't want to be fodder for community gossip. And I don't want to get this man in real trouble, she said. My former husband had just finished giving a lecture at Trinity College in Hartford. By then we were practically living separate lives, but he still had a sliver of decency about him so he took off to Rocky Hill right away at my request. He probably never saw the SUV that hit him head-on because its headlights weren't working. Nor did he live long enough to find out my mother's alleged assailant had left by then. The truth was that I was never convinced she was even in trouble that night. In my heart, I was certain she simply wanted to cause a commotion. As always, she just wanted attention.

"Why would I feel guilty about my husband's death? I'm not the one who cried for help."

My mother appeared incredulous. "I wouldn't have had to call him if you were living near me, like a caring daughter should, would I? Obviously you must blame yourself. Obviously he's dead today because of you."

I wanted to strangle her. I wanted to go to her garage, get a shovel, come back in the house, and tell her I was ready to bury her if she would just please die. I couldn't have imagined revealing the depth of my rage to anyone, and the mere thought of it inspired a new level of self-loathing. But that was the truth.

Instead of confronting her and pursuing what would undoubtedly turn out to be an illogical argument, however, I impressed myself. I stayed on point.

"Do you know anyone in the community with the initials DP?"

"What's that got to do with anything?"

I explained the entry in my godfather's calendar. At first her frown deepened with disapproval. I got the sense she thought there was something wrong with me if I was looking up entries in my deceased godfather's address book. But she'd always liked crossword puzzles, and her expression gradually morphed into one of deep concentration.

Her eyes came alive. She looked at me and shrugged. "It's obvious, but it's not what you think."

I moved forward in my seat. "It's not?"

"No. It's not the Ukrainian DP. It's the English DP."

"You know someone with those initials? Someone he was close to?"

"Yes."

"Who?"

"Dolly Parton."

"Oh, for God's sake, Mama . . ."

"He was obsessed with her. And the bigger her boobs got, the more he obsessed over her. Men are babies. Give them a good meal and show them a big tit and they'll do anything for you." She arched her back and thrust her cleavage in my direction. "You show me a so-called leg man and I'll show you a liar. You want seconds?"

No visions of a shovel in my hand this time. Just the sight of her condo complex in my rearview mirror. I gave my mother a stern look.

"The only Ukrainian I know with those initials is that blowhard former father-in-law of yours," she said. "If there were any justice in the world, he would have died at a young age instead of your father."

"That's funny," I said.

"What's funny about that?"

"Nothing. What's funny is that he said those initials might not belong to a person." I paused. My mother's eyes scrunched together as though the words had struck a chord. "He said they might belong to a ghost or something like that. And that I should ask you about them."

"He said that? That you should ask me about it?"

"What could he have meant?"

My mother thought about it some more. I could tell by the light in her eyes and the firmness of her posture that she had a notion of what Rus might have meant.

"You know something," I said.

She shrugged. "Maybe. Maybe not."

"Would you care to share it, please?"

"That depends." My mother leveled her chin at me. "What's in it for me?"

Twenty years ago her words would have knocked the wind out of me. My mother, the woman who'd protected me as best as she could, from the depth of the ocean and my father's rage, demanding payment for answering a simple question? Unimaginable. Today I simply reached for my wallet.

"All I have on me is forty-eight dollars," I said.

"I'll take a check."

"No, you won't."

I offered her two twenties and eight crumpled singles. She snatched them, folded the bills in half and stuffed them into a pocket, all in one motion.

"I really think he was writing in English," she said.

"Why do you say that?" "A DP was a Displaced Person. A refugee from Eastern Europe who ended up in Western Europe after World War II. You've heard the term."

It was true. I'd heard my parents mention it once or twice when I was a girl but it hadn't stuck in my memory. In truth, I didn't know much about my parents' lives before they immigrated to America. They were never keen on sharing the details. I had been consumed with making good enough grades to get out of town, make my own money, and cease being dependent on them.

"I was a DP," my mother said. "Your father was a DP. Your godfather was a DP, too. Most of the old-timers in the community were DPs. We lived in DP camps in Germany, France, and Austria before we came to this country. We were scattered all over the place."

"So if he had the letters DP in his appointment book—"

"It could be anyone. Most likely someone he was in camp with. A friend."

"Why do you say that?"

"Who else would you call DP? Someone who shared the experience with you. And let me tell you, it wasn't a compliment to be called a DP."

"Why not?"

My mother sighed. Her self-confidence seemed to leave her with her exhalation. Her eyes fell to the table and her voice softened.

"The world hated us."

That was the substance of what I got out of her. I followed up with a few questions about DP camps, but she clammed up and concocted some excuse about needing to do her calisthenics before one of her beaus picked her up for an early lunch. After I told her I was leaving, I loitered around the table for a few seconds to make sure she wasn't going to offer me a hug. When she took my plate and turned her back on me to head toward the dishwasher, I thanked her for her hospitality and left.

"Next time bring your checkbook," she said. "Save the crumpled singles for your brother's strip joint."

I climbed in my car, slammed the door shut, and made the tires squeal. My mother's condo was located on a road with a blind brow that led to a treacherous "S" turn. As the Porsche slithered through it, I tried not to look at the giant sycamore at the apex of the bend, where bouquets of flowers popped up now and then. People had left flowers for drunk drivers and reckless teenagers, and also a professor from Yale. I crossed myself three times, a habit from my days as an altar girl, and prayed my dead husband had successfully negotiated purgatory and had been welcomed through the pearly gates. Yeah, he was a bastard, but I held grudges against only the living. Praying and contemplating forgiveness also tended to calm me down, and by the time I'd negotiated the side streets I was focused on my mission once again.

I zipped onto I-91 headed east toward my brother's house in Willimantic. As I powered onto the entrance ramp, I spied a white compact car following me. A bend in the on-ramp offered me a sideways view of the car. It was low-slung with tinted windows, remarkably similar to the two cars that had been parked around the corner from my godfather's house last night.

But the car merged slowly into the right lane as I accelerated into the fast lane and it disappeared behind me. I tried to chalk my concern up to paranoia, but I couldn't kid myself. Donnie Angel was out there, somewhere. In truth, I was surprised he hadn't come after me yet. There was information in his absence, as though he wanted me to keep doing what I was doing.

Whenever our paths did cross again, one thing was certain. No loving mother was going to pick me up and save me from the undercurrent of the ocean.

I was on my own.

CHAPTER 15

WATER. SHE NEEDED WATER.

During the early afternoon of the second day of her survival test, Nadia ate half of her buckwheat bread and washed it down with half of her jar of honey. It took all her discipline not to finish the bread and the honey because she felt as though she was starving. Her body was sending her a signal that she needed nutrition, but she ignored it. She could deal with the hunger. Water was the key to her survival.

The one thing she knew not to do was drink from the stream. One of the boys had done that last summer camp and ended up in the hospital with a Cryptosporidium parasite and diarrhea for a week. Nadia could name fifteen parasites that lurked on the Appalachian Trail. She'd memorized them from a guidebook she'd studied as soon as she learned she was going to try to pass the survival test.

After lunch, Nadia trudged toward the stream to keep her mind occupied. Her legs wobbled a bit and she got winded much faster than usual. But the challenge of surviving a night without fire consumed her and she couldn't stand the thought of sitting around thinking about what awaited her. It wasn't the realization that she was surrounded by wild animals that scared her. She was an animal, too, and even though she was still a kid she was bigger than most of them. And she had a knife.

No, it was the uncertainty that scared her. The darkness, the noises, the openness of her camp. A fire offered not only heat and light, it issued a warning to every living thing in the vicinity. It did so not only with its flames, but with its spitting and cracking noises. Nadia had once seen a sign hanging on the shed of a house near the Uke campground in Colebrook. It said, "Fuck the dog, beware of owner." That's what the roar of a blazing fire told the animals. "Forget the fire, beware of the girl who built it."

Nadia took a circuitous route toward the stream to waste some time and see something new. In doing so, she stumbled upon a spectacular marble face. It formed an "L" on the ridge above the water. She knelt down beside the marble and swept a layer of limestone off the rock to reveal rich swirls of bronze and sapphire. When she nestled into their confines, Nadia felt like a princess in one of the corny Egyptian movies her mother liked to watch.

She closed her eyes and tilted her head toward the sky. The sun soaked her face like warm syrup. Her exhausted body absorbed the heat, and in less than a minute, she drifted to the border of consciousness. It was a delicious place, better than sleep itself.

A honk startled her. Nadia snapped upright. Scanned the horizon. A heron swooped down in slow motion from its perch on a limb across the stream and spread its wings six feet wide. As it dove, the bird's blue-gray plumes cast a dark shadow on the water. The heron landed on a rock midstream and snatched a fish from the water with its yellow bill, barely causing a ripple. It tossed the fish in the air, uncurled its "S"-shaped neck, lunged forward, and swallowed its prey midair. Batted its wings three times and soared over the trees out of sight.

Awesome.

Mrs. Chimchak had taught Nadia that the forest was no different from the city. There were two types of creatures in both places. The hunter and the hunted. Which one did she want to be?

Maybe the other kids in her neighborhood in Hartford were tough when they were in groups. Maybe they tossed bubble gum in her hair and chanted "lesbian" when she walked by because there were usually three or four of them and she was alone. Maybe they wouldn't be so strong out here, alone in the wilderness, where you had to be a hunter to survive.

An hour later, Nadia turned to head back to camp. The late morning sun shone on four bumblebees buzzing around a cluster of creeping bellflower, their open purple blossoms still wet with dew. Something about the scene struck a chord somewhere, but Nadia couldn't figure it out so she moved on.

A minute later, a wind shook a grove of beech trees and sent a shower of nuts sprinkling to the ground. One of the nuts hit Nadia in the head. She picked it up. It was as green as the skin of a lime, and totally useless. Beech nuts could be ground into soup with boiled water but they'd probably make her sick if she chewed on them raw.

The nut glistened with moisture, like the inside of the bellflower. As Nadia's fingers absorbed the wetness it dawned on her: there was water for the taking every night. Just as the bees could extract pollen from a plant, she could pull it from the ground by collecting dew.

When she returned to camp, Nadia used a sharp rock and her bare hands to dig a ditch big enough to fit the bowl from her mess kit. She pounded away at the rocky soil for more than an hour, pausing to rest every few minutes. When she was done, Nadia secured a plastic bag over the bowl with twine, poked a tiny hole in its center, and placed it in the ditch. She dropped a pebble on top so the plastic fell inside in a concave fashion. That would force the dew to stream down into the bowl.

When darkness fell, she jumped into her lean-to and crawled inside her sleeping bag. Excitement over the prospect of having water in the morning yielded to her current reality. Without the crackling sounds and blistering flames to distract her, each rustle of leaves and chirp of a cricket struck fear in her heart. How would she ever fall asleep?

She underestimated her fatigue, though, and after fifteen restless minutes she passed out.

A hoot from an owl roused her from her sleep. A flash of light pierced the darkness outside her lean-to. A second one followed quickly, and a third. After a pause, three more flashes of light followed, each of them longer than the first three.

Nadia sat up.

Five seconds later the flashes started again. Nadia rubbed her eyes. Three short followed by three long. Pause. Three more short followed by three long.

Morse code.

The SOS signal.

Someone was in trouble. Someone needed her help.

The flashes of light grew brighter as the person approached. The footsteps came rapidly.

Nadia had stored the whistle her father had given her in her knapsack. She remembered her brother getting in trouble for blowing it and vetoed the idea. Whistles were for losers.

Instead, she retrieved her knife from her lean-to and unsheathed it. Placed her thumb on top of the handle and turned the edge facing upward.

Forward grip, edge up. Forward grip for maximum reach. Edge up for finesse and flexibility.

Nadia slid behind the largest tree on the periphery of her camp, its trunk wide enough to hide her entire body, and waited for the source of the SOS to reveal itself.

CHAPTER 16

THE NEON SIGN ON THE OUTSIDE FLASHED "BRASILIA," AND the New Hampshire license plate nailed to a wall on the inside foyer read "ASS4U." My brother had built custom motorcycles for twenty-one years until Hartford real estate took a dive and never fully recovered. I'd heard he'd bought a bar but this was my first visit. It was located in a seedy section of Willimantic on the outskirts of the University of Connecticut, twenty-five miles east of Hartford. When I first learned Marko had bought a bar, I expected it to be a bare-bones watering hole consistent with his biker sensibilities. But I wasn't prepared for a strip joint. It's hard for a woman to imagine her brother making a living by serving up naked portions of any kind of ass to anybody.

Brasilia reminded me more of a bar in Deadwood than a beach in Rio, and the woman on stage looked more like a refugee from Woodstock than the girl from Ipanema. A wave of nausea washed over me while she gyrated to Joe Cocker singing God lift us up where we belong. As she arched her skinny-fat hips toward her sole pair of customers, the older one said to the younger one, "Pay attention, son. This is a preview of hell."

My apprehension about seeing Marko for the first time in six years exceeded any anxiety I'd experienced visiting my mother.

In her case, I took some comfort in my sense of self-righteousness that she was a worse mother than I was a daughter. In his case, I could find no such solace. In his eyes, I'd become the opposite of the little sister he'd loved as a child. He considered me trash and he'd disowned me, and the sad thing was I didn't disagree with his decision. I thought he was fully justified in doing so because I'd done something unforgivable.

The place was cavernous, with two bruised and battered wooden bars and a dance floor big enough for a Hells Angels' convention. It was 2:30 in the afternoon, which explained why there were only twelve losers in the entire place, human stools with shot-glass hands and thirsty stares. I pulled my jacket tight and lowered my head as their cumulative eyes fell upon me. I guessed that was to be expected in a strip club, but I still hated them for it, almost as much as I hated myself for not looking as good as I wished I did.

A waitress whose figure could have turned ketchup into Tabasco told me Marko was in the back. I found him and his wine barrel of a body aging in his office, nursing two bottles of Mickey's Big Mouth beer and watching a Red Sox game on a big old square TV. As a young man, he'd seduced women on sight. Now he looked like a cautionary tale to high school heroes who lived in the past, except he'd never even been all that.

He did a double take when he first saw me. I held my breath as I sought evidence of residual affection: a raised eyebrow, a curl of the lip. A few choice Ukrainian obscenities would have sufficed. After all, why swear at your sister if she doesn't matter to you? But he bestowed no such gifts upon me, the undeserving. Instead, he inflated his cheeks with apathy.

He looked out the window at the parking lot as though it were a portal back in time. "What do *you* want?"

He asked the question as though I were the last person on Earth he expected to see, and that my arrival necessarily meant I needed something from him, which of course, it did.

I could barely look at him. Sadness over his physical deterioration and guilt over our recent past left me in a constant state of melancholy whenever I thought of him, let alone was in his presence. If I tried to ease into the conversation, we might never get started. I couldn't even imagine him pretending to have small talk with me. To get his cooperation, I had no choice but to provoke him.

"I saw Donnie Angel the other day," I said.

It was a cheap shot of a greeting, and I almost felt guilty about it. Marko's head turned on a swivel. His expression didn't betray his emotion, but the turn of his neck made my heart sing. No matter how much he hated me, the thought of me anywhere near Donnie still infuriated him. He'd left the house by the time the Grantmoor incident took place, but I'm sure my mother had told him about it, and I wouldn't have been surprised if he'd confronted Donnie and threatened him without telling me anything about it.

"Why are you going anywhere near that psychopath?"

"It wasn't planned. Our circumstances collided in New York."

"Do yourself a favor. Next time collide with someone else."

"Why?"

It was pathetic, I knew, trying to provoke him into another display of affection, but I couldn't help myself. Marko realized it immediately. He contemplated saying something—probably a scolding for being so obvious in my search for a kind word—but turned to look out the window instead.

"Do you know anything specifically about what he does for a living?" I said.

"Sure. He's on staff at Hartford Hospital on the cutting edge of medical research. Is that why you're here? To talk about Donnie Angel?" He added a sarcastic ring to his pronunciation of the name.

"I saw Mama this morning."

He barked a laugh. "Good for you, Saint Nadia. What are you doing, some sort of lost-cause tour?"

"Thought I'd swing by and see your place."

"You are doing a lost-cause tour. Lucky me."

"What's with the name? Brasilia? I didn't hear any Portuguese out there."

He rolled his eyes as though the answer were obvious. "It sells. You take any product, mix in the Brazilian theme, and men eat that shit up. Now answer the question. Why are you here?"

I walked farther into his office, lifted a stack of fliers promoting some XXX-rated movie star's appearance at the club, and sat down. He grimaced as I approached, no doubt wishing I'd jumped out the window rather than made myself at home.

"You weren't at my godfather's funeral," I said. "Or the *panakhyda*, or the reception."

"Very observant."

"Why not?"

"Because your godfather was an asshole."

His characterization shocked me. I didn't remember him holding any animosity toward my godfather growing up. If anything, they'd been closer than Marko and my father, not that this was saying much. My godfather's presence seemed to mollify my father, which was reason enough for all of us to love him. But my godfather also had taken a special interest in Marko, buying him baseball cards, offering him a sip of Narragansett when my father wasn't looking, and making fun of his sideburns when he came back from a PLAST camp looking like Elvis.

"Why would you say something like that?" I said.

He chugged from one of the beer bottles. My eyes went to the grotesque middle finger of his right hand. It looked as though it had fallen off and had been reattached by a sleepy child. The digit protruded at an odd angle from the hand. He appeared to have two knuckles on that finger instead of one, and they both pointed sideways. I suppressed the gut-wrenching memory it summoned and tore my eyes away. That finger defined our childhood, the effect of our parents' childhoods on them, and always left me wondering what it would have been like to have had a normal American upbringing.

Marko put the bottle back down and wiped his lips with his sleeve. "Because it's true. Your godfather was not a good guy. But I believe in letting the dead rest, so let's not talk about him anymore. Let's talk about what you want so you can get out of here and leave me alone."

"No. You can't make a statement like that and not back it up. We will discuss it some more."

He bored into me with a toxic gaze that reminded me that no one told him what to do, let alone his no-good, ungrateful, bitch sister.

"Please," I said. "He's the reason I'm here. The faster we talk about him, the faster I'll leave you alone."

"You do know how to bribe a guy. Like I said, the guy was an asshole. Pick your poison. For one thing, he tried to get with Mama after our father died."

The image of my godfather making a pass at my mother flitted through my mind. It was grotesque. He was like a brother to her, or so I'd thought. "What?"

Marko nodded firmly.

I laughed. It was an uneasy nervous laugh, the kind that escapes your lips when the foundation of your life teeters and you question everything you've ever believed. "She told you that?"

"Not only did she tell me that, your godfather confirmed it when I had a discussion with him about it."

Another vision flashed before my eyes. This time it was Marko pushing my godfather down the stairs. But that was ridiculous. If Marko had wanted to intervene, a few choice words would have delivered the message to stay away. There would have been no need for violence.

"He tried to romance her," Marko said. "He took her out for the best veal on Franklin Avenue. She thought it was just a dinner with an old family friend so she said sure. She said it was real nice, mixing pasta with the past, talking about old times and all that. After dinner they stopped at Mozzicatto's to get some pignole cookies and baba al rum, and she wasn't suspicious about his motives at all. But then he tried to slip her his cannoli from behind while she was making espresso in the kitchen."

"You can't be serious."

Lines sprang in Marko's forehead. "Who would make stuff up like that about his mother?"

"He must have been drunk—"

"He wasn't that drunk. He was just an old lecher. He fooled me for the better part of my life. Fooled you your entire life. Why do you think he never married?"

"I used to think it was because he never found anyone. Then as I got older, I started to think he might have been gay."

"Wrong on both counts, though I wouldn't put it past him to have been some kind of bisexual deviant."

"Marko!"

"The guy was a swinger in his younger days. Trust me. We were naïve. He belonged to a sex club in Hartford. Used to go to orgies and shit. In a Victorian house right next to the building where we went to the dentist. What was that guy's name?"

A wave of nausea left me weak. "How do you know all this?"

"Once he hit on Mama, I asked around."

"Asked around where?"

"I asked an old friend in the Uke community. One of the guys I grew up with. He pointed me in the right direction. When you work on bikes, you get to know a certain clientele. You get to know the right people to ask about something like this."

"So what did you do?"

"I paid him a visit and told him to leave our mother alone. That I knew all about his lifestyle and if he didn't, I'd expose him for the pervert he was. Ruin his reputation in the button-downed Uke community forever, and possibly kick his ass all over town to boot."

"And I assume it worked?'

"Of course it did. Would you want to mess with me when I'm pissed at you?"

"You ever talk to him again?"

"I did a job for him."

"A job? What kind of job?"

"That's when I found out what a real scumbag he was in business, too. That's the other poison."

"Marko, what kind of job?"

He appeared to choose his words carefully. "He was doing a deal. He needed someone to watch his back."

"Watch his back? What does that mean?"

"What do you think it means? You're the college graduate. You need me to write you a definition?"

"Was it dangerous?"

He pressed his eyes shut and shook his head with disgust. My interpretation was that I should have known better than to have asked. If it hadn't been dangerous, there was no reason to inquire. If it had been risky, he couldn't or wouldn't talk about any details.

"At least tell me what kind of deal? What was he into?"

"His business. The antique business." He pronounced it "an-ti-q." "He was delivering a big package to a client at midnight. I met him at his house. He rode shotgun. A few of my boys went ahead to the delivery address and had the place staked out ahead of time."

"Where was the delivery?"

"Avon."

Avon was one of the tonier suburbs west of Hartford. Not a place dealers typically needed protection, or one where deliveries were made at night.

"Big estate," Marko said. "Lots of stone. Pool, vineyard, the works."

"Vineyard?"

"Maserati in the driveway, though. You can't trust anyone that drives a Maserati. It pretends to be a Ferrari but it's not. What does that tell you about the owner?"

"What was being delivered?"

"Big crate. Don't know what was inside. I assume it was some sort of antique."

"Big like a table, or an old piece of furniture?"

"No. Big as in the shape of a mirror."

I pictured the wooden box. "Or a painting."

Marko shrugged.

"Did you see the man who took delivery?"

"What makes you think it was a man?"

"It was a woman?"

"In tights, boots, and a ski jacket. Tights. In the dead of winter."

"And this was a one-time thing?"

He nodded. "Never heard from him again."

"Then I don't get it. Why do you say it proved my godfather was a bad man in business, too?"

"I didn't say he was a bad man in business. I said he was a complete scumbag in business, too."

"I got that. Why?"

"He tried to sell me on stealing Mama's jewelry box."

His mere mention of the box turned my body temperature up. I pictured its rubies and emeralds. They'd been the catalyst for my trespass against my big brother. My face burned.

His didn't. Instead he sat looking out the window again with puffy indignation. That mollified me a bit. Much as my act was unforgivable, his face should have turned an even darker shade of red.

"That I do not believe," I said. "There is no way he would have asked you to steal from our mother."

"Call it what you want. He took a picture of it when he was visiting her. Must have shown it to a client or something. Said to offer Mama twenty grand for it. Said he'd split the profit with me fifty-fifty. You know he was lowballing. Thing was appraised twenty years ago at what . . . seventy-five grand?"

"That's disgusting."

The thought occurred to me that my godfather would have made such an offer to my brother only if he thought he was a kindred spirit, someone with the same ethical makeup. But I decided to keep that observation to myself. I also wondered how I could have been blind to my godfather's true character all those years growing up. But I guess sometimes parents depict a person to be a certain type, and by the time we're capable of forming our own conclusions, we've lost touch with that individual.

"You ever hear him call someone DP?" I said.

Marko appeared genuinely flabbergasted. "DP? You mean by someone's initials?" His frown intensified and his tone took on a note of extreme incredulity. "In English?"

"Wouldn't matter if it was someone's initials . . ."

"I can't even remember hearing him speak English. Whenever I was around him it was always Ukes . . ."

". . . or if the letters meant something else entirely."

"I heard him say hello to that woman that bought the crate, but everything else was hush-hush in the corner—Wait. You mean DP as in Displaced Person?"

Hearing those words roll off his lips made the hairs on the nape of my neck stand up. "Why? Does that make more sense to you?"

He burst out laughing. It wasn't a complimentary chuckle in appreciation for having been entertained. It was a derisive sneer intended to insult and belittle. "Nothing you've said since you so rudely walked in here has made any sense. Just as nothing you've done in the last ten years has made any sense to me."

That made two of us. I felt some pressure behind my eyes and jumped to my feet. It was an instinctive move. An act of emotional preservation. Apparently, my brain was telling me that there was no information worth the humiliation of having Marko see tears in my eyes.

"Did you ever hear him call anyone by that nickname?" I said. "Could have been a Uke."

Marko turned pensive for a moment, as though he were contemplating my question. Then he drained the rest of one of his beers and lit a cigarette. As a plume of smoke twisted into the air, he regarded me with contempt.

"Ten, twenty years ago, I would have asked you what you're up to. I would have gone back to your first comment and wondered if Donnie Angel is involved in whatever it is you think you know, and what some DP might have to do with it. I would have wondered if you're playing Nancy Drew and sticking your nose where it might get cut off. But now, I honestly don't give a shit."

I felt hot and thirsty, as though I might faint any second.

"No. I never heard him call anyone DP," Marko said. "Now I've done you the favor of answering your questions. Can you do me a favor in return?"

A ray of hope. Of course I would do him a favor. Short of breaking the law—and even that might not have stopped me—I would have done absolutely anything for him at that moment.

I tried to form a word but couldn't. Hope overwhelmed me. The best I could do was nod in the affirmative.

"Fuck off," he said.

Leaving was an out-of-body experience. I didn't feel any of my limbs. The only sensation I had was of my brain instructing me to put one foot in front of the other, to lift my hand and grasp the door handle, to get out into the parking lot.

But before I could make my exit, the bitter stench of cigarette smoke filtered through my nostrils. It reminded me of summer camp when I was eight and Marko was a fourteen-year-old counselor. There were rumors that the counselors snuck out to the lake to smoke, but I didn't think my brother was one of them. One day he returned with the others, and when he put his arm around my shoulders, I smelled the nicotine on his breath. I had to fight back the tears. I assumed that even one cigarette would cause lung cancer, and the thought of my brother dying was unbearable. I walked around depressed for days.

I never thought I could have felt worse.

But now I did.

CHAPTER 17

THE FLASHES OF LIGHT GREW BRIGHTER AS THE PERSON APproached. The footsteps came rapidly.

"Who's there?" Nadia said. She tried to sound tough but knew it came out shaky, the way it did when Mrs. Wall made her stand up and speak in front of the whole class. Everyone laughed.

No one answered. The footsteps stopped at the perimeter of the camp behind a thicket of trees.

A voice called back from behind the trees. "Yo, Nancy Drew, how's things in River Heights?"

Nadia couldn't believe her ears. Was that her brother? Marko was the last person she expected and the one she most wanted to see. The sound of his voice made her want to jump up and down. "Marko?" she said.

Marko stepped out from behind the trees, shined a flashlight at his own head, and made a goofy face. "The one and only."

Nadia was so happy she wanted to run up to him and jump into his arms, but she didn't. Their family didn't do silly things like that. No hugs and kisses and other stupid things that weak people did.

Marko drew closer. "I said, how's things, Nancy Drew?"

"Rough," she said. "How's things with you?"

"'Bout even."

"Where's Father?"

"Having a reunion with his old friend, Johnny Walker Red. What happened to your fire?"

Nadia explained that she'd used all her matches the first night, and that the fire had died after she'd left camp to help an injured hiker.

"You lost your poncho, too?" Marko said, setting the large, square flashlight on its end so that it shone upward.

"No poncho, no matches, no water, no food."

Marko handed her his canteen. She took a long swig while he pulled a box of strike-anywhere matches out of his knapsack.

"Wait," Nadia said, placing her left hand on her hip. What the heck was he thinking? "You can't do that."

Marko gave her the flashlight while he added kindling to the ashes. "Do what?"

"Any of this. You can't give me any more matches. You can't help me at all."

"Why not?"

"It would be cheating." Nadia stomped her right foot. "I'm not a cheater."

"It would be cheating if you went outside of camp and got some matches. Got some water. Stole some food. This, this is not cheating."

What a load of crap. "It feels like I'm cheating."

"Nancy Drew, I'm tired and it's dark. So I'm going to light myself a fire here right now and make it a little more comfortable for myself. Is that okay with you? Are you going to deny a brother a fire?"

Nadia imagined a crackling fire: its warmth, comfort, and security. Marko had a point. She hadn't asked for help. If he was cold and he needed to warm up, who was she to say no?

"I guess not," she said.

"Good. Then make yourself useful and bring me some firewood. We've got to get this thing lit fast because I brought some friends with me. And they're a bit antsy to come out of hiding."

Oh, great, she thought. Had some troublemakers from high school joined him to drink beer and smoke cigarettes? Or had some hippies hooked up with him and brought pot, LSD, or some other drugs? That seemed unlikely, too, except that with her brother, anything was possible.

Nadia prayed it wasn't drugs.

When they were finished building the fire, she sat nervously on a rock. Marko stood before her near the fire with his knapsack in his hands.

"Ready to meet my friends?" he said.

Nadia wasn't sure she was ever going to be ready. Still, she nodded. "Are they in the woods behind you?"

"Nope," Marko said, pointing to his knapsack. "They're in here."

"In there? In the knapsack? Oh, no. Don't tell me you have a dead animal in there. Don't tell me you're going to make me eat snake again. That was . . . so gross. It wasn't like chicken the way you said it would be. It really wasn't."

Marko reached into his bag and pulled out a candy bar. "Say hello to my little friend, Baby Ruth," he said.

"Baby Ruth?" The mere mention of chocolate and peanuts brought Nadia to her feet. "You brought Baby Ruth with you?"

Marko reached into his knapsack again. "And her good friends and protectors, the Three Musketeers." He pulled two Three Musketeers bars out of his bag.

"Wow! What a stash!"

"Hey, I'm not done yet." Marko overturned his knapsack. Ritz Crackers, Cheez Whiz, Red Devil Chicken Spread, Pop-Tarts, and a six-pack of canned juices fell out of the bag.

"Oh my God," Nadia said, as she fell over and almost did a reverse somersault. The fat around her belly kept her from rolling over. When she straightened up, her conscience prodded her. "But it's cheating, isn't it?" she said.

Marko sat down on a rock beside her and opened the Ritz Crackers and the chicken spread.

"Well, let's talk about that," he said. "Your job is to survive in the wilderness for three nights and three days. You're supposed to

live off the land. Does the land include this knapsack and what's inside it?"

Nadia shrugged. "I don't know about that."

"Of course you do. What, it doesn't exist? It's not right here in front of you?"

"I guess so. But I'm supposed to do this on my own."

"You are doing this on your own. You didn't ask for help. But when someone offers you some food, you have to take it. Because let me tell you something, little sister, and listen good." Marko stopped spreading chicken on the cracker and looked Nadia in the eyes. "You're a tough chick. But even a tough chick can't make it on her own. Everyone needs a little help from somebody every once in a while. Everyone."

"Even the Three Musketeers?" Nadia asked, reaching for a candy bar.

"You bet."

They sat beside the fire and ate. Nadia told her brother about the hikers and that she'd used her poncho to create a stretcher for their wounded friend.

"Good job," Marko said. "Losing your poncho is not good but you had no choice. That was the right thing to do. I'm proud of you."

Nadia wasn't sure what she enjoyed more. The whipped nougat in the Three Musketeers bar or her brother's praise. One thing was certain: the combination was unbeatable. She really was going to pass this stupid test, she thought.

They ate and talked for another hour. Marko told her that he and their father had gone on personal walkabouts before joining up again at their camp, which was half a mile away. During the day, Marko had hiked nine miles to civilization and bought supplies at a 7-Eleven. He'd waited until their father had drunk his fill of scotch and fallen asleep before escaping to check up on Nadia.

"Oh, I saw Mrs. Chimchak," Nadia said.

Marko looked at her as though she were crazy. "Up here? No way. She's on vacation in Florida."

"Uh-uh. She was here. Checking up on me to make sure I was okay."

"For real, she was here?"

"Yeah, yeah. For real. One second I looked up and she was here, next one she was gone. She acted weird. Like, all emotional, you know?"

"Yeah. I hear you. She doesn't have any children. You know?"

Nadia bit into a Baby Ruth. "Yeah, I know."

When they were stuffed, Marko poured all his water into Nadia's canteen and sealed the food in kitchen storage bags.

"Remember," he said, "you're not taking these. I'm leaving them. They're part of the land. Only a fool won't live off the land when it's right there in front of him."

Nadia shivered as her brother stood up to leave.

"I'd give you my poncho," he said, "but it's camouflage and yours was puke green. If Father came by and saw it . . ."

Nadia shrugged. "I don't need it." She screwed her face tight and tried to sound as tough as she could. "I don't need no stinking poncho."

Marko laughed. He didn't laugh or smile too often, but she'd reminded him of one of his favorite movie lines from The Treasure of the Sierra Madre. *Her satisfaction over making Marko laugh, however, quickly gave way to reality.*

He was leaving.

She wanted him to stay. Better yet, she wanted to go with him, to feel safe and have fun, not be scared alone at night. But she didn't dare tell him that, lest she disappoint him and make him think she was still a weakling. She had to be strong for him.

"Thanks for the matches," she said, trying to pepper her voice with enthusiasm. "And the food. I mean, thanks for putting a lot of good stuff on the land."

He turned back and shined the flashlight on his face so she could see him.

"Keep the whistle close to you. And don't be afraid to use it. I'll be around. Not too close, but not too far away."

"That's good to know," Nadia said, fighting back the tears.

After he left, Nadia crawled into her sleeping bag and stayed there for twelve hours. She woke up constantly throughout the night, sometimes so hot she had to pop out of her sleeping bag, sometimes so cold she trembled inside it. She thought it was the sugar from the food she'd eaten, but when she woke up the next day some of the fever had stayed with her.

It didn't matter. Nothing could bring her down now. When Nadia emerged from her lean-to, the morning sun shone through gaps in the trees. Marko had visited her. Marko had taken care of her. She had water, fire, and food.

She was certain the worst was behind her.

CHAPTER 18

I ATE A LATE LUNCH AT A WENDY'S IN ROCKY HILL. IT BOASTED a highly visible parking lot surrounded by the Silas Deane Highway on one side and busy office buildings on the other. I parked near the driveway with the nose of the Porsche facing out. There was no way a van could block my exit or a couple of thugs could kidnap me without attracting attention.

After devouring a spicy chicken sandwich and a vanilla Frosty—a child's size, just enough to take the edge off my stress—I called my friend Paul Obon. He ran the Duma Ukrainian bookstore in the Lower East Village of New York. He was my source for information on all things Ukrainian. I needed his help because I knew nothing about post–World War II DP camps in Europe. Our parents and grandparents didn't discuss them, presumably to protect us from the pain and suffering of their past. But that always struck me as the partial truth. In fact, our elders preferred to keep this part of their lives shrouded in mystery for reasons unknown, or so I'd always thought.

Obon gave me the basics. After the end of World War II in 1945, five million refugees from the Soviet Union found themselves homeless in Western Europe. The United States, Great Britain, and the Soviet Union signed agreements at the Yalta Conference that required the repatriation of all Allied nationals, by force if necessary. The Soviet refugees consisted of slave labor moved to occupied Western Europe by Hitler, concentration camp survivors, and people who'd fled west during the war.

With the help of the Americans, British, and French, more than four million refugees—two million of them Ukrainian—were returned to the USSR promptly. The remaining homeless—including two hundred fifty thousand Ukrainians—refused to return voluntarily. The Americans, British, and French set up camps in Austria and Germany where they were allowed to live while the world decided what to do with them. The refugees were called Displaced Persons, or DPs for short.

The Soviets were obsessed with the repatriation of every single DP. Their fixation was rooted in two beliefs. First, they felt entitled to such a demand because of their disproportionate suffering during the war. Soviet fatalities totaled 20 million, compared with between 300,000 and 350,000 each for America and Britain. In fact, the average *daily* fatalities suffered in the USSR before 1943 exceeded the entire 130,000 deaths suffered by the Americans in three and a half years of war in Europe. The Soviet population shared Stalin's bitterness. They felt their allies owed them a debt.

The Soviets were also motivated by their insecurity over their ideology. If the Marxist state was utopia, every citizen should have wanted to return home. The presence of a dissenter would have suggested otherwise, and that was unacceptable. Hence, the Soviets deployed foreign missions to Western Europe to help with the repatriation. "The Motherland would not be a mother if she did not love all her family," they said.

The Americans, British, and French happily obliged the Soviets. Each country was dealing with its own postwar issues. None of the Allies wanted a refugee problem, but that's exactly what they got. A British Zone military order proclaimed: "HMG do not recognize Ukrainian as a nationality. No recognition can be given to any Ukrainian organization or representation as such." The Americans and the French agreed. Soldiers were ordered to use force to load refugees onto trains headed back to the Soviet Union.

Ukrainian DPs promised that they would resist repatriation "by all means." One community gathered in a church to celebrate the Holy Mass for the last time. Word spread that they were planning to commit mass suicide. When soldiers arrived to intervene, a farmer approached an officer and handed him his axe. He asked the soldier to cut off his head, that he would rather die from decapitation than be sent back to the Soviet Union. Others did commit suicide, including a twenty-four-year-old man who'd learned his sisters had voluntarily returned to the USSR and ended up in a Siberian work camp.

General Dwight D. Eisenhower and his staff understood they were legally obligated to use force to repatriate the DPs, but they had little stomach for it. There was clearly a disagreement between the welcoming message being spread by the Soviet foreign missions and future life as the DPs saw it. What Eisenhower didn't realize at the time was that the Soviet missions consisted primarily of agents from the NKVD, the predecessor of the notorious Soviet secret police, the KGB. And their agenda was altogether different from the one they advertised.

As soon as Obon mentioned the NKVD and the KGB, I immediately became suspicious they somehow had a hand in my godfather's death. Most Americans would have thought it was a silly idea, I knew, and yet I couldn't help myself. If you grew up a first-generation Uke in the free world, you heard enough horror stories about spying, persecution, and murder to believe the disciples of those organizations were capable of killing anyone, any place, at any time.

After my call with Obon, I met Roxy at a massive, crowded, and well-lit Stop & Shop parking lot. It was located five minutes from the Uke National Home in Wethersfield, the town that divided Rocky Hill from Hartford. I kept my eyes on the rearview mirror during the entire drive from Wendy's. Once I spotted Roxy's SUV, I circled around it and looked in all the vehicles surrounding it. She was the only one inside her car. All the other vehicles were empty.

I parked beside her, climbed into the passenger seat of her SUV, and nearly suffocated from the stench of bacon, garlic, and sausage.

"What the hell, Rox? It smells like Baczynsky's Meat Market in here." Baczynsky's was a popular Ukrainian store on the Lower East Side of Manhattan.

Roxy grinned. She cut a slice of Ukrainian bacon from a rectangular slab wrapped in onion paper with her pocketknife. The bacon was cured in salt and spices and commonly eaten raw. Unlike traditional bacon, Uke bacon had barely any trace of meat in it. It was almost one hundred percent fat, which is why it was called *salo*, the Ukrainian word for fat. I was never partial to the dish. I preferred to consume my fat in the form of dumplings. Roxy was eating hers with raw garlic. She was dipping the latter in salt, which she'd poured into a paper cup in her cup holder.

"This is my reward for driving to New York and back," she said.

The blast of garlic breath from her mouth overpowered me. I struggled to breathe. It was worse than an elevator packed with men the morning after they'd gorged on Korean barbecue.

"You absolutely reek," I said. "I can't believe you're doing this. I thought you were working at the Uke National Home tonight, too?"

"I am," she said with glee. "This old-timer who plays bingo likes to put his hand on my ass and remind me he has no heirs. Like he's going to put me in his will if he gets some, whatever that means at his age. I'm going to get up close and personal with him today. Ha!"

"Remember you laughed just now when he tells you he likes your perfume."

Roxy stopped chewing and frowned. "Oh, shit. You think?"

I managed a laugh under the circumstances. "No, I don't think so. Garlic breath is like body fat. Men tolerate their own but don't like it on their women." I glanced in the back of the SUV and saw a dozen or more brown shopping bags. Inside, I spied rings of kielbasas, other sausages, and breads in the bags, along with jars of condiments and boxes of mysterious delicacies. The cooperative store at the Uke National Home stocked food from New York and sold it to the Hartford crowd for Easter. But first, someone had to drive to the City and buy it.

"Since when do you do the run to New York?" I said. My father had made the runs to supplement his income—or lack thereof—when I was little. Our car would smell like deli counter for weeks.

"Since the guy who used to do it had a car accident and lost his license." She lifted the slab of bacon in my direction. "You want some of this, Diana?"

I cringed.

Roxy grinned. "It's never too late to acquire a taste."

"Great. I believe in delayed gratification, though. I'm trying to save some orgasmic experiences for my golden years so I have something to look forward to."

Roxy cut another piece of *salo*. "Saving your orgasms is a mistake. You need to live in the moment."

"I'm glad you said that. Here's what I've been living today."

I told her about my call with Obon. "Did your uncle ever talk to you about his experience in the DP camp?"

She shook her head. "He didn't talk about those days. I mean he was a kid after the war. In his teens, right?"

The DP camps had been filled with children, many of whom had been brought to Germany and Austria as slave labor for the Nazi regime. My parents had been among them.

"He was a scrounger," Roxy said. "That's all I know. We watched that movie with Steve McQueen once. The one with him on the motorcycle with all those famous actors as prisoners of war."

"*The Great Escape*?"

"Yeah. That's the one. He told me he was like the James Garner character, only more handsome."

I chuckled. "Yeah. He wished."

A black sedan rolled by. A man with dark features stared right at us. He let his eyes linger, then looked away nonchalantly. He was either staring randomly or purposefully trying to appear uninterested. Roxy must have seen him and thought the same thing because she sat silently beside me, eyes glued to the tail of the Subaru. Two men with leather jackets got out and walked into a Chinese restaurant in the mall. There was no one else in the car, and the men didn't look over their shoulders in our direction.

"Uh-oh," Roxy said.

My blood pressure spiked. I realized I must have missed something. "What?" I looked from the restaurant to the car and back to the Chinese place again. "I don't see anything."

"No. Look up. At the sky."

I glanced above and beyond the strip mall. A colorless moon hung low in the shape of the blade of a sickle, reminiscent of the symbol of the Soviet Union.

"It's a Stalin moon," Roxy said.

It was one of the first things Mrs. Chimchak had taught us at PLAST camp: beware the night of a Stalin moon, for nothing good ever happened when the symbol of communist persecution hovered over the planet.

We sat quietly for a moment. I wanted to get Roxy's reactions to what Marko had told me about her uncle, but I didn't want to offend her by suggesting he was a sleaze. In my experience as a forensic investment analyst, it's best to persuade the other person to come to the desired conclusion by herself.

"What kind of guy was your uncle?" I said.

Roxy had started to wrap up her bacon. She gave me a quizzical look, as though saying I knew him as well as she had, and it was a stupid question.

"No," I said. "I don't mean was he nice and religious and did he really care for you and all that. I mean, did he have integrity? Did you trust him?"

Roxy shrugged. "Personally, I never had a problem with him. And my parents. I think they understood what kind of business he was in and it was just in his nature to, you know, exaggerate a bit. But there was never anything malicious about it."

"Exaggerate what? Can you give me an example?"

"He was always buying and selling. Once he sold us a kitchen table he said was an antique made by some famous guy. Later when my father tried to sell it back to him, it turned out it was by the famous guy's brother and it was worth half what he thought it was. But that's how all those antique guys are, right?"

"But I thought he had a good reputation. I thought he knew his stuff."

"He did know his stuff. And he did have a good reputation. But if you knew my uncle, you knew to take it with a grain of salt." Roxy rolled down her window and tossed the rest of her salt onto the asphalt. "And if you didn't know him, I'm sure he was no worse than all the other people in his line of work."

Roxy's assessment was hardly a ringing endorsement, and disturbingly consistent with the shady picture Marko had painted.

"You ever accompany him on any strange deliveries?" I said.

Roxy twisted her body and stored the remainder of her bacon in one of the larger shopping bags behind her. "I never went with him on any deliveries. He was super secretive with all that stuff. I helped him with his groceries and with contractors for the house. You know, HVAC and plumbing, maintenance and repairs and the like. Why?"

I told her about the midnight delivery in Avon, leaving out the part about Marko providing security. There was no need to mention his involvement.

Roxy shook her head. "That's really, really weird. He didn't have a storefront because the overhead wasn't worth it. He did most of his work through auctions, swap meets, and by referral. But I never heard of any midnight deliveries."

"So what do you have for me?" I said.

Roxy started the car. "I got the name of his accountant. Gave her a call and confirmed she's got his books."

I raised my eyebrows. "She?"

Given Marko's description of my godfather's sexual tendencies, the revelation that his bookkeeper was a woman conjured more unholy visions.

Roxy nodded. "It's the Razor Blade."

My pulse picked up. She'd been my girl scout mentor. The mere mention of her name still electrified me. "Mrs. Chimchak?"

Roxy nodded again.

"She's like . . . ninety."

"Yeah. Ninety going on sixty-five. I told her you'd be calling. When was the last time you saw her?"

"Years. Decades. Last century."

"That ought to be quite the reunion then."

"Yeah." I had no idea what to expect, whether she would hold my disappearance to New York against me or not. "Yeah it should be."

I confirmed Mrs. Chimchak's address, thanked Roxy for the scoop, and returned to my car. Mrs. Chimchak lived in the south end of Hartford near the border of Wethersfield where I was parked. I wasn't surprised she hadn't moved to the suburbs even though there were more shootings in Hartford every year, and it seemed more dangerous than all the New York boroughs combined. But there was a consistency to the person who'd helped shape me into the woman I was today. I didn't picture her moving because the environment around her changed. I envisioned her personal space remaining invulnerable regardless of the changes to her environment.

I took a final look at the Subaru that had gotten our attention. The leather-clad boys must have ordered take-out because they were nowhere in sight.

Then I drove my car to Mrs. Chimchak's house along the dark streets of Hartford, my path illuminated the entire way by the Stalin moon.

CHAPTER 19

Until now, my search for clues about my godfather's death had led me to two homes and a strip bar. All three belonged to current or former family: my ex-father-in-law, mother, and brother. Entering each place had filled me with increasing dread. Knocking on Mrs. Chimchak's door should have been easier. After all, she wasn't family. In theory, I couldn't have offended her as much as my mother or brother or my deceased husband's father, but I was certain I'd done so.

I had lost contact with her. I had ceased to be an active participant in the Ukrainian-American community. As soon as I'd become an adult, I had left town and never looked back. I'd hated most of my childhood, all the mandatory Ukrainian extracurriculars. In that way, I knew I had disappointed Mrs. Chimchak. Hadn't she told me I was her only hope? Hadn't I abandoned her and shunned the ancestral heritage she loved above all else in this world, with the sole exception of the United States of America?

She lived across the street from Goodwyn Park, among a row of houses from a bygone era. Small homes straight out of Monopoly with enough yard in front of the sidewalk for a couple of kids to play. One of the houses was immaculately painted, its grass pruned by a barber, the driveway recently sealed. I recognized it as soon as I saw it.

A light deep inside the house cast a faint glow against sheer curtains in the living room facing the yard. I rang the doorbell, heart in throat yet again, and the door opened immediately, as though she'd been watching me from the moment I'd parked. *Of course she had.*

Her body had shrunken an inch, her crew cut looked like used steel wool, and she didn't hide the roadmap of lines in her face or forehead. But otherwise she looked the same. Despite the signs of aging, she didn't appear to be a day over seventy. She demonstrated her memory by planting her palms on her cheeks as soon as she saw me. There was no hesitation, no sign of uncertainty. She recognized me right away, and based on the way her eyes lit up, she was overjoyed to see me. It was the welcome I'd longed to get from my mother, and it drained the anxiety from my body.

"You've come home," Mrs. Chimchak said. "I knew you'd come home."

She kissed me on both cheeks and gave me a shockingly firm hug. We went into the living room, which was more like a small study with old furniture. I couldn't help but wonder if my godfather had furnished it with overpriced reproductions, or if there were a gem or two among her collection she'd bought half a century ago without knowing, and he'd tried to buy them from her on the cheap.

"Look at you," she said. "You look wonderful. All grown up and successful. You're a tribute to your family and the community you grew up in. I'm so proud of you."

I like to think that I hold sentiment in the lowest regard, but I'm aware that I may be deceiving myself. The truth was that I wished I'd brought a digital photographer and recording specialist to preserve the moment forever. I imagined playing it at times when melancholy and depression gripped me, upon waking and going to sleep, or at any given moment on any given day.

She went to the kitchen to make tea. The aroma of borsch and *babka* further enhanced my mood. Whereas my mother had been preparing food for suitors, Mrs. Chimchak was preparing food for Easter. I studied a series of framed photographs on the mantel above her fireplace. One of the photos caught my eye. Mrs. Chimchak, as an early teen, standing beside a strapping young man with smashing good looks. They weren't smiling but there was a pride etched in their faces and a strength to their carriage. The photo was black-and-white. They were both dressed in drab clothes and posing in front of a bombed-out building.

Mrs. Chimchak returned with a tray of tea and cookies in the shape and color of Ukrainian Easter eggs. We exchanged some small talk. Guilt gnawed at me as I perpetuated the lie that I still had a job. I quickly changed the subject, and asked her about the picture.

"That was Stefan," she said. "The love of my life."

I'd wondered why she hadn't married. Just as I'd thought my godfather might have been gay, I'd assumed she might have been a lesbian, or more likely, someone who suppressed her sexual tendencies. Mrs. Chimchak certainly cast an asexual vibe, so to hear she'd had a love of any kind was a major revelation.

"Was that picture taken before or after the war?" I said.

She cast a stern look in my direction. "That may be the first time you've ever disappointed me."

I felt myself stiffen. I studied the picture again. Apparently, I was so nervous I was forgetting the obvious. "The building is bombed out. It couldn't have been taken before the war. What happened to Stefan?"

She stared at me with a blank expression. "That is the second time you've ever disappointed me."

He was the love of her life. If he had survived, they would have been together, I thought. It had been inconsiderate and presumptuous of me to ask about him. I smiled sheepishly and tried to think of how to segue into the real purpose for my visit.

The dismay in her eyes yielded to a gentle smile. It was more than endearing, it was a provocation. *You are the child I never had*, she seemed to be saying. *All the knowledge I have is yours for the taking, if only you'd treat me with respect. If only you'd be as honest and forthright with me as I shall be with you.* All these things she expressed by merely looking at me. This was her gift. This was why she'd commanded my unswerving loyalty when I was a child even though I hated every minute of PLAST, and wished I'd been hanging out with friends like all the American girls, assuming I'd had friends in the first place.

"I think my godfather was murdered," I said. "There was an entry in his diary on the day he was killed. The letters DP were written in bold ink. Do you know of anyone my godfather called by those initials? An American, a Ukrainian, a friend from a DP camp?"

She took a second to think about it. "No. Obviously there's your former father-in-law if those were Ukrainian letters. I never heard him refer to anyone as a DP."

"Would it be possible that was his nickname for a close friend from the DP camps?"

Mrs. Chimchak considered the possibility. "DPs were the lowest rung of society in post–World War II Europe. We were the *Untermensch*, the subhumans. Being called a DP was an insult. In my experience, certain types of men enjoy insulting each other. 'Hey DP,' or 'You're just a DP.'"

"You're right. The closer some friendships, the more the men insult each other. I never thought of it that way before."

"It's just that . . . DP camps are a painful part of our past. Most people who suffered through the camps, they prefer not to talk about them. They started new lives here. They had children. Their children have had children. They don't want their families exposed to what they went through."

"That would explain why my father never talked about his life before he came to America, and, just today, my mother danced around the issue when I asked about it."

"As I recall from the New Year's Eve balls in the early days, back when the joy of being Americans exceeded all our cumulative sorrows, your mother was always a good dancer."

"Will you talk to me about the camps?"

"What do you want to know?"

"Anything you're willing to share, anything you're not willing to share, that sort of thing."

She smiled and nodded. This was more like it, she was saying. I knew I'd come to the right person. I reached for a cookie in celebration, dunked it in my tea, and ate half of it. Then I ate the rest, sat back, and listened.

She started with the salient facts. There were approximately two hundred fifty Displaced Persons camps in 1946. Most of them were located in Germany, a few in Austria, and one in Italy. The British administered approximately a hundred of them, while the Americans tended to most of the rest. Ukrainian refugees clung together.

"My camp was in the American Zone," she said matter-of-factly. "The first thing we did was get acclimated. Then we went about the business of creating our own society within the camps to help us survive as a community. We formed schools. There were about seven thousand Ukrainian children in the American Zone. We had fifteen hundred teachers. The children were battle-tested. They were used to moving and leaving home on a moment's notice. They were used to bombing and shelling. So it wasn't that strange for them to work in a classroom without tables or chairs. Without chalk or a blackboard. The children learned while standing. They wrote in pencil on window sills and on the floor."

She told me that the DPs created the Ukrainian Free University in Munich, and published a Ukrainian newspaper as well. A few men got jobs in military installations, in manufacturing plants, or as engineers with construction firms. But most sat around the camp speaking about hopelessness and dreaming of a better tomorrow. Meanwhile, a black market and barter system evolved.

"Cigarettes were the gold standards in the *Schwarzmarkt*," Mrs. Chimchak said. "One pack bought you illegal entry into Berlin. Two packs got you some bread, potatoes, or meat from a German farmer. Twenty-five packs might have won you a German radio, and thirty bought you a bicycle."

"Was my godfather a good scrounger?"

"He was the best. Anything you needed, you went through him. The second-hardest thing for him to acquire was fresh fruit and vegetables. Food was scarce but we got our hands on it. But the diet wasn't varied, and we all looked gray and lifeless. That didn't stop us from being productive. We organized a theatre. Uncensored productions without the watchful eye of the NKVD. What joy! We focused on our religion, too. Orthodox, Catholics. Most Catholic priests made it out of the USSR alive. In the camps, most people attended Mass every Sunday."

She paused to sip her tea. Her hand trembled as she lifted her cup to her mouth. I hadn't noticed any tremors beforehand, and was left wondering if this was an ailment or an indication of the emotional toll of recalling her past.

"Did my godfather develop any enemies back then? Something personal, that may have lingered for decades?"

Mrs. Chimchak laughed. It was a full, open-mouth laughter that showed her teeth. They were small, slightly stained, and ferocious looking. "Enemies? My God, child. It's hard for you to understand, isn't it? It seemed like we were the enemies of the entire outside world. But in the camps themselves? Please . . . You know what they say about Ukrainians. Put two in a room and you'll get three political parties. Sure, there were politics. There were always politics. But we were too consumed with our survival to create grudges among one another."

Something had struck a chord but I couldn't place it. I took a few breaths and remembered.

"You said the second-hardest thing for him to acquire was fresh produce. What was the hardest thing for him to get?"

"That which could not be scrounged. Freedom. A destination. A new home for everyone who refused to go back to the old one."

I nodded.

"That is what we lived for," she said. "And we dreamed our dreams in a constant state of fear. The ghosts of concentration camps loomed large. There was residual fear from the war—the fighting—but mostly there was constant fear of repatriation. It was there, in the back of our minds, from the moment we arrived. But then the Americans and the British authorized the use of force to send DPs back to Ukraine toward the end of 1946. The stories of their violence spread and we knew things would only get worse.

"Violence? What kind of violence?"

"The British and American soldiers were given orders to herd people onto trains to send us back to Ukraine. When we refused, they hit us with their rifles. In our stomachs, our backs. They cracked foreheads open. They told us we were going back one way or another. They had orders."

"And they beat DPs? Allied soldiers actually beat refugees?"

Mrs. Chimchak nodded solemnly. "There were two types of soldiers. The men from the European campaigns who'd fought the Germans were horrified. I watched battle-scarred veterans with tears in their eyes slugging DPs with their rifles. A black American doctor by the name of Washington. I will never forget him. I saw him leaning against a shed as they herded us on board crying uncontrollably. Tears rolling off his cheeks. You see, these were the same trains that had been used to bring survivors from the concentration camps back to civilization. Back to freedom."

Neither of us spoke for a few seconds. Her words sank in.

"Who was the second type of soldier?" I said.

"The new recruits. They had no wartime experience. They bonded with postwar German society, the people who hosted them, provided them services. To them we were DP scum and while there were exceptions, most of them didn't shed any tears when they were ordered to use force for repatriation. The new American soldiers hated us as much as the locals did."

I imagined an American soldier happily slugging a malnourished refugee to force him or her to board a train. A knot tightened in my stomach. I loathed the thought of any American having done anything evil, especially during the war when our country had helped liberate Europe. It was silly, naïve, and unrealistic, and I didn't care. We were the lucky ones. We were Americans. We were supposed to stand for absolute good at all times.

Then the image took on a new dimension. Mrs. Chimchak entered the picture.

"You saw this Dr. Washington?" I said. "If you saw him, it means you were there. It means you were one of the DPs loaded onto the train. It means you were repatriated."

She looked at me with her signature expression—sheer and utter inscrutability. I sat waiting for a segue to more personal revelations, but instead she smiled again. "I was very young, and very naïve." She reached across the table and took my hand in both of hers. Donned an earnest expression, the kind I'd never seen her wear before. "Now . . . Your godfather was murdered. Let's talk about how you're going to find the killer."

CHAPTER 20

I FIRED A SERIES OF QUESTIONS AT MRS. CHIMCHAK ABOUT MY godfather and her belief that he'd been murdered. The queries came streaming from my mouth in no particular order. Why was she sure he'd been murdered? Did she have any suspicions about who might have killed him? Did my godfather have any enemies? When I paused for a breath, she cut me off with a raised hand, and said she wanted to get some more tea before we talked further.

"Don't be too eager, dear." She patted me on the shoulder as she stood up from the table. "There's an old Ukrainian proverb: He who licks knives will soon cut his tongue."

While she went into the kitchen, I savored a most pleasant adrenaline rush. My former father-in-law was certain his brother had been murdered, and now Mrs. Chimchak had revealed that she thought he'd been killed, too. Not only that, she'd volunteered her belief. My childhood mentor, the woman I respected more than anyone else in the world, had come to the same conclusion. *Sweet validation!* I wasn't imagining a crime to keep myself occupied because I'd lost my job and hadn't found another after six months of searching. I wasn't suffering from delusions and fantasies. My instincts had been spot-on.

Mrs. Chimchak's revelation, however, wasn't the only reason

for the uptick in my spirits. She'd expressed no disappointment over my absence, showed no evidence of harboring a grudge for my failure to communicate with her for more than twenty years, and hadn't hidden her joy in seeing me. She was, as she'd always been, inscrutable yet real and true. She was the complete opposite of my mother. For the first time since I'd returned to Hartford, I had an urge to linger in someone's home.

She returned with more tea and cookies. As she refreshed the table, I decided to lob a grenade, the kind I threw at company executives to keep them on their toes. In this case, I wanted a spontaneous reaction to a question that bothered me.

"Was my godfather a good man?"

She lifted her eyebrows a smidge, enough to reveal the question surprised her. She thought about it for a moment.

"To my knowledge, he had no family. And there are no friends in business. Solitary people can become a bit self-absorbed. 'The church is near but the road is icy. The tavern is far but I'll walk carefully.' That was your godfather. His life was about him and his pleasures. Not an evil bone in his body but if I had to pick three people to share my foxhole, he wouldn't have been one of them."

Her depiction was consistent with my brother's revelations, except for the part about no evil in his body. I considered his plan to buy my mother's heirloom for a fraction of its worth to be pretty darn evil.

"Something changed fifteen months ago," Mrs. Chimchak said. "I knew from his lifestyle. I knew from doing the accounting for his business. I did his books, you know. Of course you know. That's why you're here. I once had twenty-one clients, small Ukrainian businesses, but most of them have died. Three of the children who inherited their father's trade kept me. A plumber, an appliance repairman, and a beekeeper. I have three clients left. One of them was your godfather. Did you know he was my client?"

An awkward silence followed. I didn't know what to say. It was the first time Mrs. Chimchak had shown a momentary memory lapse, repeated herself, or digressed. Although they were minor observations, they reminded me of her true age.

"How did his lifestyle change?" I said.

The question snapped her out of her stupor. She rubbed her thumb and forefingers together. "The fancy televisions, the Cadillac—"

"But he bought it used, didn't he?"

"He may have bought it used, but it was new to him. It was still a Cadillac. That wasn't all. He took several trips out of the country. And he had a table at Fleming's in West Hartford. He had a whole new wardrobe, too. I told him some of the clothes made him look like Liberace but he didn't care."

Fleming's was the area's top steakhouse. It was notoriously expensive, frequented by those with expense accounts, deep wallets, and a taste for the finest. I tried to picture him at his own table, dressed like Liberace, being served by an elegant waitress intent on emptying his wallet.

"Godfather had a table at Fleming's? You've got to be kidding me."

Mrs. Chimchak's expression didn't change. "I know this only because he mistakenly included a month's worth of receipts with his business receipts. I say it was a mistake because he was very upset when I asked him about it. He paid cash for his meals and didn't want anyone to know about it."

"Why the secrecy?" I said.

"And where did the money come from?"

"I thought his business might have taken off."

"He made between twenty-one and thirty-six thousand dollars during each of the last three years. He owned his house so there was no mortgage, but still . . ."

"Thus the secrecy," I said. Donnie Angel's words rang in my ears yet again. *Tell me what you know about your godfather's business.* "He had an alternative source of income."

"I should say so."

Perhaps that explained why he paid my brother, Marko, to watch his back during a midnight delivery to Avon.

"Any ideas?" I said.

"He knew only one business. He had to be selling something old. Something precious. Something people wanted that only he could get them. But I don't have a clue exactly what it was."

"And you never saw any receipts for anything unusual?"

"No. Nothing out of the ordinary. Nothing that profitable. The one thing I can tell you is that it all started after he took a trip to Crimea."

Crimea was an autonomous republic in the south of Ukraine surrounded by the Black Sea.

"Why Crimea?" I said.

She shook her head. "I don't know. When he first told me he was going on vacation to Sevastopol he looked tense and anxious. He didn't act like someone going on vacation. But when he returned six days later he was a bit more relaxed. And within a month, I'd say, he turned downright cheerful."

Sevastopol was a port city in Crimea. It was a tourist attraction, and the home of the Ukrainian and Russian Black Sea naval fleets.

"Then it seems logical to assume that whatever he sold," I said, "the arrangements were made there and then. Which suggests he was selling something from Ukraine, if not Crimea itself. I didn't see anything extraordinary in his house. Though there was all that furniture . . ."

"That had been around forever. They're nice pieces but not enough to stop renting the attached house, buy a Cadillac, travel to Europe, and eat steak four times a week."

"Four times a week?" I shook my head. "So we don't know what he was selling, whether he was accumulating inventory, or selling these pieces one by one."

I thought of the heist of the Isabella Stewart Gardner Museum in Boston, and recent suggestions that a Hartford-based mob had done the job. That was the type of inventory that could change a middleman's life. Perhaps my godfather had been selling stolen decorative arts or furnishings from Ukraine. It was a natural deduction given his line of business, Donnie Angel's interest in what I knew, and the job my brother had done for him.

"We also don't know what he did with his cash," Mrs. Chimchak said. "He didn't trust banks. He kept a minimum balance in his checkbook for expenses, tax payments, and the like. For appearance's sake. But you can bet he kept the majority of his profits in cash in his house. Did you check under the mattresses when you visited his home with Roxanne?"

Someone who didn't know the Ukrainian immigrant community might have been surprised, but I wasn't. Most people, like my parents, managed their funds like every other citizen. But some didn't. A friend of my deceased father's had kept his life's savings under the floorboards of a closet. When a fire broke out in his apartment building, he ran inside to rescue his money and burned to death.

"No," I said, and to my own surprise added, "but we should have. I should have thought of that."

Mrs. Chimchak nodded and I knew she was thinking of the same incident involving my father's friend. "Yes. You and Roxanne probably should give the house a thorough once-over."

"Would you come with us?"

"No. It's not my place. This is a family matter. Roxanne was his niece. You were his goddaughter. That's not a place for an old spinster. Besides, my back and my knees . . . I can't move around as well as I used to. I have a hard time with stairs, you know."

I raised my eyebrows. "You guys had that in common, too."

"Indeed."

We stared at each other with blank faces. I knew we were thinking the same thing.

"No way he went down those stairs on a rainy night," I said.

Mrs. Chimchak shrugged. "Rainy night, silent night. I don't care if the Stalin moon was shining the path down his stairs.

There is no way he went down them of his own accord. Someone pushed him. Someone killed him."

I marveled at her conviction. "You're so certain."

"Of course I am."

"Because he suffered from bathmophobia?" I pronounced the affliction in English but with a Ukrainian accent, as though that would somehow make it a Ukrainian word. I did that when my Uke vocabulary failed me, which was inevitable when the discussion included technical terms.

Mrs. Chimchak, thankfully, understood what I meant. "No. I'm not sure he was killed because of his fear of stairs. I'm sure he was killed, because the only reason he went down them was to get a bottle of wine. And he didn't need to do that the night he died."

"Why not?"

"Because I brought it up for him."

Her words echoed in my ears. "You were in his house the day he died?"

"I came by to discuss his invoices for March. We met once a month to go over the books. And before I left, he asked me to bring him up a bottle of French wine. There were many cases of wine. They looked expensive. I forgot to mention it. That's another place he parked some money."

"What time of day was this?"

She considered the question. "Midafternoon. About three o'clock. Right before your brother showed up."

A lump formed in my throat. I had to clear it to speak. "Marko?"

She nodded, not a hint of emotion about her.

"Marko was at my godfather's house that day?"

"He was walking up the sidewalk as I was leaving. He said hello, he was very polite. He never smiles, your brother. I feel sad for him because I wonder if he's ever experienced joy. But he does speak beautiful Ukrainian."

"Yes," I said, my head reeling from the revelation. Why hadn't Marko told me he'd been there? "He's a fanatic. He's obsessed with his Ukrainian heritage. His fluency is a point of great pride."

Mrs. Chimchak slid a folded piece of paper toward me. "That is a copy of a receipt for your godfather's airplane tickets for his first trip. Notice that he didn't pay for the tickets. A third party was billed."

I studied the receipt. Round-trip from New York to Crimea via Frankfurt and Kyiv. The cost of the tickets had been billed to the Black Sea Trading Company. The address given was in Sevastopol. There was also a phone number.

I pocketed the receipt, thanked Mrs. Chimchak, and got up to leave. She stopped at an alcove on the way and pulled a box out of a desk drawer. She turned and handed me a tin of Altoids. It was the same white box she'd given me during my survival test more than twenty years ago, with the teal piping around the edge. I smiled and tried to say no, but she insisted.

"Take them. Keep them close to you. When a person doesn't feel well, a mint will always improve her spirits."

I'd heard that line before. The Altoids helped save my life back then. The circumstances were different now, and there was no way they'd save me this time. Still, I changed my mind and took them. It was a spontaneous decision rooted in the knowledge that Mrs. Chimchak was giving them to me for a reason. She was reminding me that I was going to have to be as resilient as I'd been when she'd given a similar box to me last time. With this small gesture, she was also telling me to expect the unexpected, and to remain diligent at all times.

She asked me about my plan of action and I told her.

"You'll keep me informed?" she said.

"Better than that. I'll be back tomorrow. And the day after. And the day after that. Until we've solved the murder. Until we've solved it together."

She gave a slight nod of satisfaction and hustled me out the door.

I got back on the highway and headed toward Brasilia. Once I was safe in the left lane cruising at a comfortable seventy-nine-mile-per-hour pace, I flipped open the box of Altoids. I remembered the unexpected taste I'd experienced the last time I'd popped one of her mints into my mouth. This time I licked it first.

It really was a mint this time.

CHAPTER 21

On the morning of her third day, Nadia woke up to find her fire had survived the night. The log-feeding mechanism Mrs. Chimchak had taught her to build had actually worked. The sight of the low burning flames boosted her spirits, as did the realization her fever had broken.

She climbed out of her lean-to. The red sun rising in the East told her it was still early morning. She still had the rest of the food Marko had brought, and enough juices and water to last her through the night. With the fire burning and the extra matches he'd left her, nothing could go wrong. All she had to do was waste time and survive one more night.

Nadia ate a Baby Ruth candy bar for breakfast. It was the smart choice. It had peanuts for lasting energy and caramel for an instant pickup. Then she hiked to the stream and washed up. After she was done washing her face, however, she had to sit on a log to rest. The short walk and the simple act of splashing water with her hands had tired her out. By the time she returned to her camp she felt feverish again. Nadia cursed her bad luck as she fed the fire.

She wished she had some Sucrets throat lozenges or some Vicks cough drops to ease the pain in her throat. It hurt every time she tried to swallow. Then she remembered Mrs. Chimchak had given her the box of Altoids. Maybe a mint really could make a person feel better when she had no better options.

Nadia popped one into her mouth. Instead of a burst of mint, however, she choked on a bitter explosion. Nadia bolted upright and spit out the tablet. What was it? A salt or iodine tablet? Was it another test? Was she supposed to survive with some sort of strange substance in her body? Maybe the KGB had interrogated Mrs. Chimchak back in Ukraine. Maybe this was her sick way of toughening Nadia up. All the immigrants were wacko that way, Nadia thought. They had a different mentality about what made a person strong from regular Americans because they'd been through so much themselves.

The residual aftertaste of the tablet lingered on Nadia's tongue. Thirty seconds after she'd spit it out, she recognized the taste. It was aspirin! The kind adults took, not the baby kind her mother used to give her. She'd taken only one tablet about nine months ago when she'd had a terrible headache. Mrs. Chimchak had pretended to give her mints, but she'd filled the box with aspirin. It was a real wonder medicine, and Mrs. Chimchak cared about her so much she wanted her to have some in case she got sick. Either that or Mrs. Chimchak could already tell she was getting sick when she'd visited her camp. She knew things about people they didn't even know themselves. She was a strange, bizarre, spooky woman. She was the best.

Nadia took a fresh aspirin and washed it down with some pineapple juice. Then she slipped into her sleeping bag to rest. Her mind wandered, and she began to get scared about being sick all alone in the wildness.

Marko had taught her how to deal with unpleasant situations like these. Don't be scared of getting scared, he said. It's normal to be frightened in unusual circumstances. Make fear your friend. Let the fluttering in the belly and the pounding of the heart remind you to be alert and not do anything stupid. Then focus your mind on something else, Marko said. Picture yourself doing something you enjoy, and imagine you're really doing it.

And that's what she'd trained herself to do when she got scared or nervous. She did it when she had to recite a poem in front of the entire Uke community on stage at the National Home. The community put on half a dozen banquets during the year to commemorate a person or an event like Uke independence day. Sometimes a Uke dance troupe would perform, other times a Uke choir would sing.

And then there was the obligatory Nadia Tesla poetry recital. That was her punishment for being the best Uke student in school and having the best Uke diction. There was nothing she hated more than being volunteered by her father to commit eight stanzas to memory and stand in front of five hundred people and perform. She didn't even know what half the words meant or what she was getting all emotional about.

As the recital approached, her nerves got so tight she thought her head would explode. To ease the tension, she pictured herself eating her reward at McDonald's, a cheeseburger with fries and a vanilla shake. The key moment was when she sipped the shake with a mouthful of food, and the sugar in the shake blended with the salt from the burger and fries. Except she didn't get any reward after the last recital because she forgot a line and had to be prompted by her teacher from behind the stage. Her father got so mad . . .

But not as mad as he got when he learned Marko had doctored his report card, used a typewriter to turn an F into an A. As soon as he'd taken his belt off, Nadia had raced upstairs to her bedroom, hidden under the blanket, and covered her ears. Then she pictured herself reading The Adventures of Sherlock Holmes *in the living room, her father smoking a pipe, her brother watching baseball on the TV as their mother pared apples for them to share. They were happy. So happy . . .*

But there were times when the trick didn't work. Like when her father and mother screamed at each other, when he told her marrying her was the dumbest decision of his life, and she said she regretted having had his children. There was one time in particular, when they went totally ballistic and her father picked up a kitchen knife and pointed it at Nadia's mother, and Marko jumped in and stood in front of their mother to protect her. The anguish in Nadia's soul had been so intense she thought she would never get out of the moment, that she would never recover from the incident, that she would be incapable of experiencing happiness again.

Much to her surprise, she did recover from that incident. And her family went on pretending there were no problems, that they were a normal family. And so she would survive her final night here on the Appalachian Trail, too, Nadia thought.

She drifted in and out of sleep for hours. When she woke up to the sound of spitting and cracking, she thought she was seeing things because giant orange flames were raging against the black of night. That was impossible, she said to herself, because she'd been sleeping and hadn't fed the fire. Then she felt a gentle hand on her forehead and heard a voice that made her realize she was no longer sleeping and this was not a dream. It was the sound of a voice that might have instantly calmed other girls, but for Nadia it was the voice of holy terror.

It was the sound of her father's voice.

CHAPTER 22

THERE IS A PARADIGM IN THE FINANCIAL MARKETS CALLED the greater fool theory. In such a scenario, a person buys an investment knowing she is paying too much for it, with the underlying assumption she'll be able to sell it to someone else at an even higher price. In essence, the person knows she's exercising poor judgment but thinks she's smarter than everyone else. She believes she'll unwind her investment in time.

Such was my current situation. I knew Donnie Angel and his organization were out there. Maybe they were tracking my every move, or perhaps they simply kept watch on the motel where I was staying. But there was no doubt they knew I was in Hartford and understood exactly what types of questions I was asking. I had no doubt of this because if that weren't the case, I would have been already punished for breaking his leg.

I was certain this was the case as soon as I walked out of Mrs. Chimchak's house. In fact, I probably knew it earlier, the moment she implied my godfather had dealt in stolen art or antiquities, and that he hadn't trusted banks with his money. Those revelations meant that my godfather had probably left something valuable behind him. And by inquiring into my godfather's death, I was providing Donnie Angel an invaluable service.

I was leading him to the prize.

I doubted there was any cash in my godfather's home as Mrs. Chimchak had suggested. The house was protected with an alarm, but a criminal like Donnie Angel would know how to acquire a code or get past it, wouldn't he? If he'd found what he was looking for, he wouldn't have lifted me off the sidewalk in New York. It was as though he knew that my kidnapping assured him that I would continue to ask questions. I wondered if it were possible that Donnie Angel was so smart that he was playing me, or if I was simply thinking too much. Either way, there was no doubt in my mind that he was using me now.

The Uke community knew his reputation. People in the community wouldn't answer his questions. But he knew they would answer mine. That was the reason I'd remained unscathed since breaking his leg, I thought. In fact, it suggested that Donnie wouldn't have exercised his threat of breaking mine, that strapping me onto his leg-breaking machine was just a scare tactic. Why break my leg and risk that I would stop pursuing what he wanted?

Even if that were true, his mercy was calculated and temporary. Eventually, I'd discover what he wanted me to find or I'd cease to be useful. When that time came, he'd have his vengeance. By going on with my investigation even though I knew what awaited me, I was assuming that I would be able to extricate myself like the aforementioned person who'd overpaid for his investment.

As a result of my actions, I had become what I'd always deplored. I was playing the part of the greatest fool. Even worse, I was playing the role consciously and willingly, which surely made me the greatest fool of all. And yet I persisted. The thought of quitting was a nonstarter. I wasn't exactly sure why I was so committed, nor did I care to stop and hyperanalyze my motives. I had a mission and I was determined to complete it.

I called Paul Obon, my friend in New York, and asked him to see what he could learn about the Black Sea Trading Company. Then I called Brasilia and found out my brother wasn't working tonight. I tried him at home but got his answering machine. I didn't bother leaving a message.

Searching for him would have been futile, so I drove to the Ukrainian Catholic Church in Hartford instead. I had been planning to visit with Father Yuri to see if he could help me. Now I had even more questions to ask him. When I arrived, the church was open. Nine people stood waiting in line across from the confessional. Father Yuri kept the church open the Friday night before Easter to provide a longer window for people to cleanse their souls. That he was still doing so didn't surprise me. Sin was a perpetual growth industry.

Two banks of wooden pews faced a rich altar dressed in gold trim with colorful stained-glass windows above it. I dipped my right finger in a bowl of holy water resting on a sconce in the vestibule and crossed myself Eastern-style, thumb, index, and forefinger pressed together to represent the Holy Trinity. The openhanded gesture the Roman Catholics favored never made sense to me.

Tension melted from my body. The Church had been an emotional shelter where nothing could hurt me when I was a child. Time hadn't erased its magic despite my prolonged absence. I considered getting in line for confession myself but I wasn't prepared to bare my soul. Instead, I sat in a pew and waited half an hour for the church to empty and Father Yuri to emerge from the confessional.

Most priests looked older than their age, and the man who'd taught my catechism classes was no exception. The belt that encircled his waist could have secured a cargo container. He wore the toll of his profession on his body. Giant bags drooped beneath his eyes as he walked with a limp. When he saw me, he lit up. I smiled back but he screwed his face tight and nodded toward the exit instead. His frosty transformation filled me with dread.

I followed him outside. He looked around as he locked the church. I did the same. Cars lined both sides of the street, but they appeared as empty and harmless as the sidewalks.

"We have to talk," Father Yuri said. "Don't get me wrong, it's good to see the only altar girl I ever had, but we have to talk. Let's go inside the rectory . . ." His gaze fell on my Porsche. "Is that yours?"

"What do we have to talk about?"

"Zero to sixty in what—six seconds?"

"No. Under five. What do we have to talk about?"

"By God, that's better than sex. Especially for a man in my profession. Not that I'd know but even a priest has an imagination. Forget the rectory. We'll talk in the car."

"We will?"

He waddled toward the street. I hustled to catch up, still fixated on his prior sense of urgency to talk.

"I didn't remember you to be a car guy, Father."

"New hobby."

"Since when?"

"Since now. Let's take it on the highway and blow the doors off some minivans. They're constantly leaving my hybrid in the dust. I must have my vengeance."

"But I remember you preaching forgiveness from the time I was five years old."

"They didn't make minivans when you were five years old, child."

Father Yuri climbed behind the wheel and pushed the seat back to accommodate his huge belly. He was known as the gourmet chef, one who also received weekly platters from devoted Ukrainian spinsters.

"The Women's League has been spreading rumors about me," he said. "They say I emerged from my mother's womb with a Heineken in my right hand."

"Well, we know they're wrong about that. It was Lowenbrau. I always saw you drinking Lowenbrau at summer camp. Lowenbrau Dark, wasn't it?"

"You scoundrel," he said, laughing.

"Why did you say we have to talk?"

"Why do children remember what we wish they'd forget?" He pointed at the shifter, looking confused. "What is this thing?"

I couldn't have cared less about my car at that moment, but I did value our lives. "Wait. You've never driven a car with a manual transmission?"

He frowned. "What's a manual transmission?"

"You're kidding me, right?"

"No, I'm not kidding you. But how hard can it be?"

I stammered through an incoherent answer.

"Of course I'm kidding you," he said. "Buckle up, Danica. I did the two-day course at Lime Rock. It was a gift from a parishioner. He supplies them with tires. Let me show you how this thing's supposed to be driven." He wiped the traces of good humor from his expression. "And then we'll talk."

Fifteen minutes and an equal number of hairpin turns later, I was almost searching for a sick bag. The engine wailed as we raced down I-91 toward New Haven, carving up every minivan in sight.

"And she's on the cell phone too," Father Yuri said, as he passed one of them, finger pointed at the driver.

I clung to the armrest on the passenger door.

"What a machine," he said, as he slowed down to sixty-five. He merged into the right lane and blended with traffic. He took a deep breath and exhaled with satisfaction. "Thank you for that, Nadia." Then he glanced at me with the look of a man who was used to standing in God's place. "Now tell me, exactly what do you think you're doing?"

His question knocked the breath out of me. "What do you mean?"

"Don't play with me. This is your health and welfare we're talking about. Why are you digging around into things that are none of your business?"

A shiver ran through me. "How do you know what I'm doing?"

"It's an insular community, Nadia. You know that."

"Who told you I was asking questions?"

He cocked his head at me as though I should have known better than to ask. The priest-penitent privilege protected any communication between Father Yuri and anyone who'd confided to him in confidence. He didn't need to reveal what he knew to the police, and he certainly wasn't going to share the source of his knowledge with me. I couldn't even be sure it was only one person involved. There could be multiple degrees of separation between his source and one of the people who knew what I was doing.

"I presume you called me because you have some questions of me," Father Yuri said. "I may know the answers to some of them. I may not be able to answer others. But I will not be party to putting your life at risk."

I could hear my heart pounding as though someone had stuck a metronome behind my ear. "Is my life at risk?" I knew the answer, of course, but hearing someone else state the obvious was far more terrifying than believing it myself.

"Is Bohdan Angelovich using crutches?"

Father Yuri knew about Donnie Angel. He knew what I'd done to him, which meant he must have known that Donnie had kidnapped me. Only three people knew about that incident: Donnie, Roxy, and me. Except that was a guess. I had no idea how many people knew about it. Roxy, Donnie, the two guys in Donnie's van, or their boss could have been the source. I couldn't infer anything with certainty.

"I don't know," I said. "I haven't seen him for a few days. Is my life at risk?"

"Didn't your mother teach you to keep matches away from straw?"

"No. She sent me to PLAST camp where I learned how to put matches to birch bark. It burns just as fast."

"Why are you doing this?"

"Someone has to."

"Nonsense. Prying into an unlikely death will not bring back the departed. Why do you care so much?"

"I honestly don't know," I said. "I just know I have to follow this through to the end."

"Nonsense. You have a choice. You can walk away now."

"You of all people, Father Yuri, should understand the concept of a calling."

He slipped into the lane for the last exit in Hartford. It would deposit us at the border of Wethersfield, a mile away from the Uke National Home.

"Fair enough. We're about ten minutes away from church. For those ten minutes, in appreciation for allowing me to use this sublime piece of machinery, I'll discuss those things I'm permitted to discuss with you. I won't discuss anything else, and you won't mention this subject ever again once we get back to the church. And we will do so against my better judgment, as tribute to your generous heart and kind soul. The parish and I remain grateful for your donations."

His thanks only served to remind me I was unemployed. I was glad it was dark and he couldn't see me blush. I wondered if my financial situation would ever allow me to be generous again. Then I asked him if he'd seen any evidence of a surge in my godfather's disposable income or a change in lifestyle.

"The church never saw any of that money, if that's what you're asking me."

"So you knew he'd become rich?"

"He took me to Fleming's Steakhouse once."

"Where he had a regular table and the waitress knew his name."

Father Yuri looked shocked. "How did you . . ."

"The church never saw the money?"

Father Yuri shrugged. "I didn't say I didn't get a free meal out of it. Porcini-rubbed filet mignon. Definitely heaven-sent. I think he wanted me to know he was doing well. Which meant he wanted the community to know he was doing well, but I didn't see any increase in our collections."

"That was rather inconsiderate of him."

"I should say so."

"You'd think he'd understand even spiritual enterprises run on cash."

"You would, wouldn't you?"

"I love a pragmatic priest."

"As well you should. Believe me when I tell you, religion is a business, too. Prayers don't pay the electricity bill. You mind if I pass this lollygagger?" He downshifted into third and blew past a late-model BMW, glaring at the driver as he passed. "Why buy a sports sedan if you're going to drive ten miles below the speed limit?"

"Did you ask him how he'd come by his good fortune?" I said.

"I don't pry. I remember telling him, 'Business must be good,' and he said 'Never better. If you live long enough, anything can happen. Ukraine can gain independence, you can turn a profit on the past, and even an old scrounger can get lucky.'"

The last two lines caught my attention. "You're sure that's what he said? 'You can turn a profit on the past and an old scrounger can get lucky?'"

"My memory is infallible once fortified by a steak and a good Napa cabernet. He wanted to order French but I told him it was unpatriotic."

"Says the priest driving the German car."

"It's not my name on the registration."

The light turned, he mashed the pedal and turned right onto Wethersfield Avenue headed toward Hartford.

"Did he offer any other clues?" I said. "About how he was earning the money."

"No, but there were rumors."

"What rumors?"

"It's hard to keep a secret in a small community."

"Such as?"

"There were rumors he was making money along the lines of his usual business. Art and antiquities. But that he had a connection in Ukraine. And he was getting rare artifacts into the country with the help of some questionable characters and selling them for big money."

"Questionable characters?" I said. "Anyone I know besides Bohdan Angelovich?"

"You have enough to worry about with him, don't you?"

I couldn't argue with Father Yuri on that score. The rumor he'd shared with me jibed with Mrs. Chimchak's revelation about his life changing since he'd visited Crimea. I imagined a dispute arising about profit. I could picture my godfather demanding a higher cut, or Donnie Angel insisting on part of my godfather's cut. Donnie could have pushed him down the stairs himself, or had an accomplice do it. The horror was that I couldn't be sure my brother wasn't that accomplice.

A minute later, Father Yuri pulled into my original parking spot in front of the church. He slid the gear into neutral and lifted the emergency-brake handle, but left the engine running. It was his way of telling me he wasn't inviting me into the rectory to answer any more questions. Instead he turned toward me with a stern look.

"Walk away," he said.

I avoided his eyes and stared at the glove box.

"Walk away while you still can and go to the police. Ask for their protection."

"I can't."

"Why not? I'm still not clear on that. I know you loved your godfather and all, but please. Be real."

"I can't walk away. That's all I know."

He sighed, closed his eyes, and said a quick blessing, making the sign of the cross in my direction as he spoke. It was a quick request for God to watch over me. I crossed myself and thanked him.

He pushed the seat back as far as it would go and flung the driver's door open. I stepped out of the passenger seat while he hauled himself out of the vehicle.

"Anything else you can tell me, Father?"

He hesitated.

"Anything?"

Father Yuri considered my request. "I still remember when we were left with one altar boy. When your father suggested a girl, I thought, why not? You, with your excellent Ukrainian, perfect manners, and that boyish haircut. Will I see you at the blessing of the Easter baskets tomorrow?"

I hadn't even stopped to think about it. I remembered Donnie Angel telling me he used to attend with his mother. Of course, his mother had passed away and he was now a completely unrepentant criminal. The odds he'd be there were zero. Still, I couldn't see how attending the ceremony was going to help me find my godfather's killer.

"I'm sure your mother would be thrilled if you and your brother came," Father Yuri said, before I could answer. "And it would be a great opportunity for you to talk to your brother."

Father Yuri's words struck fear in my heart. I'd asked him if he could tell me anything else that would help me, and he'd just done so. He'd told me to talk to Marko. It was the advice I needed but didn't want to hear.

"Yes," I said. "You'll see me tomorrow."

CHAPTER 23

I TRIED TO FIND MY BROTHER BEFORE RETURNING TO THE motel. First I called Brasilia. A woman told me he wasn't working, which I found strange. I assumed Friday night was a profitable night in the strip club business, and that an owner-operator would want to be present. When my call to his house rolled to the answering machine again, I decided to drive to Willimantic and see both places for myself. My drive was for naught. The lights were off in his house and no one answered the doorbell. Meanwhile, Brasilia overflowed with breasts, butts, and beer-guzzling revelers, but Marko wasn't among the men maintaining order.

On Saturday morning I called my mother at 7:00 a.m. sharp. I had a personal rule not to call anyone before 8:00 a.m., but I'd long since passed the point of worrying about etiquette. Much to my shock, my mother welcomed the call. She'd been up all night baking *paska*—the special Easter bread—and *babkas*. Yes, she said, Marko had promised to be at the school hall behind the church for the blessing of the Easter baskets at 2:00 p.m. I told her I was coming over to her house and driving her to Hartford, and hung up before she could answer.

I got to within a mile of her house when I saw the white Honda parked discreetly beside a Dumpster at a twenty-four-hour food mart. It was one of the two modified cars I'd seen idling outside my godfather's house. Then, after visiting my mother, I thought I'd spied it again as I'd raced up the entrance lane to the highway. The suspension had been lowered close to the ground, fiberglass skirts had been added to the body, and the wheels were black. I suppose there could have been a third such car in the Hartford area, but it would have been an incredible coincidence.

I could see two figures inside the car as I took my turn perpendicular to the corner where they were parked, but the windows were tinted and I couldn't make out their faces or bodies. By the time I reached my mother's house, I'd deduced that either Donnie Angel had multiple teams of men covering my likely destinations, or he knew where I was going this morning. The only way he could have known where I was going was if my mother had told them. No one else knew I was coming to pick her up. No one.

I was prepared for some verbal punishment for hanging up on her, but when I stepped inside she hugged me as though we were soul mates. For a brief moment, all my concerns vanished. The white Honda, Donnie Angel, my godfather's death, Marko's possible involvement in his business or murder, my job loss, and the personal dissatisfaction I had to overcome every morning to get out of bed. None of it mattered as my mother held me. Only when she let go did a voice of reason remind me she had to have had an ulterior motive for her most uncharacteristic display of affection.

"I'm so happy to see my beautiful daughter," she said. "You know, my children are my pride and joy. I'm so thrilled you'll both be with me at the blessing today. The entire community will see us as the family we are. The other women will be so jealous of me. Come in, my kitten, and help me arrange the basket."

I realized her enthusiasm was a function of appearances. Or perhaps a combination of love and appearances. Yes, I thought. This sounded more logical. I understood it might have been a delusion, but I settled on it nonetheless. After all, it was the day before Easter.

We went to the kitchen.

"You said both of us will be joining you. Did Marko call? Did he call to confirm?"

"He told me a few weeks ago he'd be there today."

"You mean he didn't call to confirm?"

"Your brother's a con artist, a bum, and a degenerate sinner, but he's my son and I have no reason to doubt his word. You want some green tea?"

I shook my head. "So you didn't call him."

My mother looked at me as though I were an idiot. "Do I ever call my children? I don't want to bother either of you. I don't want to be one of those old women who's a pain in their children's butts. You think we should take all these colored eggs or leave the black one out?"

"You painted an Easter egg black?" I'd never heard of or seen such a thing.

She held it up. It was black as tar.

"My hairdresser has all the magazines," she said. "Black is the new black, didn't you know that? I'm just trying to bring fashion into the Easter basket. I thought you, Miss New York, would understand."

Only the Black Widow would put a black egg in her Easter basket, I thought. "Of course, Mama. You're right. Take the black egg. It works for you. But we're going to leave my car and take your Buick, okay?"

Her face fell. "Why?"

"I'm low on gas. I didn't have time to stop at a station, and I don't want to take any chances. I know how you hate it when a car isn't fully fueled and there's a risk of running out."

"Shame on you for not planning ahead. The one time your mother gets a chance to drive in a sexy car . . ." She bit her lip. "Pity. I would have looked so good in it pulling up to the church."

It was a lie, of course. There was plenty of high-octane in the 911; I wanted to switch cars. I doubted it would be of much help.

Even if I lost the boys in the white Honda, I was headed straight to the heart of the Uke community. I couldn't have made myself more conspicuous. Still, the mere thought of being in another vehicle lowered my blood pressure. At least I was changing my routine a bit. At least I was doing something differently.

We arranged the breads, colored eggs, ham, sausage, a mixture of horseradish and beets, butter, cheese, and salt in a wicker basket decorated with an embroidered cloth. My mother spent no less than fifteen minutes rearranging the items until the presentation met with her approval. Afterward, we packed the car and I drove us to church.

I held my breath as I approached the food mart where I'd seen my followers, but the Honda was gone. It was also nowhere to be seen in the rearview mirror. I wondered if a second car would pick up my trail any moment, and if there were even more than two vehicles following me. Then I wondered if they knew my mother drove a Buick. Perhaps I was alone for the first time in days. Perhaps I'd actually lost them.

My mother may have liked the idea of sitting in a sports car, but she didn't enjoy traveling at high speeds in any car. She scolded me twice and told me to slow down before I ever got on the highway. I apologized and reduced my speed. I needed her to be cooperative. I also wanted to ease into my intended topic of conversation but couldn't figure out a way to do so quickly. I had no time for small talk.

"We were talking about the DP camps the other day," I said. "Someone told me quite a few priests made it out of Ukraine during the war and ended up in the camps. I imagine Easter had special meaning back then. The resurrection of Christ, the Savior. It was probably a big deal in camp, wasn't it?"

She glanced at me as though I was trying to poison her. "You're going back there again? Give me a break. I thought I'd be sitting pretty in that little Porsche of yours. Like James Dean's girlfriend. But no. You want to go cruising down memory lane in my old American jalopy instead."

"That makes two of us. Wanting to cruise down memory lane."

"What are you talking about?"

"We're going to the blessing of the Easter baskets. Together. Where all your friends will see us, Mama. And remember us as a family growing up." My mother was the world heavyweight champion of quid pro quo. I was certain she'd understand. "Was Easter a big deal in the DP camps?"

She turned away from me and looked out the window. I glanced in her direction and saw her fidgeting in her seat, her head bobbing sideways and making little circles the way it did when she was irritated, digesting bad news, or contemplating something serious. In this case, it was all of the above, I suspected.

She turned back toward the windshield. She leveled her voice and sounded eerily calm. "Of course it was important. I was just a child but the adults did everything they could to give us structure and keep our spirits up." She talked about the day-to-day struggles and tedium for a minute. "Fear lingered in camp. From the war, from the Holocaust. And eventually, from the screenings."

"The screenings?"

"The screenings were a time of terror."

"What screenings?"

"We all felt the tension. Even the children. It hung in the air like a noose waiting to fall on anyone's head. You just prayed it wasn't your parents."

"What screenings?"

"People weren't simply allowed to enter the DP camps. They had to prove they were legitimate refugees. Everyone in camp was interviewed. The interviews took upwards of a year. The interviews were conducted in Russian, English, and German, regardless of whether the people being interviewed spoke any of those languages. It was chaotic. There wasn't enough room for all of us. Of course, the Russian officials were NKVD. Their real mission wasn't to help administer the camps. Their purpose was to persuade the Americans and British to reject as many people as possible. Anyone whose story didn't check out—anyone who changed a date from a previous interview, any charge of collaboration with the Nazis—and the person would be thrown out of camp."

"And then what happened to them?"

My mother fired a look of disapproval in my direction, as though with each question I was making her delve further into a topic she preferred to forget. "What do you think happened? Most of them ended up on trains going back to the Soviet Union."

"But I thought forced repatriation lasted only for a short time. I was told Eisenhower and his generals put an end to it."

"I didn't say anyone forced them to get on the trains."

"You mean they went voluntarily? Why? I thought that was the last place they wanted to go?"

"It was. But the NKVD rounded them up one by one. They kidnapped them off the streets if they had to, and then made them offers they couldn't refuse."

"What kind of offers?"

"Go back to the Motherland where you belong and the family you left behind will not be sent to a labor camp. Or murdered."

"Extortion? The Americans and the British allowed that?"

"The Americans and the British didn't understand the Russians. Plus they had their hands full managing the camps and trying to figure out where all the hard-core DPs would go. The ones who survived the screenings. The Americans and the British had no idea that SMERSH even existed."

"Did you say SMERSH?"

"Vindictive men with a vindictive spirit."

"I heard that name in a James Bond movie once. That was real? I assumed that was something Ian Fleming made up."

"You did? Well, so much for your college education. Stalin thought of the name. *Spetsyalnye Metody Razoblacheniya Shpyonov.*" Special Methods of Spy Detection. "He created SMERSH to prevent the Gestapo from infiltrating the NKVD. In the camps, SMERSH used bribery, blackmail, and threats to repatriate as many DPs as possible to the Soviet Union. After the camps were disbanded in 1950, they stayed in Europe and became the foundation for the Soviets' European spy network."

"And the DPs that went back because they were threatened. What happened to them and their families?"

My mother snickered. I could tell it wasn't directed at me. She was staring out the windshield remembering a scene from her past, or one that she'd imagined.

"The Soviet officers would gather around the trains that were leaving and make it look like a big party. They would clap and cheer and wish all the DPs a pleasant journey back home. But when the train crossed the border into Russia, all their bags would be seized and they would be greeted as traitors."

I darted into the exit lane for Hartford. It was the same exit Father Yuri had taken last night in my car, but we were coming from the opposite direction. It occurred to me that ever since I'd started digging into my godfather's death, I was increasingly discovering the truth to be the opposite of what I had thought it had been. In this case, my mother didn't sound like my mother. She sounded lucid, logical, and authoritative. She sounded like someone else's mother. That thought shook me to the bone.

"How do you know so much about this, Mama? I mean, I know you lived it and all, but you sound . . . You sound incredibly knowledgeable on the subject."

My mother looked out the side window again. "What? Your mother isn't the idiot you thought after all these years?"

We sat in silence for a minute as I negotiated some gridlock. I took a right onto Wethersfield Avenue and headed toward the church. I tried to connect what I'd learned to the DP entry in my godfather's calendar.

"Did SMERSH or the NKVD ever try to turn one DP against another?"

"It wouldn't surprise me if they tried it, but I never heard of anything like that. Our community was our strength. It's how we survived. Where is that coming from?"

"I found out my godfather was a bit of a scoundrel." I remembered my brother's assertion that my godfather had made sexual advances toward my mother. "Where business is concerned," I quickly added. I didn't want to embarrass her. "Do you think he could have discovered something about someone? Someone who was a DP but pretended he wasn't, or someone who was a DP and hurt the community. Do you think he could have been blackmailing someone? I know it's a stretch but it is possible."

"That sounds like nonsense to me. I knew your godfather pretty well. He was a drunk and a pervert, but he was not a blackmailer. He wasn't mentally strong enough for that sort of thing. Try to get a corner parking spot. I don't want some fat Ukrainian kielbasa-lover swinging his door open and denting my vintage Buick."

Until that moment, I'd assumed my godfather's murder was related to his business. Now, for the first time, I realized that wasn't necessarily the case. He might have been murdered as a function of his involvement in some other scheme. Something related to his experience in a World War II Displaced Persons camp.

The Uke school was located behind the church. I drove around the lot like a zombie, still dwelling on my mother's revelations. All the parking spots were taken. Families marched toward the school hall in their Sunday best carrying Easter baskets. My mother became frantic that the school hall had filled up and there would be no vacant spots on the tables for her to place her basket. She told me to drop her off and go find a parking spot on the street quickly, but I was barely listening. I was focused on the image of the letters DP on my godfather's calendar.

I pulled over. My mother got out of the car and removed the basket from the back seat. Then she stuck her head back in the passenger-side door.

"One ride. One conversation. Don't ever ask me about the past again. I know what this is about. I know how your mind works. Trust your mother. You're not going to get any satisfaction trying to find out what your father did and didn't do before he came to America. So take my advice, and let it go."

With that, she slammed the door shut and left me shell-shocked.

My father had died when I was thirteen. He'd never spoken to me about his life in Ukraine before he immigrated to America, and I'd been too scared and young to express any curiosity. I'd never thought about his past. Now, thanks to my mother, I had another mystery to solve.

I parked on the street along the sidewalk facing Colt's Park, and hurried to the school hall. I climbed the stairs to the auditorium on the second floor. It teemed with people. There had to be hundreds of them. The cumulative noise of their conversations was deafening. I wedged my way through a group of men I'd never seen before in my life and caught a glimpse of one row of Easter baskets. They sat atop a series of rectangular tables that had been arranged along the perimeter of the basketball court. Families huddled beside their baskets waiting for the priest to arrive.

At first, I didn't recognize anyone. Then I bumped into my former geography teacher from Ukrainian school. She gave me a quick hug and told me someone had saved a spot for my mother near center court. I spied my mother farther down the column of tables, smiling lovingly and in animated conversation with a broad-shouldered man. His head was obscured by a father of four, who was standing beside his wife. I knew immediately that the broad-shouldered man was Marko. A combination of excitement and dread filled me as I pushed my way toward them. I vowed not to let him out of my sight until he answered all my questions truthfully this time.

My mother was the first to see me. She smiled. Her children had accompanied her to the blessing of the Easter baskets. It was every mother's dream, and it gave me some satisfaction to have helped fulfill it.

"Look who stopped by to say hello," my mother said.

I stepped around the father of four but it wasn't Marko's face that I saw. Instead I looked straight into the smiling eyes of Donnie Angel.

CHAPTER 24

It was a surreal moment. Donnie Angel stood leaning on crutches beside my mother, the two of them beaming at each other as though they were about to be nominated for sainthood. I couldn't believe I wasn't prepared for this event. I'd considered it, of course; I wasn't an idiot, at least not usually. I'd heard Donnie Angel admit how much he enjoyed this particular ceremony. I'd noted the sincerity in his voice when he told me how much it meant to him to return to his community and be welcomed, if only for a day. But there was no reason for him to be here. None whatsoever. His parents were dead, and he needed me doing his dirty work for him, namely, looking for the cash and the inventory. That's why I'd banished this possibility from my mind.

There was no rational explanation for Donnie's presence. And yet, there he stood, two feet away from me, a cast on his left leg, the one I'd proudly broken.

"You remember my daughter," my mother said, "don't you, Bohdan?"

She asked the question in Ukrainian, but Donnie answered in English. He'd had limited Ukrainian language skills growing up. My mother undoubtedly knew this but to a Uke Mom, a Uke kid was forever a Uke kid.

"Of course I remember her," he said.

He extended his hand. I had no choice but to take it. It felt like snakeskin plucked from the fridge. I tried to slip out of his grip as soon as his fingers tightened, but he held my hand firmly, braced himself on the crutches, and kissed it. I'm sure my mother thought he was being a classy European fellow, but that was only because his back obscured her vision, and she couldn't see his tongue linger on the back of my palm before his lips engulfed my knuckle.

I cringed. It was a full-body shiver that started at my wrist and spasmed down to my toes. It was as discreet a rejection as my mind, body, and soul could demonstrate under the circumstances, given I was surrounded by men, women, children, and Easter baskets.

My mother didn't notice my reaction. She was too busy cooing.

"What a gentleman," she said.

I regained my composure. "Good to see you, too, Donnie," I said.

My mother frowned. "Donnie?"

I managed to keep smiling. "How long has it been?"

"Who's Donnie?" she said.

"Sixteen . . . eighteen years?" I said.

His lips turned down. "What do you mean? We ran into each other in New York a few days ago. Don't tell me you've forgotten?"

"Will someone explain to me who Donnie is?" my mother said.

She knew he preferred to be called Donnie instead of Bohdan. Such a rejection of one's proper Ukrainian name was a sore point with the older generation, and I knew she simply wanted to tease him.

"Bohdan is Donnie," I said.

"Oh, really," my mother said. She glanced at Donnie. "How did you manage that translation?"

"You know how it is in America, Mrs. T. It's easier to conduct business when someone can pronounce your name real easy."

"It's easier? Who said easier is better? Would you rather be the man who made it easy, or the one with the different name that everyone remembers?"

"Geez. That's a good point, Mrs. T. I never thought of it that way."

My mother nodded with satisfaction before frowning again. She glanced alternately from Donnie to me. "Who ran into whom in New York?"

"I bumped into gorgeous, here, on the Upper East Side," Donnie said. "Same neighborhood where you live, right?"

I didn't want my mother to get suspicious and start asking questions about how and why we bumped into each other. I needed to change the subject as quickly as possible.

"We never got a chance to talk," I said. "So what have you been doing with yourself all these years?"

"Yes," my mother said, clearly intrigued by the question. She knew Donnie's reputation and probably couldn't wait to hear what lie he was going to spin. There was no reason for her to be afraid of the conversation, even though she knew he was a criminal. After all, she had no idea he'd kidnapped her daughter and she'd broken his leg. "Tell us, Donnie. What do you do for a living?"

Donnie dazzled us with a smile. "I own a chain of rental shops."

"Rental shops?" my mother said. "Like tuxedos and dresses for weddings?"

Donnie laughed. "No, Mrs. T. Like furniture, televisions, and microwaves."

My mother looked incredulous. "People rent microwaves?"

"Sure," Donnie said. "It's big business. I have stores in Bridgeport, Norwalk, and Waterbury. And I'm opening up a new one in Newark. My first store outside Connecticut." He leaned back on the crutches and thrust his chest forward.

This was news to me but it made sense. Rent-to-own schemes charged huge interest rates and repossessed property. It was as close to criminal as a legitimate business could get.

"Good for you," my mother said. She seemed genuinely impressed. "We hear all these rumors about you, you know. But you're telling me you've cleaned up your act."

"Absolutely, Mrs. T. A man gets to a certain age, he's got to take a good look in the mirror. It ain't no fancy job like a doctor or nothing, but we're providing an important service to folks who can't afford the basics."

My mother nodded. "It's an honorable profession. You're doing good for your community. Yes, you are."

Donnie chuckled and nodded in my direction. "Tell that to your daughter. I offered to buy her a glass of champagne that night we ran into each other, but I don't think my bubbly was good enough for her."

My mother scolded me with a glance. "You refused a glass of champagne from an old friend?"

"Kicked her heels up and ran away from me like a gazelle," Donnie said. "All I saw was legs. She looks great, though, don't she?"

My mother shrugged as though he were stating the obvious. "She's my daughter, isn't she?"

Donnie burst into laughter.

A bustling young woman with two little girls dressed like pink bunnies knifed past us. She searched in vain for an empty space on the table. I realized we were completely surrounded. Bodies were packed tight and deep. I couldn't have made a run for it if I tried. We were trapped at the center of the gym. My mother, the charming sociopath from the Ukrainian-American gutter, and I.

"Truth is, I shouldn't be laughing," Donnie said. "A close friend of mine died yesterday."

My mother touched him on the shoulder. "I'm so sorry. Anyone we knew?"

"He'd just moved up north. Decided to go ice fishing. Lake's still frozen this time of year. Or so he thought. He fell right through."

"That's awful," my mother said. "And he was alone? There was no one there to save him?"

Donnie shook his head solemnly, and then planted his eyes on mine. "Only his two dogs. Loyal to a fault. They jumped in after him. The three of them drowned together."

My mother offered more sympathy.

Donnie didn't take his eyes off me. "It just goes to show you. You can never be sure how solid the ground is beneath your feet."

I doubted Donnie had a friend who'd died. In fact, I doubted Donnie had any friends at all. His fiction was a message. I was the friend in his story. My assumption of safety was the ground beneath my feet. But who were the two dogs?

"Speaking of feet," my mother said. "What happened to your leg?"

Donnie held my gaze and smiled slowly. In the time it took him to spread his lips and flash his teeth, the ice began to melt beneath my feet. Both my legs were shaking. What would he tell her? And exactly what was he telling me?

"Sports injury," Donnie said.

"I didn't know you were a sportsman," my mother said.

Donnie wiped the smile off his face. "My cleats got stuck in the carpet."

"What kind of sport were you playing indoors?"

Donnie paused. I could picture the knife-edge of my shoe connecting with his tibia, hear the sound of the paint stick cracking in half. In retrospect, I couldn't believe I'd done it. And now he was here to tell me he was going to kill me. My legs wobbled so badly I feared everyone around me would notice them.

"Soccer," Donnie said. "It was an indoor stadium in Waterbury. AstroTurf."

"Afro-turf?"

Donnie chuckled. "No, Mrs. T. AstroTurf. It's fake grass. Like a carpet over concrete."

"I've never heard of such a thing. Sounds like a rug from another planet. Who plays soccer on a carpet?"

"If I ever see the guy that pushed me when my cleat got stuck . . ."

My mother gasped. "Someone pushed you?"

Donnie bored into me. "Yeah."

"You'll get even the next game. Forgiveness is overrated." My mother raised a fist and screwed her face tight. "You stick him where it hurts."

"I love your style, Mrs. T. But I doubt I'll ever see him again. He knows me too well. I'm sure he's left town. Left town for good."

The crowd hushed. Father Yuri appeared at center court, inside the perimeter of tables. A cassock with golden hues hung like a tent from his shoulders. The two altar boys behind him were dressed in black.

Donnie held both crutches in his left hand and gave my mother a hug. "It's so great to see you, Mrs. T," he said. "You'll always be my Mrs. Robinson." He pulled back, left his arm around her, and smiled at me. "Your daughter is so lucky to have you and her brother. Alive, and well, and close by. You can't put a price on family, can you, Nadia?"

The people behind us were craning their necks to see Father Yuri, but when a man in crutches begged their pardon they listened. A narrow gap formed in the crowd. As Donnie Angel disappeared among them, the people returned to their places and sealed the gap. The evil Moses, I thought, was leaving the building.

"Still a handsome devil," my mother said. "Just like his father. He had a crush on me. The father, that is. You know, if he has turned himself around, you could do worse. Don't those rental places make a lot of money?"

Father Yuri began the ceremony with a prayer. My mind swirled. The dogs who died in Donnie's imaginary story were his supposed friend's closest companions. They were the equivalent of family. When Donnie told my mother how lucky I was to have a mother and a brother, he was making it clear to me that he'd kill them both if I didn't leave Hartford immediately and stop asking questions.

There was a more logical analysis to be made but I was incapable of making it. Donnie Angel knew that my mother and brother meant more to me than anything or anyone else in my life, and he'd left no doubt in my mind that he would shatter the ice beneath their feet without any hesitation. As Father Yuri walked around the basketball court blessing the Easter baskets and sprinkling holy water onto each and every one, I plotted my exit. I needed to get out. For my mother's and brother's sakes, I needed to leave Hartford immediately.

But before I could depart I had to wait for the ceremony to end and the crowd to disperse. It took less than ten minutes but the delay was excruciating. I passed the time by watching the altar boys and remembering when I was one of them, young and invulnerable, protected by my belief in a just God and eternal salvation. Back then, I couldn't wait to leave Hartford and start a new life, away from my parents, their expectations, and the ethnic traditions that constrained my youth. Now here I was, two decades later, desperate to escape again.

I knew my mother would become inveigled into multiple conversations with her friends after the ceremony. She'd want me by her side. It would take her close to an hour to get to the car. She wouldn't realize, of course, that each minute I lingered, her and my brother's lives were increasingly at risk.

I had to get away immediately.

I spotted an acquaintance of my mother's from Rocky Hill, Mrs. Smith, and a solution sprang to mind. I walked over to her, said hello, suffered through a minute of small talk, and then asked her for a favor. Afterward, I hurried back to my mother, who was receiving compliments on her Easter basket from a handsome, elderly man I didn't recognize. One of her suitors, no doubt.

"Mrs. Smith is going to drive you home," I said. "Something's come up. I have to go back to New York now. I'm going to switch cars on the way home." I leaned into her ear. "I'll leave the key on top of the driver's side rear wheel."

My mother pulled her neck back, disappointment etched in her face. She glanced at her friend, who stood by expectantly.

"But I wanted to introduce you to some people."

"I'm sorry, Mama. I'd love to hang out with you, but I can't."

She studied me again. Her expression turned serious. "What's wrong?" she whispered.

"Nothing. Just business. Go home with Mrs. Smith."

My mother hesitated as though she wanted to ask more questions. But then she cleared her throat and raised her voice so everyone could hear her.

"I understand, my kitten," she said. "It's not easy being a top financial executive these days. I appreciate that you came. You go, take care of yourself." She leaned in and kissed my cheek.

Her kiss disoriented me. Even though it was for show, under any other circumstances it would have made my day, year, or quite possibly my life. But now it simply reminded me how arrogant I'd become and how close I was to ruining the lives of the two people who mattered to me the most. I wanted to climb into a time machine and go back and change things, or jump into a vat of acid and dissolve my entire being.

I started to leave but she tugged on the sleeve of my coat.

"One more thing," she said, leaning into me. "Ignore what I said before. Stay away from that Bohdan Angelovich. He was bad news from the moment he came out of the womb. His mother was a pathological liar and so is he. Don't believe a word he says. Promise?"

"Yes, Mama. I promise."

"Good. Now don't forget. Send me that big check soon."

Kisses and advice in exchange for money. That was a new one, I thought.

I kept my head down as I headed for the stairs for fear someone would recognize me and call my name. I couldn't imagine stopping to reminisce and wasting more time, but I didn't want to be rude to good people. I held my breath until I got to the door and exhaled when the sunshine hit my face outside the school hall.

My relief didn't last long.

Donnie Angel's van sat idling in front of me.

CHAPTER 25

EXHAUST BILLOWED FROM FOUR TAILPIPES, ACCOMPANIED BY an intermittent rasp. The two men who'd snatched me off the streets of Manhattan stepped out of the van. One of them threw a cigarette butt onto the ground and stomped it out. The parking lot was filled with people carrying Easter baskets. Some were milling about chatting; others were climbing into their cars. A line of vehicles was waiting by the exit. There was no way for the van to leave the parking lot, and they couldn't kidnap me right behind the church in front of a hundred people.

Could they?

I turned and headed toward my car. Their appearance was so audacious, the sight of the van so disturbing, that I began to run. I sprinted down the sidewalk from the school past the church. When I caught up to a dozen people headed for their cars on the street, I stopped and looked over my shoulder.

I didn't see the two men. They weren't on my heels. A wave of relief washed over me. Then I spotted them, leaning against the back of the van, staring straight at me. As soon as our eyes met, they climbed into the van without saying a word to each other. The brake lights flashed red. The driver was shifting into gear, I thought. They were going to follow me. They were coming after me.

The rectory obscured the school parking lot, but I could see traffic backed up at the intersection to the main road where I was parked. The van couldn't have followed me if it wanted to. I had an advantage. I could escape.

Only after driving away in my mother's Buick and seeing no van in the rearview mirror did I remember the white Honda parked a mile away from my mother's condo in Rocky Hill. I realized there was no need for them to follow me closely. They knew exactly where I was going.

I powered through a yellow light and cursed the car's lack of acceleration. I considered driving directly to New York City in my mother's car. That would have allowed me to escape whatever Donnie Angel had planned for me at my mother's condo. But then what? My mother would have been stuck at home with no car. She couldn't have operated the Porsche's manual transmission, and even if she could have driven it, the keys were in my pocket.

I took the exit for Rocky Hill and rounded the twenty-four-hour supermarket. But the white Honda was nowhere to be seen. My car was right where I'd left it across the street from my mother's home. I circled around the block three times. Two men were fixing the roof. One of my mother's neighbors was washing his SUV in his driveway. I tooted my horn and waved. He waved back.

That gave me all the confidence I needed to make the switch. I parked the Buick, got into my own car, and drove to the Super 8 to check out of the motel. Fifteen minutes later, I merged onto the Merritt Parkway, my preferred route to New York City. It snaked through western Connecticut via valleys, dips, and blind brows. Trucks were not allowed on the parkway, and in a worst-case situation, the van couldn't have kept pace with my car.

After an hour of driving, I pulled into a rest stop to use the facilities. I bought a Diet Dr Pepper and a Three Musketeers bar, and only after medicating with some chocolate did the obvious occur to me.

My mother was not at risk. My brother was not at risk.

I was perfectly safe.

My mother's final words were prophetic. Donnie Angel was a pathological liar. *Don't believe a word he says.* Donnie Angel had implied he'd kill me and my family if I didn't leave Hartford immediately, which was to say, if I didn't stop asking questions. In fact, per my mother's assertion, he was lying. He had no plans to kill any of us.

Another death or disappearance would be bad for business. Three more deaths would be infinitely worse. Donnie couldn't afford any adverse attention from the police or the community. There was too much money at risk. The art and antiquities smuggling ring in which my godfather had participated was too profitable. The last thing Donnie wanted was more trouble. What Donnie needed more than anything was a return to normalcy. And if he wanted a return to normalcy, it meant I was no longer useful to him. He no longer needed me to ask the questions no one would answer for him.

The conclusion was as clear as the whipped nougat was delicious: Donnie Angel had found the money. Whether it was my godfather's cash, or some art or antiquities that hadn't been sold yet, I wasn't sure. But in either case, I'd accomplished his mission, even though I hadn't achieved my goal. I still didn't know who'd killed my godfather or why.

I threw the wrapper in the garbage can in the parking lot and sipped my Diet Dr Pepper in my car. After liberating myself in Donnie Angel's van, I thought I'd never act on emotion again. I assumed I'd crossed a threshold of cumulative adversity such that I'd remain calm and analytical under any circumstances. Now I knew that was wishful thinking. My wiring had not changed. I was no action hero. I didn't relish conflict or confrontation, and the threat of violence still scared me. It always would. I was still the same person as I'd always been with one exception. I'd proven to myself that I could do the unimaginable if it was necessary to complete my mission.

Donnie Angel's use of leverage was unoriginal and unsurprising. He'd threatened my family. The effectiveness of his threat was equally unsurprising. I cared so much about my mother and brother that I'd lost my composure, did exactly what he wanted me to do, and ran. In a way, that infuriated me. My relationships with both my mother and brother were frayed or broken. The more I tried to mend them, the worse they got. My mother had told me I was to blame for my husband's death. My brother had asked me to do him a personal favor and fuck off. I wanted to care less about both of them. Yet no matter how hard I tried to detach myself from them, I couldn't.

Time passed. Fifteen minutes, half an hour, and then a full hour. I listened to some classical music and sought inspiration as to what to do next. I used the facilities again. When I returned to the car, the logical course of action was obvious to me. A change of scenery would clear my mind and help me think more rationally. The smart move was to return to New York City.

I pulled out of my parking spot and headed toward the entrance ramp for the parkway headed south. When my cell phone rang, I considered ignoring it, but then a vision of Mrs. Smith having a car accident flashed before my eyes. It's illegal in Connecticut to hold a cell phone and drive at the same time, and I hate steering a car with one hand, so I pulled over before getting on the ramp, and answered it.

It was Paul Obon, my booksmith friend and walking encyclopedia on all matters pertaining to Ukraine.

"It took awhile," he said, "but I finally heard back from an old colleague in Crimea."

"Crimea?" The events of the day had dulled my memory. I'd forgotten I'd asked him to make some inquiries regarding the company that had paid for my godfather's tickets to Ukraine.

"The Black Sea Trading Company is an export company specializing in floating crafts."

"Boats?" I said.

"Fishing vessels, commercial and recreation. It started as a state-run enterprise and was eventually bought by a man named Boris Takarov. He was a career foreign service officer for the Soviets. When basic industry was privatized in 1996, he had the necessary connections as an insider to get control of the business."

"Foreign service officer. What does that mean?"

"Takarov was stationed in West Berlin from 1946 to 1950, and then spent twenty-one more years in Vienna, Amsterdam, and Rome."

"He was a diplomat?"

Obon chuckled. "Yes, in the Russian sense. He was a spy. He was NKVD and KGB."

"If he was NKVD from 1946 to 1950 and stationed in West Berlin . . ."

"He was one of the Soviet officers assigned to the administration of Displaced Persons camps."

I made an obvious deduction from my mother's insight. "He was SMERSH."

"It's impossible to know for certain, but yes, Takarov may have been SMERSH. The Russians began installing the infrastructure for their spy operations in Western Europe immediately after the war. And they did so with the full cooperation of their European and American allies, unwitting as it may have been. The Soviet officers assigned to the DP camps were handpicked not only to help repatriate the refugees considered to be traitors and collaborators, but to burrow into the fabric of European society. Takarov may have been one of them."

Whether he was SMERSH or not, Takarov had been stationed in the DP camps. That meant he might have known my godfather. That explained their connection, but not their personal history.

"Is the Black Sea Trading Company involved in any other exports?" I said.

"Such as?"

"Arts and antiquities."

"Not on record. But a business like this . . ." Obon hesitated as though he were searching for the right words. "It wouldn't be a surprise if the shipbuilding was now a front for other businesses as well."

"Why do you say that?"

"Because Takarov died six months ago. His sons inherited the business. His sons are the subject . . . the subject of rumors."

"What rumors?"

Obon paused. This time I had the sense he was more concerned about what he was about to reveal than finding the right words. A note of caution peppered his voice. "There have been accusations that they have a more profitable family business on the side. That they are colleagues of a man named Milanovich."

"Never heard of him."

"Of course you haven't. That's how he likes it. Milanovich is the most dangerous man alive that no one has ever heard of. Number three on the FBI Most Wanted list. He is the global head of the so-called Russian mafia."

Marko. All I could think of was my brother. At a minimum, he'd taken a job as protection for my godfather during a delivery, not knowing he was getting involved in mob business. The more frightening scenario was that he had lied about the depth of his involvement, and he was either my godfather's silent partner or the man who'd murdered him.

"Now I want to emphasize," Obon said, with a note of urgency, "that both the Takarovs have vehemently denied such rumors, and to date they remain just that. I'm telling you about them just in case . . . so that you understand . . . if you are involving yourself in their business in any way . . ."

I had no interest in their merchandise, money, or business.

All I cared about was finding out what happened to my godfather and my family's safety. I thanked Obon for his concern and thoughtfulness.

"The Black Sea Trading Company's floating craft business," I said. "Do you know where their top three importers are located?"

His voice turned faint as I heard the sound of papers shuffling. "I have that here somewhere." A ten-second pause followed. "Thirty-two percent Russia. Seven point eight percent Turkey. And five point five percent of their goods are imported by buyers in the United States of America."

Black Sea Trading had an established exporting process to the United States. They knew how to package, ship, insure, and deliver. I imagined they had connections at ports in the United States as well as Crimea. I wondered how hard it would be to hide stolen arts and antiquities in a boat.

I thanked Obon and told him I'd be in touch. After hanging up I remembered my mother's unexpected warning not to dig into my father's past. I'd meant to ask Obon to do some research on him, but in the heat of the moment I'd forgotten all about it. Just as well, I thought. That was a matter for a later date.

With my engine still idling, I hit *67 on my cell phone to block my identity and called Brasilia. I let it ring eight times but no one answered. It was approximately 5:30 p.m. and I knew their business didn't pick up until later in the evening. Still, it was a Saturday, and I was surprised someone wasn't manning the entrance, collecting cover charges, and answering the phone. Then, as I was about to hang up, I heard a quick, coarse hello. It was a familiar voice and tone, one that told the caller he hated to answer the phone for any reason, and he enjoyed surprise phone calls even less, which is why he refused to carry a cell phone.

Marko hadn't worked last night, but he was working tonight.

I hung up without saying a word. By not identifying myself, I'd preserved the element of surprise. The latter was necessary because there was no reason to expect my brother to be more welcoming this time. Our discussion wasn't going to be a colorful and cordial affair like the blessing of the Easter baskets. This meeting was going to be the essence of familial darkness, the stuff that led one to close the curtain behind him, kneel before God, and confess one's transgressions. The stuff that left emotional scars forever and ruined lives.

I zipped down the parkway, took the first exit, looped around to the north side, and gunned the engine.

Fear, prudence, and Donnie Angel be damned.

I was headed back to Hartford.

CHAPTER 26

NADIA'S FATHER KEPT HIS PALM ON HER FOREHEAD AND studied her eyes. It would have been hot a couple of hours ago, she guessed, but thanks to Mrs. Chimchak's aspirin it probably wasn't that hot. She didn't feel as though she was burning up inside anymore.

Marko stood beside him. The flames from the torch burning in his hand prevented Nadia from seeing his eyes. She wished the torch had died.

"Not that bad," her father said. "A bit hot. Light fever. Not heavy fever. Not that bad. Is it, Nadia?"

Nadia shook her head right away. "Uh-uh. Not that bad. Not that bad at all."

Her father patted her on the head. "That's my girl."

Marko cleared his throat. "Um, I'm not so sure about that. Looks pretty bad to me."

Their father ripped Marko a new one with a single glance. "What do you know about the human body, slacker? Except how to abuse it with drugs and alcohol."

An excruciating cramp wracked Nadia's stomach. She hated it when her family didn't get along. Hated it more than anything in the whole world. More than all the girls who picked on her at school and camp put together and multiplied by a hundred.

Her father turned back to her and smiled. "So do you want to stay here through the night and earn your merit badge, or do you want to go home?"

"I want to stay," Nadia said, knowing this was what her father wanted to hear.

"Good girl," he said, beaming at her.

Nadia was so happy he smiled at her she was prepared to stay in her lean-to alone for as many nights as necessary, even if it killed her.

Nadia's father told her he was proud of her. He told her they'd be back to get her at 8:00 a.m., and until then, in accordance with survival test rules, she was on her own.

As they turned to leave, Nadia tried to make eye contact with her brother but it was impossible. She could tell he was looking at her, probably trying to encourage her somehow, but she couldn't make out his face. Then he turned and followed their father into the woods, and for the first time in her life Nadia felt truly alone.

She crawled back into her sleeping bag and counted bobcats to fall asleep. By one hundred seventeen, a light rain started to fall. By two hundred ten, she drifted asleep. An hour later, she woke up covered in sweat. She felt delirious so she took two aspirin and washed them down with a fresh can of pineapple juice. She ate some Ritz Crackers, too. Ritz Crackers were some of the finest food known to mankind. They never failed to give her a boost and make her happy. But this time she couldn't taste them. No matter how hard she focused, she couldn't taste that sugar and salt combo she loved so much. She closed her eyes and counted imaginary bobcats again. They were cute, like kitties but with an extra edge. Her kind of edge . . .

The two aspirin did the trick. Nadia fell into a deep sleep. So complete was her slumber, she didn't feel the rain when it fell in sheets from the sky and pelted her sleeping bag. Nor did she hear the crash of thunder, its echo among the trees, or hours later, the sound of unfamiliar footsteps approaching her camp.

CHAPTER 27

Brasilia's parking lot overflowed with vehicles, from an ancient Chevy pickup to a late-model Maserati sedan. A stretch limo in the shape of a Hummer idled by the side entrance. Six college-aged men bounded toward the front door joking with one another, faces bursting with anticipation.

The building pulsated to the beat of some old heavy-metal song, a raspy voice begging someone to pour some sugar on him. I approached the bouncer at the door, a thirty-something beast with a pleated and puckered face, dressed impeccably in a navy suit that might have been sewn from the fabric of three of Brooks Brothers' finest.

He sized me up the way an auctioneer might have done in centuries past and flashed me a smile boasting four gold teeth. I was already fired up for my encounter with Marko, and I wasn't going to swallow any insults from some misogynistic thug. I sharpened my tongue.

"Are you here for a job application, ma'am?" he said.

I hesitated, uncertain if I'd heard him correctly. His eyebrows remained raised, his expression earnest. He wasn't patronizing me, I realized. He was being serious. Sometimes I had to remind myself I'd lost all that weight and wasn't entirely hard on the eyes.

"And what if I am?" I said.

"The boss does interviews in the afternoon on account of it gets busy at night. You want to leave your name and come back tomorrow?" There wasn't a hint of facetiousness about him.

I knew there'd come a moment when I'd be rewarded for staying out of the Two Little Red Hens Bakery on the Upper East Side, and curbing my addiction to their Brooklyn blackout cupcakes. And here it was, at a time when I least expected it. In fact, I was so happy, I wished I had one of their cupcakes in my car so I could celebrate.

"If you read minds by any chance," I said, "please forgive me."

He looked confused. "Excuse me?"

I put my hand on his shoulder. "No matter what you may have heard me think, the truth is you're a kind man with impeccable taste. I'm going to have a look inside, okay? My name is Nadia. My brother, Marko, he owns the joint."

I blew past him and walked inside.

The place smelled of coconut, not disinfectant as before. The refugee from Woodstock had been replaced by six nubile young beauties. Two of them actually looked Brazilian, with bronzed bubble butts so big you could have gotten loans to build condos on them in the days of zero percent financing. The seedy stragglers had been replaced by one hundred or more men, from newbies to geriatrics, some with dirt on their Wranglers, others with pinstripes on their Armani suits.

I found Marko with his back to me behind the bar mashing lime and sugar in a muddler beside a long bottle of Brazilian cachaca. Four suits were laughing at the counter opposite him. I spied a grin on his face and deduced he'd just told them a joke. If there was one thing I was certain my brother knew how to do, it was empty a man's pockets.

When he turned around and saw me, he froze. Shock and anger spread across his face. Without saying a word, he had told me that I was the last person on Earth he expected or wanted to see. He quickly served the caipirinhas, made his way around the bar and motioned for me to follow him to his office. He didn't do so with a casual and friendly wave. Instead he pointed a finger, first at me and then at the office, like an angry trooper motioning to a speeding driver to pull her ass over.

We went into his office. I felt as though I were following the headsman to the town square to receive my just punishment. I counted five open bottles of Mickey's Big Mouth in the room. Marko didn't sit down this time. We stood in front of his desk facing each other. His expression was one of contained fury.

"I thought you left town," he said.

How could Marko have known what I'd revealed to only my mother? "Did Mama call you?"

"No. I called her."

"When?"

"When I didn't show up for the blessing of the Easter baskets. I called to apologize. Answer the question."

"What question?"

"Mama said you went back to New York with steam coming out of your ass. That something important had come up. But instead you're here." He spat the last word out as though he'd chewed on something bitter.

I could sense my self-confidence waning. This is the problem with guilt. More than any other human emotion, it weakens the knees. "Mama misunderstood. The something that came up has nothing to do with my job."

"How could it when you don't have a job anymore?"

My face flushed. I feared it would burst before I figured out what to say. "Who . . . who told you I lost my job?"

"You did."

"What?"

"You just told me you lost your job."

I understood what he was telling me, but I couldn't believe it. He'd bluffed me into revealing myself. That was a result I, the forensic securities analyst, usually secured when I interviewed people. Not the other way around. Yet it had just happened. Guilt did more than weaken your knees, I thought. It blinded you.

"Why did you ask?" I said, as I regained my senses enough to sustain a logical train of thought. "What made you suspect I'd been let go?"

"There's smarts, and then there's street smarts. One might get you a job in New York City. The other one might let you know when someone's lost one."

"Meaning?"

"You're around here all the time. Not in New York where your job was. Real rocket science, huh?"

"I could have been on vacation."

"Sure. Hartford just passed Bora Bora on the top ten list of vacation hot spots for the hoity-toity. Though you should be asking yourself why you're here even if you lost your job. Why aren't you in New York looking for a new one?"

"Because I want to find out what happened to my godfather."

Lines sprang to Marko's face. "Why?"

I still didn't have an answer to that one, nor did I try to think of one. All I could think of was how hot it was in the room and how desperately I needed to reverse the trajectory of the conversation. I was the one with an agenda. I needed to ask the question. I had to impose my will on him. It's what I did for a living, or at least what I used to do for money.

"Why couldn't you make it for the blessing of the Easter baskets?" I said.

"Something came up."

"Something related to my godfather's business?"

"No. Something related to my business. We have a special guest. She flew in from LA. I had to pick her up at Bradley. Not that it's any of your business."

"When did you tell my godfather to leave Mama alone?"

Marko rolled his eyes. "Oh, for God's sake . . . You're back to that again? Who cares?"

"Humor me."

"A year ago. No, maybe less. More like nine months."

That was after my godfather's trip to Crimea and the profitable turn in his business. "Did you agree to do that job for him—when you rode with him to Avon for protection—after you told him to leave Mama alone, or before?"

He circled around behind his desk, sat down, and drank from one of the open bottles. When he answered my question he looked straight at the wall to my side, not in my eyes.

"It was right after that. He came by a week later."

"And it was a one-time thing. You never did a job with him again?"

Marko drank from the bottle again, puffed his cheeks out, and stared at the wall.

"Why won't you answer me?"

He shook his head. "You're embarrassing yourself. You're making a complete fool of yourself in the community and you don't see it. The guy was a stinking drunk. He fell down the stairs going to get a bottle of wine. Everyone knows it."

"You're still not answering my question."

He grunted. "I don't have to answer your question. You don't mean nothing to me."

I ordered myself to ignore those words. That's all they were, I told myself. Words. He didn't mean it. I was his little sister. I was his little sister and he loved me unconditionally.

"Why were you at my godfather's house on the day he died?"

Marko glanced at me. The quick turn of his neck and the burst of light in his eyes told me I'd surprised him. The shift in his Adam's apple and the hesitation that followed suggested he was about to lie.

"Who told you that?"

"You did," I said. "Just now."

There was no need for him to know Mrs. Chimchak had seen him. The less I told him, the more power I gained in the room. He let his eyes slide off mine slowly. I could sense his resentment that I'd returned the favor and used my experience to get the better of him. I savored a quick adrenaline rush. Just as quickly, however, an overwhelming sense of foreboding gripped me. The next question was obvious. It needed to be asked almost as badly as I needed to make amends for the past.

"Did you kill him, Marko?"

He let out a snort, something between a laugh and a dismissal. Then his face began to turn the color of eggplant. I turned to make sure I knew the precise way to the exit. When I looked back at Marko, I realized I'd looked for the door out of fear that he was going to stand up and hit me. Clearly the question had insulted him. Relief washed over me. He looked angry, not guilty. He hadn't killed my godfather. It was cause for minor celebration.

Then I saw something previously unthinkable. Tears welled in my brother's eyes. The anger, machismo, and bravado completely evaporated from his face and carriage. For the first time in my life, my brother looked vulnerable. I wondered if I'd erred in my deduction that he hadn't killed my godfather. Whatever the reason for his tears, the sight of him showing emotion rendered me incapable of further thought. I had survived my childhood because I'd drawn strength from my brother. Without it, without him, I would not be alive. The sight of him on the verge of tears paralyzed me.

His voice crackled with emotion as he spoke the words I'd been dreading to hear.

"You hit me," he said.

I knew what he was talking about right away. I knew it as soon as I heard the uncharacteristic quiver in his tone, before the words left his lips.

The thud of my knuckles connecting with the side of his head reverberated around my memory banks and rendered me speechless. I kept my eyes on his out of pride, but didn't say a thing. What could I say?

"You—hit—me," he said.

"Yeah, well, shit happens," I said. "You were stealing from our mother."

He was barely audible. "Yeah, but you hit me."

Six years ago, in one of those spurts of good will, Marko and I had organized a birthday party for our mother at her house. A few of her friends brought food, others brought beer and scotch. People drank and reminisced, and as the evening wore on, Marko began drinking. By the end of the evening, he was the drunken fool of the party. After the guests left, our mother told him he was a no-good bum that would never amount to anything, and that she regretted bringing him into the world. I never forgot his answer to her after he took another swig of Rolling Rock.

"That makes two of us," he'd said.

Under other circumstances, I would have been sympathetic to him. After all, we suffered from the same depression and anxiety from all the trauma we'd endured as kids. But that night we'd agreed to sacrifice ourselves for our mother, and I was livid he couldn't restrain himself for one evening. After walking our mother to bed, I returned to find my inebriated brother pulling the rubies and emeralds out of our mother's precious jewelry box, her one priceless possession.

"What the hell are you doing?" I said.

"Being the bum she says I am," Marko said.

And then I hit him. Closed fist, full force, I stepped into the punch and pummelled, with all my might, the only person who'd ever shown unconditional love for me when I was a child. His head hit the carpeted floor with such force I feared I might have killed him.

Now, as I stood before him in his office, it was as though a stranger had lifted her hand to him. It simply could not have been my fist that had hit him. I prided myself on being the exact opposite type of person. I hated violence and strived to be forgiving in all things. I'd comforted myself through the years by believing that we are all capable of regrettable actions under the wrong set of circumstances. And yet, that offered me no solace today.

The thought of apologizing occurred to me now, as it had for the last six years. To understand my inability to do so, one would have had to be a witness to my upbringing. My father never apologized for berating, hitting, or humiliating us. My mother never apologized for at least partially creating the circumstances that resulted in my husband's death. Every family had its own culture. In ours, words were for weaklings. People were defined by their actions. Apologies meant nothing.

Still, I tried. I stood looking at him through bleary eyes desperately trying to summon the words. But the harder I tried, the more futile was my attempt. It was so awkward as to be incomprehensible. I didn't say another word to my brother. I stormed out of the office and slammed the door so hard a mirror with the Michelob beer insignia fell off a wall. It smashed into pieces, scattering shards of glass in every direction on the floor.

In the absence of grace, a woman may resort to anger or cruelty to suppress her guilt. The only benefit of such actions is to inform her that she has hit rock bottom.

I had hit rock bottom.

CHAPTER 28

I NOTICED A POSTER HANGING ON THE WALL ON MY WAY OUT. IT was a blown-up image of the one I'd seen on a pile of leaflets inside Marko's office promoting the appearance of some XXX film star. The actress's boobs looked like genetically enhanced cantaloupes stuffed in a bra, so it was impossible not to notice the poster. Once it caught my attention, however, my eyes drifted to the date. The woman was appearing for one night and one night only next Saturday. Not tonight, I noted. Next Saturday.

Outside, twelve people stood in line waiting to pay cover, among them two middle-aged women. After the two men in front paid, I darted ahead of the next couple and put my hand on the bouncer's shoulder. He lifted his eyebrows. I leaned in so only he could hear me. Not because I was going to ask anything sensitive, but because I was too embarrassed for anyone in line to think I cared about the answer for entertainment reasons.

"You have anyone special on stage tonight?" I said.

"Special?"

"From out of town?"

"There's Raquel and Rafaela, the sisters from Rio."

"And they're actually from Rio de Janeiro?"

"No." He lowered his voice to a whisper. "Loretta and Janice from Sturbridge, Mass."

I shook my head. "I mean from out of state. Los Angeles?"

"Miss Twin Peaks. She's from LA. But that's next week."

"No one from LA on stage?"

"Only in their dreams."

I returned to my car. I was parked in the deepest part of the parking lot the farthest from the entrance. Rows upon rows of cars, pickup trucks, and SUVs obscured my car from the door to the club. I'd picked my spot purposefully to afford myself some cover in case I needed it. My concern at the time was that my brother might refuse to talk to me and might have me physically removed from his establishment. In that case, I was going to stay put the entire night and follow him home. Now a combination of uncertainty about my next move and curiosity about my brother's blatant lie were going to keep me stationary for a while.

He'd told me he'd missed the blessing of the Easter baskets because he had to pick up a special guest from LA at Bradley Airport. He'd also said the guest was related to his business. I'd assumed he was referring to his strip club. But the XXX actress wasn't appearing in his club until next Saturday. That left two possibilities. One, Marko had told a complete lie. He hadn't picked up anyone at the airport. He wasn't prepared for my question and it was the best answer he could concoct on the fly. Two, Marko had told a partial lie. He'd picked up someone else at the airport who was relevant to a different business. The other business might have been my godfather's business. I considered it a noteworthy coincidence that Donnie Angel had found what he was looking for at the same time that Marko had lied to me. My gut told me my brother might have been involved in Donnie's discovery.

Marko's lie only increased my commitment to my mission. My problem was I wasn't sure what to do next. I sat in the car for fifteen minutes and let my pulse slow down to normal, my vision clear. A thought dawned on me after reviewing all my moves since I'd first started looking into my godfather's death. Sometimes there was no substitute for a second pair of eyes. What I needed was someone to talk to. I'd promised Mrs. Chimchak I'd keep her apprised of my progress. It was the perfect time to call her.

She answered on the third ring and immediately told me my call was a most pleasant surprise. I asked her if it was too late in the night—it was only 8:30 p.m., and she laughed saying it was never too late for a phone call from her favorite *Plastunka*. She asked me if I was making any progress. I gave her a brief update on the essential developments.

"Did Marko tell you why he was at your godfather's house the day he died?'

"No. He avoided the question."

"And what do you conclude from that?"

"I don't conclude anything but I have some strong convictions. First, he didn't kill my godfather."

"Why do you say that?"

"Because I asked him and when he answered he was mad that I'd even considered it. I know my brother. He's not that good an actor. Plus, I've known him all my life, and I don't think he's capable of killing a man in cold blood."

"We're all capable of things beyond our comprehension under the right conditions. But no one knows your brother like you do. If you're sure you're not letting your wishes become your deductions, then I trust your judgment."

"I'm sure. My second conviction is that my brother was my godfather's partner. If not partner, then business associate, at a minimum. Marko admitted he did one job for him. He probably got paid good money for a few hours of work helping deliver an object of beauty. I know my brother. He's always looking for easy money. I can see him trying to turn it into a steady thing, and then an even more lucrative thing."

"That would explain why he was at his house the day he died."

"He was either getting paid, or there to arrange the next job."

"But if it were the latter they could have done that over the phone, no? Doesn't a face-to-face meeting suggest there was something more urgent involved? Something so important to your brother that he was willing to invest the time to go all the way from Willimantic—or divert from wherever he was—to East Hartford."

I sighed. "Money."

"A man's living is an urgent and important thing."

"That was it then. My godfather was a louse and a cheat. Maybe he didn't pay Marko on time. Maybe he owed him money. Whatever the reason, Marko went over there to have a confrontation about their business."

"Good. That's logical," Mrs. Chimchak said. "And this is a perfect time to tell you that I found something late this afternoon that might be of help to you."

"I need all the help I can get."

I heard the sound of paper crinkling in the background. "I found the copy of a lease for a warehouse in Hartford."

"A warehouse?"

"On Ledyard Street."

Ledyard Street was a mile away from the Ukrainian National Home.

"I thought he kept all his stuff in his house," I said.

"So did I. This is the first I'm learning of it."

"How did he pay the bills?"

"Probably the same way he paid for his meals at Fleming's. With cash."

"When was the lease signed? And what was the term?"

More crinkling noises followed. "It was a one-year lease. Signed almost a year ago." Mrs. Chimchak paused. "If I'm reading this right . . . wait . . . let me check the calendar. Yes. I think I am reading this right. There's only three weeks left on the lease. Three weeks from Monday."

"The time period—when he signed it—coincides with the timing of the Crimean business."

"Which makes me wonder . . ."

"Is there anything in the warehouse now?"

"Indeed."

I also wondered if Roxy knew about the warehouse. She hadn't mentioned it to me. Was it realistic that her uncle would keep it a secret from her? She rose to the top of my list of potential coconspirators. Per her own admission at the Uke National Home, she needed the money, too.

"Did you make any progress on the other front?"

I heard her question but didn't focus on it. Instead I was imagining myself skulking around a warehouse trying to get a look inside. I doubted there would be a window in front. "The other front? You think there might be a window in back?"

A pause. "I'm not talking about the warehouse," Mrs. Chimchak said. "I'm talking about the other mystery. The letters in your godfather's calendar. DP."

I apologized for not understanding her question. "It must have something to do with his connection. With the man in Crimea. The man who used to run the Black Sea Trading Company before he passed away. Have you ever heard of a man named Takarov?"

There was another pause. This one was longer and much heavier. "Yes." Always the inscrutable one, Mrs. Chimchak couldn't quite control the volume of her voice. It was a touch quieter, more solemn, as though she were desperately trying to hide the emotional resonance of my mere mention of the name. "I know the name. Is that the man who bought your godfather the plane tickets?"

"His company did."

"Then it all makes sense now."

My pulse picked up. "How does it all make sense?"

"There was a man named Takarov in the camps. He was NKVD. He was the man who had me repatriated."

This was the second time she'd mentioned her repatriation. I was so curious I had to pursue the story this time. I did so gingerly, praying I wasn't offending her because she'd been reluctant to discuss it further the first time.

"I don't want to dredge up bad memories . . . but if you don't mind my asking . . . how did he do that?"

"He showed me a picture of my family. My mother, father, and sister. It was a picture of them at our farm in Ivano-Frankivsk." I knew from my geography lessons that the latter was a region in western Ukraine. "He said they were looking forward to my return home."

I waited for Mrs. Chimchak to follow up but she didn't add anything else. "That's all he said?"

"That's all he needed to say."

"And you believed him?"

"No. He was very charming. Very persuasive. Of course he was. That's why he was picked for the job. Anyone else, I would have known with one hundred percent certainty my family was either dead or in Siberia. But Takarov had a gift, he knew how to win your trust. He won it by not trying to win it. He did not sell. He was like a priest. He told you what you wanted to hear with a gentle voice and a soothing touch. I knew with ninety-five percent certainty my family's fate was sealed, which means I knew. I knew, and yet . . ."

"And yet you went. You went because you had to go. You had no choice."

"I had no choice. If there was a sliver of hope my family could be saved, I had to go. Truth be told, I knew deep down there was no hope. And yet still I had to go."

"Because you couldn't live with yourself if you didn't go."

Mrs. Chimchak didn't answer, and I stayed mute. I imagined she was reliving the excruciating. I counted to six slowly before asking my next question.

"What happened to you after you got on the train?"

"Once we entered Ukraine, I was arrested and taken to a government building. I was brought to a room with wooden floors. It was empty except for a desk and a spotlight. The man behind the desk was courteous. He asked me to stand at the opposite end of the room facing the desk. He told me there was an *X* painted in white on the wood. He told me to look at my feet, find the *X*, and make certain I was standing on it. He was very particular about that detail. I remember him asking me to be certain I was standing on the *X*.

"Then he pressed a button on top of the desk. There was a loud explosion—like a rifle shot—and I felt myself knocked backward. At the same time, the floor fell out from under me. I dropped into an abyss. I don't know how deep it was. Ten, twenty feet. I'm still not sure. I landed on top of bodies. They were buried deep, one on top of the other. The floorboards closed high above me, but before they did a flash of light illuminated the bodies. They had red stains on their chests. I reached up and touched my chest. It too was bloody, but not over the heart. My wound was just below the shoulder. And then the floorboards closed and it turned dark.

"I heard several men moaning, talking incoherently. Not everyone around me was dead. Later, after I'd made my escape, I realized what had happened. The NKVD had created a device where a button on top of a desk fired a rifle that was hidden somewhere else in the room. Probably in the desk. The bodies fell under the floorboard. If the shot didn't stop the heart, the prisoner would bleed to death. There was nowhere for him or her to go. Or so they thought.

"I am much smaller than the average man. That is what saved me once, when the shot was fired. The bullet went through my chest near the shoulder. It didn't touch any vital organs. And then it saved me again, when I crawled around the entire basement of the building and found a water pipe. There was the tiniest sliver of light where the pipe went outside through the wall and it hadn't been sealed properly. It turned out it was a makeshift building made of cheap wood, which was to be expected. The war had just ended. I was able to loosen the nail on one of the wallboards and slip out of the building. I managed to get back to Europe through the kindness of a few friends. They maintained an underground route from Ukraine to Germany via Czechoslovakia and Poland. This time I went to Austria, to a different camp, where I used my mother's maiden name to create a new identity for myself."

It was a surreal story, the kind you read about in history books or saw at the cinema, not the kind your childhood mentor tells you she lived. It took me a moment to digest it, accept the images of her being shot and landing among a pile of murdered men, and those still clinging to life with no hope of escape. There was one question, I realized, that still needed to be asked.

"Why did the NKVD sentence you to death?"

"The Soviet government considered all DPs traitors. If you were in Europe, in their minds, you were a collaborator. Didn't matter if you were forced labor brought to Germany against your will by the Nazis, or you simply had no other place to go and you were trying to survive. One woman was sentenced to death when the NKVD found her shoes wrapped in an English newspaper. She'd picked it up off the floor in a camp and used it to protect her shoes. Once she was repatriated, her luggage was examined, and her choice of wrapping was found, she was executed.

"My sentence was a bit more justified. The Ukrainian Insurgent Army fought the Nazis and the Soviets. It had a unit of women who carried out missions of guerrilla warfare. I was one of those women."

This was not a surprising revelation. There had been rumors that Mrs. Chimchak had been a soldier. A real soldier. But to hear the admission from her lips stunned me nonetheless. I remained quiet. I didn't know what to say. I didn't have anything to say to something like that.

"Remember how I told you that when your godfather came back from Crimea he looked depressed?" Mrs. Chimchak said.

"And how he perked up only when he started spending more money a few months later?"

"It's as though Takarov had something on him. As though he coerced him to be an American distributor for his stolen arts and antiquities—I'm assuming they're stolen—and then once the money started flowing in—"

"And Takarov died."

"My godfather became a willing participant. But how could Takarov blackmail my godfather at his age? What could be so embarrassing to an old man with a poor reputation to start with?"

Mrs. Chimchak took a moment to consider the question. "Ambition blinds a man to his age and reputation. So don't assume your godfather understood how others viewed him. He probably thought he was the only person in the community that knew he once frequented houses of ill repute. And as for the basis for Takarov's blackmail, we must remember. Time heals all wounds but guilt never expires."

"Unfortunately, I'm all too familiar with the concept." I pulled out a pen and pad from my glove box. "Would you please repeat the exact address for that warehouse on Ledyard Street?"

Mrs. Chimchak gave me the number. She told me to be careful and call her after I took a look at the warehouse. She also gave me a final word of advice.

"Remember," she said. "Black souls wear white shirts."

CHAPTER 29

NADIA ENJOYED THE TRIP TO THE CONNECTICUT SHORE WITH her family. Her father was in a good mood. She and her brother dug up soda bottle caps from the sand and tried to get as many different brands as possible. Their mother had made capicola and ham grinders with provolone cheese. She served them with giant pickles the size of zucchinis and chilled cans of Fanta Root Beer. Everyone was happy. On the way home they stopped for hot dogs, french fries, and butter pecan ice cream cones for dinner.

They listened to the Red Sox in the car. It was a close game, tied 2–2 in the ninth inning when the lights went out in Fenway. Why did the lights go out in Fenway? And why was her hair wet? Most importantly, why was she upside down?

The next thing she knew she wasn't at Fenway anymore. Wait, she thought. She hadn't been at Fenway. She'd been listening to the game on the radio, hadn't she? It was so confusing. All she knew now was that someone was carrying her through the forest and rain was pelting her face. She was slung over a man's shoulder. A woman with the face of a wild boar and the shape of a mutant pear swung a lantern as she marched behind them, a massive knapsack resting on her hunched back. Nadia could hear the man's lungs heave with each step.

A few steps later Nadia understood. She understood that she'd been dreaming. She hadn't been to the beach with her family, and she hadn't gone to a baseball game at Fenway or heard it on the radio. She was still near the Appalachian Trail in the middle of her final night of the godforsaken survival test.

And two strangers had taken her.

CHAPTER 30

Ledyard Street was a half-mile road on the commercial outskirts of Hartford. It was as cozy as the fringe of any urban area, with shot-out lights hanging from abandoned factory buildings and chain link fences surrounding auto body shops and vacant lots.

Access to Ledyard came via the exact same route Father Yuri had taken when he'd whipped my car around the greater Hartford area. I'd driven it by myself and with my father hundreds of times. A left turn beyond Ledyard would point the driver toward Wethersfield and the Ukrainian National Home. A right turn put him a block away from Franklin Avenue and the Italian section of town. That is where Mozzicatto's Bakery beckoned with fresh cannoli filled on the spot. It was the same bakery my godfather and mother had visited after he'd taken her to dinner. It seemed fitting that the warehouse where he'd stored his coveted merchandise was right smack in the middle of it all.

I took a left onto Ledyard. My car twisted through a ninety-degree curve. The streetlights behind me faded into darkness. A sign for Jarosz Welding on a giant building's façade appeared to have been stenciled by an intoxicated blacksmith. The road straightened. A custom motorcycle shop, a rivet manufacturer, and a space for lease followed. I couldn't find a street number on any of them.

I approached a massive quadrangle surrounded by a towering chain link fence with barbed wire. The gate was open. I counted five separate buildings inside the compound. One was a car detail shop. I couldn't see what the others were. I was about to roll past it when I spotted a row of mailboxes with a series of numbers above them. One of them matched the one Mrs. Chimchak had given me.

The warehouse was one of the buildings in the quadrangle and the gate was open.

I wondered if someone was there right now.

Butterflies swirled in my stomach. I drove through another bend and pulled into the parking lot for Lindo's Bodywork. I parked behind a row of bigger cars waiting for repair to keep my vehicle out of street view.

I retraced my path along Ledyard Street, hugging the chain link fences. When I got to within one lot of the gate to the quadrangle, I looked around. It was too risky to get any closer. I needed elevation to improve my line of sight.

Rectangular buildings with smooth walls surrounded me. Not a foothold to be found. I glanced across the street. A metal shack housed Pawliczko's Salvage. A rusty camper stood tall among a parking lot of decaying vans and cars. I darted across the street to the RV, a GMC Eleganza, with peeling white paint and sea foam trim. An uninspiring metal ladder offered me a boost to its roof.

I scampered up the rungs each step faster than the previous. The ladder creaked, groaned, and swayed. When I got to the top I saw human figures across the street. I dropped to my stomach on the roof of the camper. My hands felt as though they'd fallen onto a sheet of used sandpaper. Rust, dirt, and grime surrounded me. Empty cans of Tecate beer formed a pyramid to my right. There had to be fifty of them, or more. A pair of metal beach chairs lay folded beside it. Apparently, the proprietors were salvaging cars at the expense of their livers.

I focused my attention across the street. A door to a prefabricated metal warehouse was propped open by a giant cinderblock. A faint light inside the warehouse illuminated a white, unmarked delivery truck with its back to the loading dock. Donnie Angel's van was parked beside it. I recognized it by the modified twin tailpipes and the memories they inspired. A German shepherd sat in front of the vehicles, tongue hanging out.

I waited for more than fifteen minutes. Then a man came out of the warehouse and opened the door to the delivery truck. Two other men wheeled a crate out of the warehouse to the edge of the loading dock. Donnie Angel emerged from the warehouse on crutches. One of the men climbed into the truck and helped the other maneuver the crate inside.

Another figure emerged from the warehouse. A dark beret and turned-up coat collar obscured the man's head, while a bulky winter coat did the same to his physique. It was hard to measure height precisely from my distance and angle. Donnie Angel was six feet tall. That much I knew all too well. The strongest conclusion I could draw was that the man with the turned-up collar was about the same height, perhaps a bit taller. He was remarkable only in the way he moved. More like a mountain lion than a human being, bounding on his haunches with a profound confidence bordering on arrogance.

The two men who'd loaded the cargo climbed into the delivery truck. The third assistant helped Donnie Angel into the back of the van. The German shepherd followed. The assistant closed the door behind them, circled around to the driver's side and got behind the wheel. The man with the turned-up collar got into his own car, an older American sedan. One by one, they started their engines.

I hurried down the stairs. I watched the vehicles turn toward the gate. As the headlights of the delivery truck swung in an arc toward me, I hid behind the RV. I waited for the second and the third pair of lights to shine, and when I heard the sound of the engines grow faint, I knew they'd driven off in the direction from which I'd arrived.

I ran to my car, started the engine, and raced to the highway entrances on Airport Road. I came up on them so quickly I had to break to make sure I didn't overtake them. The sedan was in the lead, the delivery truck in the middle, and Donnie Angel's van brought up the rear. It was the van and its gaudy aftermarket tailpipes that I recognized, yet again. They took the ramp onto I-84 East and drove the speed limit in the far right lane.

I followed the three vehicles into Avon, the tony suburb on Talcott Mountain west of Hartford. It took us an additional twenty minutes to get to their final destination. Two lefts off Route 44 at the top of the mountain left us in a heavily wooded area and off the beaten track. A gate made of cherry wood opened, and they pulled into a massive stone castle.

I continued onward so as not to arouse suspicion, and parked three hundred yards away from the house. Gently pressing my doors shut, I high-stepped it over a guardrail along the curb and descended into the forest that abutted the property. Then I squatted down to my haunches and checked my watch. I needed to wait for rhodopsin to be released in my retina and improve my night vision. Another lesson learned long ago from Mrs. Chimchak during one of the excruciating summer PLAST camps I'd all but purged from my mind.

Five minutes later I began to advance toward the main house through the vineyard. I cupped my hand over my nostrils so the steam fanned out. I hugged the tree line so that the mulch surrounding the trees muffled the sound of my footsteps. A cottage stood on the left, where I guessed they made the wine. A tennis court appeared on the right. I was halfway to the main house when a cat darted across my path, hissing and yowling at me for trespassing. Not a good sign, I thought. Even the cats were on guard for prowlers.

A spotlight burst to life. It shone from my right beside the tennis court. I stayed low and sprinted left across two rows of vines. The spotlight followed in my wake but didn't shine directly on me. I pressed my back against the far wall of the cottage facing the access road.

A man approached. His footsteps grew louder. He was walking along the far wall. The pace was determined but not urgent. Diligent, but not panicked. This suggested he hadn't seen me. Perhaps the buyer or Donnie Angel had sent one of his men to walk around the entire property to make sure they were alone. It would have been a worthwhile security measure.

I looked around for a weapon of some kind in case I needed one. I found a rock the size of a baseball. I didn't see any other option so I grabbed it. It felt ridiculous in my hand. I couldn't imagine using it to hit a human being. I returned to my spot against the wall of the cottage. The man continued along a path between two columns of trees. He scanned the horizon to each side as he walked like a patrolman. When he got close enough for me to see his face, knots formed in my stomach.

He was one of Donnie Angel's men. He was one of the men who'd grabbed me, thrown me into the van, and kidnapped me a block away from my apartment.

I pulled my head back, kept my back against the wall. I didn't move or make a sound. I counted to twenty slowly, each second consistent with one step. My guess was it would take him ten to fifteen steps to walk past the cottage. The five additional steps were insurance. Once I counted to twenty, he would be safely past me and I could take a peek at him from behind.

I finished counting, slid around the cottage to the opposite side, and stuck my head out to catch a glimpse of him.

The man rounded the corner. We collided. Shock registered on his face.

I smashed him in the forehead with the rock. I didn't think. I simply hit him. Not as hard as I could. I pulled back at the last minute. A dull thud was followed by a muted groan.

Blood trickled from his forehead. I stood there horrified, praying I hadn't killed him. I checked his pulse. A strong heartbeat mollified my fears as did my memory of what he'd done to me. This man had kidnapped me.

I was about to turn and head toward the house when I caught a glimpse of something stuck in his belt. The item was exposed because his waist-length jacket had hiked up a few inches when he'd fallen. It was a small black gun. I knew nothing about guns. I'd never even touched one. They scared the heck out of me. But I grabbed it anyway. When I reached for the grip, it was an out-of-body experience. I could see myself from afar. Mouth agape I wondered, is she really going to take that gun?

It felt sleek and light and fit perfectly in the palm of my hand. More than that, it felt disturbingly good. It felt right. It weighed less than a pound, I guessed, and was about five inches long. The letters "M" and "P" were etched in the black matte barrel beside the words "Bodyguard 36." The word "safe" was visible beneath a small button that was pushed up on the left side of the gun. Logic suggested the safety was engaged. The gun would not fire. I could not shoot myself by accident.

To my utter shock, I slid the button down. The word "safe" disappeared beneath the button. Now I could shoot someone, or myself. My nerves stood on edge. I put the safety back on, but to my surprise, I didn't drop the gun. I kept it. If I needed to ditch it for whatever reason, I could wipe my prints off and toss it into the woods.

A combination of fear, dread, and empowerment possessed me. The feeling was as powerful as the one that had overtaken my senses after I'd cracked Donnie Angel's tibia with the heel of my foot. I was not going to be intimidated. I was not going to be pushed around by anyone. I'd been a soldier in my mind as a girl scout, and I could be one now, too.

I checked the man's breathing and pulse again. His lungs filled and his heart beat regularly.

I took off toward the main house, gun in hand.

The van and the delivery truck were parked in a circular drive flanked by two separate three-car garages. It amazed me that someone would need six garages, but I decided that might be exactly the type of person who was interested in stolen art. The rear door of the truck was open as though the crate had been removed. Distant voices echoed from the back of the house. There was no sign of the German shepherd, Donnie Angel, or the mysterious man with the turned-up collar.

I wound my way along a fence made of bushes that lined the far edge of the driveway. The back of the house opened up onto a veranda that led to an expansive pool area. A pair of double glass French doors was open. The voices grew louder as I approached. I snuck around the pool and edged up to the window.

The two deliverymen stood beside an empty crate. An impossibly fit woman of indeterminable age sparkled with joy. Marko had told me that a woman had taken possession of the delivery he'd supervised. They had come back to the same client. The source of her adulation was a five-by-six-foot icon of a medieval knight in a colorful cloak spearing a dragon from atop his black stallion.

A priceless relic, I thought.

The man with the turned-up collar stood next to the proud owner with his back to me, still camouflaged by a coat and hat. I willed him to turn around. He didn't. Instead, Donnie Angel hopped into the room on crutches. He nodded at one of his men to indicate he needed to speak with him. The nod was in my direction. They both started toward the window beside me and had a brief exchange before they came within earshot.

I ducked down so they couldn't see me.

Their voices gradually rose as they came closer.

"Where are the shovels?" Donnie Angel said.

"I left them there," his man said.

"What if someone steals them?"

The man chuckled. "No one's going to be there this time of night."

"I hope not."

"What about Marko?" the man said.

"He's going to meet us there."

"You sure he's going to show?"

"I just got off the phone with him. He's on his way now. He hasn't gotten paid. He's going to show."

I heard a sound behind me. It was the suppressed sound of a man in agony. Or was I imagining things? I heard it again. I caught a glimpse of a man stumbling toward the main house through the vineyard.

It was the man I'd hit with the rock.

"Donnie," he said with a weak voice. "Donnie, she's here."

I kept my head low, slipped around the corner away from the window above me, and raced around the other side of the pool toward the front gate.

The German shepherd leapt from behind the van. I jumped to the side. The dog's teeth came within inches of my leg but snapped backward before they could connect. A leash prevented him from stretching farther. He was tethered to a door handle of the van. He began barking furiously. I had a gun in my hand and I'd taken it to defend myself, but even at the moment it appeared I was going to get bitten, I hadn't raised my arm. I could not imagine shooting an animal. Not unless it was rabid and charging me with saliva dripping from its mouth. Would I be able to pull the trigger at a human being if I had to?

I sprinted out the driveway and down the access road. After a hundred yards my lungs were heaving. I slowed down to a jog, glanced over my shoulders, and saw no one behind me. I ran the rest of the way to my car, started it, and peeled out of the neighborhood. Once I'd driven a mile away along the same route we'd taken to get to the house, I diverted onto a side street, turned my car around, and parked by the curb. The side street dipped down into a valley allowing me a decent line of sight as any cars drove by. They would have to drive past me to get to the main artery, Route 44, which led to the highway. My biggest concern was that one of the neighbors might call the police because some stranger had parked beside his house.

As soon as I killed the lights and the engine, I called Brasilia and asked for Marko. The woman who answered the phone told me he'd gotten sick and gone home for the evening. I knew it was a bogus excuse and that he had left to meet Donnie Angel, but I called him at home nonetheless. It was a futile attempt. I prayed that he would pick up so I could warn him that Donnie Angel had shovels, and shovels were used to dig holes, and those shovels had been left in a place where no one else went on a Saturday night. I prayed that my brother would pick up so I could warn him that the man who'd kidnapped me was going to kill him. He was going to kill my brother tonight.

But I was too late. Marko didn't pick up. He had no cell phone, of course, and there was no way to reach him.

I sat and waited, wondering if I should call the police. I didn't know where we were going nor was I absolutely certain a crime was going to be committed. At least not yet.

Less than fifteen minutes later the sedan, van, and delivery truck drove past me on the road above. I counted to ten to let them get ahead of me, and then I pulled out and followed them. They took a different route this time, circling the mountain peak and looping around Simsbury, through Bloomfield and onto I-91 headed for Hartford. It was a longer but less taxing route on the driver. The road was less serpentine, the ascents and descents less steep.

Eventually we merged onto I-91 headed south. I stayed ten car lengths back the entire time. When we approached Hartford, they got into the far left-hand lane for the entrance ramp to Route 2 headed east over the Connecticut River.

Many Ukrainian-Americans now lived east of the river, but that hadn't always been the case. Growing up, most folks lived in Hartford or the surrounding towns west of the river to stay close to the church and the Ukrainian National Home. When I was a child, we'd taken this road for one purpose and one purpose only. Given the conversation I'd overheard between Donnie Angel and his man, there was no doubt in my mind where we were going.

My ex-husband was buried there, as was my father. It was a place where picks and shovels came in handy.

We were headed for the cemetery.

CHAPTER 31

The ride was interminable. The driver never surpassed the fifty-five-mile-per-hour speed limit on Route 2. Meanwhile, I relived memories of tossing the first handful of dirt over my father's grave, the unpredictable gush of tears as my abusive husband's casket was lowered into the ground, and Father Yuri telling me both times that it was God's will.

The Ukrainian Cemetery of the Holy Ghost was built in an undeveloped forest thirty miles outside Hartford because the land in Hebron was cheap. When I rounded the bend toward the entrance and saw that all three vehicles' taillights had disappeared, I continued past the cemetery for a quarter of a mile. Then I pulled onto the edge of the woods and parked on the side of the road.

I climbed a small embankment to even ground and hiked two hundred yards through the woods. The property appeared to be four acres in size with a thousand graves. The high ground on the northern side was filled, but there were still plenty of unfilled lots on the south side closer to the main road. The sedan was parked in the northwest corner of the cemetery by the groundskeeper's hut. I'd been in that hut many times. It contained a storage shed and an office with cedar siding on the inside. I'd stood beside Father Yuri as his altar girl while he prepared for more funerals than I could remember over a five-year span. Maybe that's why I associated the smell of cedar with tears, mourning, and closure.

A light came on in the office. A shadow moved against the walls. It was the man with the turned-up collar. He was removing his hat and coat. I still couldn't see his face or figure, only an amorphous black silhouette. The light in the office would prevent him from seeing out the window. There was no risk that he could see me. I guessed Donnie Angel and the other three men were in the shed or digging my brother's grave, but I didn't take it for granted.

I weaved my way up a modest incline toward the hut, choosing the path with the highest tombstones, the ones that afforded me some cover. I hunched as I walked to minimize my exposure. My gun—yes, it was my gun now—felt cool and lethal in my hand. It gave me a sense of omnipotence. I'd been striving to become emotionally invulnerable, to cease to be affected by my relationships with my family. The gun imbued me with a different form of self-confidence. The kind that could get me killed or land me in prison for life if I wasn't careful. I took some solace in knowing that I was still self-aware enough to understand that.

Somehow, I still ended up walking past my husband's grave first, on the low ground, and my father's grave second, on the high ground. I didn't know if this was a function of familiarity, guilt, or a tug from the afterlife. I found myself speeding through "Our Father" twice, one prayer for each of their souls. I didn't believe in the afterlife anymore—did I?—but I was programmed for prayer from youth. There was nothing an altar girl could do about it.

I heard noises coming from the storage shed. Donnie Angel and the other three men emerged laughing about something and headed to the office. I assumed Marko's grave had been dug. Meanwhile, the mysterious man in the office disappeared from sight. Another light had come on in the western side of the hut, where the bathroom was located. As soon as the other four men entered the office, I sprinted the final fifty yards from the window to the eastern side of the hut. I wondered if I should have called the police now, or waited for Marko to arrive. I still had no evidence of a crime having been committed, other than my assault on the man in the vineyard. I reminded myself that Marko's safety was my primary concern. As soon as I saw his car approaching, I would race toward him and warn him it was a trap. That they were going to kill him.

I knelt down behind a tall headstone and caught my breath. Thirty seconds later, I lifted my head around the granite block enough for my right eye to see past it. I scanned the area surrounding the hut and found what I was looking for. A mound of dirt was piled high beside a grave. But a headstone stood in front of that plot, implying someone was already buried there. I glanced toward the office. One of the men had pulled out a bottle. Another was passing glasses around.

I crawled on my hands and knees and read the inscription on the headstone.

Renata Clara Zen. Born 1917, Died 1979. I didn't know the name or understand the significance of the headstone, but I knew there was one. Donnie Angel hadn't chosen it at random. I glanced in the unearthed lot. A layer of dirt covered the casket but I could make out its outline. And then it hit me.

It was a woman's grave.

Marko's body wouldn't fit in the hole atop the casket. But mine would.

Marko wasn't coming. The grave wasn't for him.

It was for me.

I suppressed a sense of doom and scurried back to my hiding place. I put my gun in my pocket and whipped out my cell phone. I managed to punch in a nine and a one before I heard the metallic snap of a pump-action shotgun.

The man I'd hit with the rock stood above me. He told me to give him the phone. I did.

"Where's my gun?" he said.

I gave him the gun. When the polymer grip slipped out of my hands, some of my confidence went with it. But not all of it. I still had my wits about me.

I stood up.

He punched me in the jaw.

Pain shot through my nose. My eyes watered. I staggered backward but a gravestone kept me upright. Good, I thought. I hadn't fallen. I'd kept my balance. That was a victory. A small one, but nevertheless a victory.

"That's for hitting me in the face," he said.

He escorted me to the hut. When I stepped into the office, Donnie Angel was seated in a folding chair sipping an amber liquid from a masonry jar.

"Home girl," he said with his trademark smile. "Been waiting for you."

A briefcase stacked with bills lay on a desk to his left. Two other men flanked him. They were also drinking.

Water gushed through pipes. Someone had flushed the toilet.

The doorknob turned. The bathroom door opened. The person who'd been wearing the coat with the turned-up collar stepped out and revealed himself.

CHAPTER 32

Nadia hung upside down over the man's shoulder. She'd patted her pockets in search of her whistle, but it was gone. It must have fallen out when the man threw her over his shoulder, or when she got dizzy and fell by the stream earlier in the day. It wouldn't have mattered if she'd found it. No one would have heard the sound over the thunder and the rain, and either the man or the woman would have taken it away within seconds.

Blood pressed against the skin of her forehead as though her insides wanted to spill out. A bitter taste filled her mouth.

Blood? Was that blood in her mouth?

She stuck her tongue between her lips.

Not blood. Aspirin. Regurgitated aspirin leaking down her throat.

Nadia bounced off the man's body with each step. When the lantern swung forward, it illuminated the path in front of them. When it swung backward, however, it lit up the area directly beneath her.

Ferns, leaves, a dead branch.

The woman's orange high-top Converse All Star sneakers.

Nadia had already replayed Mrs. Chimchak's lessons in hand-to-hand combat ten times in her mind. She knew what she had to do. What was the problem?

It was so gross, that was the problem.

She had to reach around with her hand and yank the man's eyeball out. He'd fall to the ground. The woman would freak. Nadia would kick the lantern with her boot and kill the lights. She'd do it all so fast these assholes wouldn't know what hit them.

So why wasn't she doing it?

Mrs. Chimchak had taught her that the person willing to do anything was the one who had the advantage in a fight. The one who would survive.

Nadia repeated the mantra Mrs. Chimchak had taught her for such a situation:

There are no rules in a real fight.

There are no rules in a real fight.

There are no rules in a real fight . . .

CHAPTER 33

THE MAN WHO EMERGED FROM THE BATHROOM WAS ALL TOO familiar to me. The only shocking thing about him was his sudden mobility. He was Danilo Rus, Roxy's father, and my former father-in-law. The man who'd hit me in his home, the one who'd hated me from the moment his son had started dating me. Now he was going to get his ultimate revenge for his son's death. After all, if his son hadn't been married to me, he would have never received a distress call from my mother, and he wouldn't have driven headfirst into a tree.

"You're looking well, father-in-law," I said, in Ukrainian. "What happened to the Parkinson's?"

"It's like my recollection that you were once my daughter-in-law. An affliction that will eventually kill me. When my brother came to me for help, I decided to accelerate my decline. To take any suspicion off me. No one ever worries about the gimp."

I turned to Donnie Angel. "How did you know?"

"Know what?" Donnie said.

"At the house. You told your man my brother would be coming. And asked him where the shovels were. That was for my benefit."

"You think?"

"But how did you know I was there?"

"Memo to Nadia. If you see a house with an infinity pool, a tennis court, and a vineyard—a fucking vineyard—assume security cameras are watching you."

"You saw me—"

"From the minute you stepped foot on the property."

"But the grave. It's dug out already. All prepared. As though you knew that I wasn't going to New York. As though you knew I was going to find you at the warehouse."

"The gravedigger is on my payroll. It's the type of connection that comes in handy in my line of work. The hole in Mrs. Zen's resting place was dug a few days ago on account of my knowing that you'd eventually show up again. And by the way, Mrs. Zen has no living family so no one's going to show up and ask questions why the dirt on her grave's been messed up. I knew you wouldn't let it go, especially since you were worried your brother was involved. Didn't know it would be tonight. Real sorry it worked out this way. I gave you every chance, Nadia. I gave you every chance to walk away."

My head spun. My body temperature soared as though the invisible jaws of death had grasped my body and squeezed. But of course they had. The grave really was for me. I'd mentioned it nonchalantly, ever the cool and calculating analyst, subconsciously hoping Donnie would laugh and tell me I was out of my mind, that he wasn't going to snuff out my final breath and toss my body into a casket containing another woman's bones . . .

Unless he was planning to bury me alive.

The jaws of death squeezed tighter. All the moisture in my mouth evaporated. I felt like a useless ball of cotton candy.

He wouldn't do that, would he?

Donnie was so insane I couldn't rule out the prospect. I imagined him tossing a shovel full of dirt onto my mobile body, covering my head and filling my nostrils as I struggled to breathe . . .

I took a deep breath as though I was lying in that crypt. The focus on my lungs snapped me out of my spell. A voice sounded in my head.

There is always a way out of trouble.

When in doubt, I reminded myself, ask questions.

I took another breath and turned back to Rus. "Were you involved in this from the beginning? Because I don't get it. If you were, why was my brother hired to provide protection for your brother?" I glanced at the three thugs. "Looks to me that, between Donnie and his guys, there's plenty of muscle here."

Rus was busy trying to remove his belt from around his waist. "When the call came from Crimea, my brother was too scared to see the opportunity. He came to me for advice and I became his silent partner. I was the one who suggested he use your brother as protection for his first big delivery."

"Silent partner," I said. "I get it." I looked at Donnie. "You're the connection to Crimea, but you kept your distance to minimize your legal risk. But when my godfather died, you had no idea where the inventory was. You had to get involved. And when you couldn't find out on your own, you let me ask the questions and followed where I went."

"You were always a smart cookie," Donnie said. "I knew you wouldn't let me down."

"How did I lead you to the warehouse?"

"You didn't," Donnie said. "You led me to him." He nodded at Rus. "You searched your godfather's house with Roxy, then went straight to his house. Alone. Everyone knows the two of you hate each other, so you weren't going there to say hi to the old father-in-law. I figured you must have found something that made you wonder. So after you left, I went in and asked a few questions of my own and found my silent partner. Once he understood that the inventory wasn't going to be his for the keeping, that he had partners here and in Ukraine whether he knew them or not, we got along just fine. Didn't we, Danilo?"

Rus cringed at the sound of Donnie using his first name. There was no love lost between the partners that I could see. I wondered how I could use that to my advantage. Rus slipped his belt from around the last loop in his pants.

"What was Roxy's role in this?" I said.

Rus's head snapped in my direction. "She had no role in this. My daughter is a good girl. She understands her place is by her husband. He's useless but that's not her fault. And now her inheritance will provide for the rest of her life."

"My godfather's cash," I said. "You took it from his house before Roxy and I ever searched."

He confirmed my suspicion with a stoic glance. I was momentarily pleased to hear that Roxy wasn't involved. My circumstances, however, prevented anything more than a fleeting thought in that direction.

"The letters DP in his calendar," I said. "They were your initials after all. Danilo Rus. Except the "R" is a "P" in Ukrainian."

Rus stared at me stone-faced. He kept one end of the belt in his right hand and grabbed the other end with his left.

"You killed him," I said. "You killed your own brother."

"Oh, for God's sake." Rus rolled his eyes. "The smartest people understand themselves the least. My brother fell down the stairs. You made up some theory about him being murdered to come back here. To make amends with me, your family, your community. Everybody can see that. It's a small community. We all know each other. I played with you when you came to visit me that night for sheer entertainment purposes. Just to watch your massive, overgrown ego get even bigger. The police said it was an accident, but you, the great intellect among us, you, Nadia Tesla, knew better. What a farce. Nobody thinks he was murdered. Nobody but you."

My head spun again. Rus's words sounded like a dart hitting the bull's-eye. Had I concocted everything for my own subconscious purposes?

Of course I had. The room turned sideways. Then it hit me.

"That's not true," I said. Mrs. Chimchak believed me. Mrs. Chimchak had brought him his wine that night. "I'm not the only one who thinks he was murdered."

Rus made small circles with his wrists around the ends of the belt to shorten its length. "Oh, right. Mrs. Chimchak. The accountant. I forgot about her. You do realize she's suffering from dementia? Three months ago they found her wandering half-naked at Naylor elementary school. Scared the hell out of the boys."

Mrs. Chimchak suffered from dementia? I remembered her rambling incoherently on the phone. The signs had been there, but I'd refused to see them. I felt my confidence and my life slipping away from me. Had I deluded myself so badly? Was I such a wreck? Visions of my childhood survival test flooded to mind again.

Yes. I was such a wreck. After everything my brother and I had been through. How could we not be wrecks?

Rus stepped forward. "Grab her," he said.

Two of the thugs grabbed me by the shoulders, one on each side. I tried to break free but could barely move. It wasn't only their strength. I seemed to be operating at half power, as though I was accepting my inevitable fate. Then I felt warm breath in my right ear, and the sickly-sweet smell of Brut aftershave in my nostrils.

"Love you, baby," Donnie Angel said.

Rus's jaw tightened. A look of unadulterated hatred spread over his face. "I've been dreaming of this moment since my boy died. Good-bye, bitch."

He raised the belt over my head. My pulse quickened but I didn't feed my fear. I let the moment pass, and I thought to myself:

You are not a fraud. A man is going to kill you but you can prevent it. You can prevent it because you are smart, tough, and resourceful. What do these men covet? Money. What is their weakness? They don't trust each other.

Rus slipped the belt over my head.

I twisted my neck so that I could look into Donnie Angel's eyes. They shone with the perverse anticipation of watching a woman be strangled.

There is almost always a way out of trouble. The woman who keeps her emotions at bay can find the way.

"You don't want the nativity scene?" I said.

I choked on the last word. The belt strangled me. My airway shut. The blood from my throat surged to my face. I could smell Rus's wretched breath, see the glint in his eyes as he pulled the leather taut and held it. I waited for Donnie Angel to tell Rus to release the belt. He would want to know what I meant by my question. Surely he would.

Black clouds blinded me. I needed air. Why wasn't Donnie doing the logical thing? Why wasn't he stopping this so he could ask me what I meant?

I needed air. I needed oxygen now.

I struggled with all my remaining might to break free from the grip of Donnie's thugs. My struggles were for naught. I felt myself passing out.

Good-bye, Marko.

I heard some noise. It sounded like a man speaking. A struggle of some kind ensued. It happened right in front of me. Then I felt my head falling back . . . gently, gently . . . my back landed on the ground.

My airway freed.

I gulped air. Choked and swallowed air repeatedly.

Panic overtook me. I could not control it. I needed oxygen. Were they going to choke me again? Was I going to die? I couldn't get the air into my system fast enough. I couldn't keep my mind from racing, or my lungs from heaving—

Something touched my shoulder.

My vision cleared.

Donnie Angel was kneeling beside me, belt in hands. He wore a look of genuine concern. "You okay, baby? You need some water?"

He made calming noises and patted my shoulder like the doctor he'd emulated in his van. Then his men helped me into a chair. My limbs trembled. One of the men brought me a cup of water. I could barely keep my hand steady enough to lift it to my lips. My throat was so dry I choked and spit out the first mouthful. The second one went down, however, and the third restored some of my equilibrium.

Rus stood steaming in the background, hands open by his side as though they were ready to finish the job his belt had started.

Donnie bent over so he was at eye level. "Better?"

"Peachy," I said. My voice sounded like nails on a chalkboard. "Ready for the debutante ball."

Donnie doubled over and laughed. No one else bothered to even chuckle, and Donnie's reaction was so over the top it left no doubt he was pretending to be amused for profit's sake, and that I was a dead woman if he didn't believe my story. But he would believe my story, I thought. He would believe it because I was going to give him my confidence. It's what I did as an analyst. I ripped companies apart, understood them, and imparted my confidence to investors who paid me.

"What nativity scene?" Donnie said.

"The one your partners in Crimea sent my godfather. Direct. As a special bonus. I found it in his house the night Roxy and I searched it. Then I went back and took it the next day."

"That's a lie!" Rus said. "There is no such thing. All the goods were delivered through the shipyard in New London. If there was a bonus of some kind, I would know about it."

Donnie stared at him through slits. "Maybe you do know about it, but I don't."

"Nonsense," Rus said. "Can't you see she's making it all up—"

"Shut up," Donnie said. He cocked his head to the side and pointed a finger at Rus.

Rus shut up.

Donnie turned back to me. "How did you get into the house alone when Roxy had the key?"

"Roxy doesn't have the only key. I borrowed the other one from my godfather's best friend and accountant. From Mrs. Chimchak."

Donnie glanced at Rus. The old man didn't say anything, implying he either knew Mrs. Chimchak had a key or it was a safe bet.

"Tell me about this nativity scene," Donnie said.

"Adoration of the shepherds," I said. "It's a standard Byzantine theme. Common in Eastern Orthodox icons. Shepherds behind your basic nativity scene. Except this one is circa 1685 by a student of Rembrandt's. It's about yea big." I estimated a width of fifteen inches by twenty-five inches with my hands.

"What a pack of lies," Rus said. "You couldn't get something like that past customs—"

"It came as a ghost on the back of a cheap reproduction of a harbor scene print," I said. The lies were coming quickly and furiously to me. Any one of them could get me killed but I had no choice. I was already a dead woman. That realization emboldened me even more.

"A ghost?" Donnie said.

"The harbor scene was painted on top of the nativity scene. Kirtch Bay. No one in customs would ever know. To them they would have looked like a set of cheap posters. How would they know what was painted under one of them?"

"You lying little whore," Rus said. "This is the stupidest story I've ever heard." Rus glanced at Donnie with pleading eyes. "Why? Why would our friends possibly alter the delivery process to send my brother some sort of bonus? Bonus for what?"

"For maintaining your arrangement," I said. "When Takarov died six months ago, his sons assumed control of all his businesses, including this one. My godfather—your dear and loyal brother—immediately demanded a token of good faith to transfer his partnership from the man he'd known since DP camp in Germany to two young men of questionable integrity he knew nothing about."

A lie depends on the voracity of detail behind it, and the quality of its delivery. I knew I'd nailed it. I knew it even before Donnie Angel's eyelids shot up to his forehead, and Rus's jaw dropped. The momentary silence that ensued told me I'd won a reprieve. It might last a minute, an hour, or a day, but I was still alive. And if I could get them to New York, anything could happen. A doorman, a fire alarm, a cop. A cop! There were more cops in New York City than coffee houses in Seattle. All I had to do . . .

"Where is this nativity scene now, Nadia?" Donnie said. "And be honest with me, or you and your family are gonna pay dearly."

"In my apartment building," I said.

"In New York?" Donnie said.

"Every tenant has a storage locker. For bicycles and luggage and stuff. It's in the basement. Only the super has the key to the basement, and only I have the key to the locker. It's there, wrapped in a blanket and sealed with duct tape."

The more truth to the detail behind the lie, the easier it is to sustain it. That's why most frauds inevitably reveal themselves. They become lies built on lies. The lockers existed, my super and I had the keys as discussed, and my storage space contained a framed object wrapped in a blanket. It was a limited edition print of a winter scene from Hunter Mountain in New York. I loved it to death, but it had been a gift from my husband and I didn't want his memory hanging on my wall.

"All right then." Donnie pointed to one of his men. "You take him home," he said, motioning toward Rus. "And stay with him.

Don't let him out of your sight, not even to the bathroom. Nobody goes out of our sight until I figure out what's what."

"You're a fool," Rus said. "My son was a fool for trusting this ugly harlot, and you're the biggest fool of all."

Privately, I had to agree with him. For the moment, at least, I was no longer the greatest fool.

"Watch your mouth," Donnie said. "She's not ugly and she's a friend of mine. I go back a lot longer with her than I do with you." Donnie gave me another gorgeous, psychopathic grin. "Don't we, babe?"

One of the thugs put the whiskey and masonry jars in a corner. After Donnie gave logistical orders—one of the men would drive while the second would keep a gun pointed at me during the entire trip—the other thug opened the door.

An object came whipping around out of nowhere. The glint of steel, a wooden handle, a pair of hands. It happened so quickly, that's all I saw. The object crushed the man's face. He collapsed to the floor. I could see at the last second that it was a shovel that had hit him in the face. The hands pulled the shovel back out of the doorway.

The crunch of bone beneath the shovel sounded like sweet salvation. The hands that had swung the shovel couldn't belong to a cop. The police didn't announce themselves with earth-moving equipment. Neither did disgruntled clients from tony suburbs like Avon. And the hands couldn't belong to someone I knew because there was no one left who cared—

Two men burst into the office. Both of them looked vaguely familiar but I couldn't place them. One held a gleaming silver revolver in his hand. The other aimed a shotgun at Donnie Angel.

"Don't move," the man with the shotgun said.

Marko stepped into the office, shovel in hand. It was a brand new shovel. The promotional sticker was still affixed to the blade. Kobalt, made in America. Heavy gauge, tempered-steel blade for increased strength and durability. I could not for the life of me understand why I read that sticker or why it mattered to me that the shovel was new. But it did. My brother had come to save me and he'd brought a brand new shovel for the job. It was amazing what we noticed when we were under duress, I thought. Only then did it dawn on me that this was an unlikely observation under the circumstances, and that I might be in shock from the events of the last half hour.

Marko scanned the room without emotion, pausing only on Rus's face. Evidently, his presence was the only surprise to my brother. When he was finished appraising Donnie and his crew, he stood before them.

"My associates are licensed to carry firearms," Marko said. "They're also veterans of the United States Army which means they're trained and know how to use them. I'm guessing you're not and you don't."

Marko told them to remove their weapons and put them on the floor. They followed his instructions. Afterward, he had one of his boys search four of the men. He tended to Donnie Angel himself. After patting him down, Marko looked him in the eye.

"I thought I told you to leave my sister alone."

Donnie grinned as though he didn't have a care in the world, and shrugged.

Marko slugged him in the jaw and knocked him to the floor.

We stood there for ten minutes until two state police cars arrived. Most conflicts were resolved within the community, but the prospect of a second murder—my own—was too much in Marko's opinion. He'd call the cops himself. I didn't disagree with his decision.

When I thanked Marko for rescuing me, he looked at me and waited, as though expecting me to follow up with something else. I didn't. I wanted to say more, but I simply couldn't. Even in light of what had just transpired, the prospect of sentiment streaming from my lips made me nauseous. As a result, what should have been a time of celebration became an experience of physical and mental relief coupled with extreme emotional anguish. I thanked God I was alive and prayed for his forgiveness for the indomitable Tesla pride that defined me.

During the entire wait, Marko never said a word to me. He didn't ask me how I was feeling or if I was hurt.

That was okay with me. Sometimes a makeshift weapon in a brother's hand is all the love one needs.

CHAPTER 34

NADIA TRIED NOT TO THINK OF THE IMAGES THAT CAME TO mind, but the more she wished them away, the more vivid they became. What sound would her fingers make when they pulled the man's eyeball out of his head? How mushy would it feel?

She felt the urge to puke. She waited. The wave of nausea crested, and then nothing. She waited some more but nothing would come out. She understood why. There was nothing left in her stomach to throw up.

Her body heaved up and down in cadence with the man's lungs as he took one long step after another. Sweat rolled down Nadia's forehead. She had to do it. She had no choice. PLAST had taught her self-reliance. Who else was going to come rescue her?

Nadia brought the first three fingers of her right hand together to form an adjustable clamp. Grabbed the man's T-shirt with her left hand for ballast. Yanked herself up, reached around and jammed her fingers toward the man's right eye.

He turned his face toward the woman behind him to say something to her.

Nadia's fingers connected with his cheek instead of his eye.

"What the hell." The man shouted and cursed.

Nadia stabbed at his eye. Got a handful of slimy hair instead.

The man tossed her to the ground. Nadia landed in a bed of ferns.

"You little brat," the woman said.

The lantern swung toward Nadia's head illuminating the woman's orange sneakers. The right sneaker reared back, its toe aimed at Nadia's head.

A strong wind shook the pine trees to either side of her. Nadia was reminded of the night she'd first arrived, when dusk came and the trees began to whisper and move as though they were human, capable of pulling her to their trunks with their branches and devouring her with hidden mouths. The next morning, she'd thought how silly she'd been when she'd thought a tree could come alive, but now she realized she hadn't been silly at all. Trees had faces. Maybe most people didn't know this because the trees revealed themselves only at night. Like the one she was staring at right now.

And then, the tree came alive. She could make out its face clearly. The eyelids batted once, twice, three times, right at her. The trunk sprang a limb and raised it to its lips. The tree was going to save her. It was telling her to be quiet. If only she could keep quiet, the tree would come to her rescue. That it would do so didn't come as a surprise, Nadia thought. She was always one with nature. She'd never chopped a live tree for kindling, she didn't leave garbage behind her, and she stepped on bugs only if they were near her lean-to. She loved nature and nature loved her. Of course it would save her. Of course it would.

The face of the tree moved. It grew a human body. She could see its outline within the tree itself. It was the body of a young man. It sprang from inside the trunk—a hollowed-out, dead tree trunk. The man's face was caked with mud the same color as the tree. The golden locks that had been tucked behind him were released. They fell to his shoulders and bounced off his back. He gripped a homemade bat carved from a thick tree branch. His ferocious blue eyes were glued to their target.

Wait, Nadia thought. She knew those eyes. They didn't belong to a tree.

They belonged to Marko.

He swung the bat into the man's knees. The man fell. Marko pummeled him in the head once, twice. The woman lunged at Marko with a knife. Marko darted away. Not quick enough. The blade stabbed him in the side. He let out a muted groan.

Nadia screamed her brother's name.

Marko and the woman squared off. Bat against knife. She backpedalled, pointing the blade at his chest. Put the lantern down to free her left hand.

Take two more steps, woman, Nadia thought.

One.

Two.

Nadia leapt from the bed of ferns and grabbed the lantern. Turned it down until there was only a spark left.

Everything went black.

A shuffle of feet. A yelp and a thud.

Five seconds later Marko told her to turn it back on.

"You all right?" he said.

"I'm good," Nadia said. In fact, she wasn't good. Her teeth wouldn't stop chattering and she felt light-headed, as though she might faint any second and never wake up. But she couldn't let Marko think she was a weakling so she pretended she was okay. "What about you? You got stabbed. You must be bleeding. Let me take a look."

"There's no time for that, Nancy Drew. We need to tie these two up. Get the hell out of here."

They bound her captors' wrists and feet with rope from Marko's backpack.

Afterward, Marko carried Nadia three miles to a ranger's station, where a man in a gray uniform drove them to a hospital in his pickup truck. Nadia thought of fun things during the entire ordeal. There were plenty of them, she realized. Life wasn't so bad. There was Fanta Red Cream Soda, her best friends Nancy Drew and Sherlock Holmes, and there was Marko. He was her brother and as long as she had him there would always be joy in her life.

When the nurse in the emergency room took Nadia's temperature it was 102. The doctor feared she was coming down with pneumonia so he admitted her for the night. Marko's wound needed twenty-one stitches but otherwise he was okay.

Two policemen came and listened to Nadia's story. They told her the man and the woman had concussions but were going to live, and spend most of their lives in jail. The man had escaped from the Coxsackie Correctional Facility four days earlier. It was a maximum-security prison in New York State. He and his girlfriend were making their way to a farm she'd inherited in Canaan, Connecticut. They both had a history of doing bad things to children.

Nadia stayed in the hospital for one night. Then she went home and recuperated without catching pneumonia.

Two months later at a PLAST summer camp, Nadia was awarded her merit badge. The pride in her father's eyes made the entire ordeal worthwhile. She'd pleased him. He was happy. There would be no yelling or screaming for at least a few days.

When Nadia held the cotton badge in her hand at the awards ceremony, she knew there was nothing in this world she could not do.

CHAPTER 35

THE LOCAL POLICE ARRIVED TO HELP THE TROOPERS RE-store order at the cemetery. Then more troopers arrived, and we were driven to the eastern district headquarters of the Connecticut State Police in Norwich. A detective from the Major Crimes Unit debriefed us individually. During my stay, I learned that Marko had gotten to know some troopers over the years through his business. I wasn't sure if that was his motorcycle or strip club business, and I didn't think it was appropriate to ask. Perhaps both. He'd called them after his two men let him know I had followed Donnie Angel and his crew to the cemetery.

I found the white Honda that I'd seen following me parked near the cemetery entrance. It turned out it belonged to one of Marko's men, the one with the handgun. Behind it was the black Subaru I'd seen the night I'd met Roxy at the Stop & Shop parking lot. That's how I knew the men who'd burst into the office with Marko to save me. I'd caught glimpses of their faces through their windshields.

The state police released us at 6:00 a.m. Marko and I walked to the parking lot. A team of cops and troopers had driven all the vehicles from the cemetery to Norwich. Marko used his long stride to try to forge ahead of me. I hustled to keep up with him.

"When did you start having me followed?" I said.

He gave me a sour glance as though trying to wish me away, but I refused to leave.

"Well?"

He shook his head. "As soon as you told me you'd run into Donnie Angel, and that you had some cockamamie theory that your godfather had been murdered. First, you don't run into scum like Donnie Angel unless you're dirty or he wants you to run into him. And you're not dirty. Second, I figured one was related to the other."

"What do you mean?"

"Donnie Angel and your theory that your godfather was murdered. It was too much of a coincidence. Them happening at the same time."

"Yeah," I said. "That it was. Why did you go to his house that day?"

"The bastard hadn't paid me."

"Did he pay you then?"

"Yeah. He was all apologetic and what not. He wanted to sit on the money for as long as he could. A lot of people are like that when it comes to business. Even though you don't earn anything on your money these days."

"So he was fine when you left him?"

"I left him watching reruns of *American Pickers* on TV." He let a moment of silence pass. "He died like the cops said he did, right?"

"Yup. Whatever else he was, Rus was his brother. He knew him better than anyone, and when he said it was an accident at the cemetery there was no lying in his face. He must have fallen down the stairs going for more wine, to check for flooding, or for whatever reason we'll never know. I guess I was looking for something to do. I guess I got myself all riled up for nothing."

"How about that."

"What about the blessing of the Easter baskets?"

He glared at me. "What about it?"

"The reason you couldn't make it. You said you were meeting someone at the airport. Someone who was coming from LA related to your business. But the bouncer told me that woman wasn't coming in until next week. Why did you lie?"

He looked incredulous. "I didn't. She's not appearing at the club until next Saturday, but she's touring the other clubs in the area during the week. Hartford, Vernon, Springfield, and the like. I'm coordinating her gigs, showing her some hospitality, if you know what I mean."

Not only had I deluded myself into believing a murder had been committed, I'd made simplistic assumptions, too. An effective forensic analyst did not necessarily make an effective investigator.

"Why did you go to the cemetery alone?" Marko said. "What were you thinking?"

"I thought you were meeting Donnie's crew there. I thought they were going to kill you." A sense of pride washed over me. I'd gone to the cemetery to protect him, and now Marko knew the truth.

Marko leaned toward me, face etched in fury. If he hadn't rescued me, I would have thought it was sheer hatred. And maybe it was. Maybe I was still deluding myself.

"Get this through your thick skull," he said, spittle flying from his lips. "You don't protect me. I protect you. You understand? It was that way, is that way, and always will be that way. Now once and for all, will you please fuck off?"

He climbed into his truck and left. I stood there, eating his exhaust.

Nothing had changed. My brother still cared.

Nothing had changed. He never wanted to see me again.

CHAPTER 36

I DROVE BACK TO ROCKY HILL AND ATE ANOTHER SHORT STACK of pancakes for breakfast. It was Easter Sunday, but my mother wasn't planning a family meal. She'd stopped doing that after the incident with Marko. Instead, she was having a traditional Easter breakfast with one of her boyfriends. She'd told me his sons were in town, and she was eager to charm them into not minding if their father added her to his will. That's why I asked the waitress to sprinkle some chocolate chips into the pancake batter. In the absence of familial bliss, we always have chocolate. I washed the pancakes down with a cup of tea and waited another half hour until it was 8:00 a.m. Then I called Mrs. Chimchak and told her I was coming over to give her an update. I analyzed her words, delivery, and comportment. She sounded perfectly normal to me.

Still, I dreaded my arrival even more than the first time. Would she be lucid when I got there? Had she been in control of her faculties when she'd encouraged my delusion that my godfather had been murdered? Did she know she was suffering from dementia? How, in the name of all that was decent, could I even broach the subject with her? If the topic of her dementia didn't come up, I had no idea how I would explain that we'd been wrong about my godfather. I'd fostered suspicions for my own emotional needs. Evidently she'd done the same.

The first time I'd shown up at her house, she'd been waiting for me as though I were her long-lost daughter. This time was only slightly different. Once again the door opened and her smiling face appeared before I climbed to the top of the stoop. But instead of calling me by my name, she spoke someone else's.

"Stefan," she said. "Is it really you, my love? Oh my God. It is you."

She let me into her home and then reached out with her arms to welcome my embrace. I hugged and held her for a long three count, and then tacked on another three count for good measure. Afterward, I pulled back but kept my hands on her small, narrow shoulders. They were hard as stone.

"It's not Stefan, Mrs. Chimchak," I said. "It's Nadia. It's your favorite *Plastunka*, Nadia Tesla."

She stared at me with a vacant expression, her eyes glazed over as though she were looking right through me onto a celluloid screen. I wondered if she actually saw her childhood love in my place, or if she was watching a movie in which they were the stars. And then, the glaze disappeared. Her focus sharpened instantly, as though someone had turned the projector off and the lights back on in her head.

"Nadia," she said, sharp as the razor blade that she'd earned as a nickname. "Come in, dear. Come in."

She led me into the sitting room where we'd talked before. I reminded myself to be gentle, and to avoid being the sledgehammer whose image I sometimes invoked. She told me she had hot water and offered me tea. I declined and told her I'd just finished breakfast. We sat down and faced each other. She eyed me curiously.

"There was a note of finality in your voice when you called this morning," she said. "You have some news for me? You've learned something important, yes?"

I told her everything that happened last night and this morning. She listened in her typically inscrutable fashion. She raised her eyelids and shifted in her seat when I recounted the most dangerous moments, in the vineyard and later in the gravedigger's office. I told her the state police were calling in the FBI, and that they suspected I'd broken up a multimillion-dollar arts and antiquities ring that may have spanned the entire Northeast, and included other middlemen besides my godfather. I told her everything except the bombshell Rus had dropped on me. The one that had shed light on my overly active imagination. That he had not killed his brother, nor had Marko. That I'd invented the story for my own purposes and that she'd encouraged me for her own reasons, whether because of her illness or in a desperate stab to be part of something meaningful as she watched herself deteriorate.

"And what did Rus say about your godfather's death?" Mrs. Chimchak said.

"He said he didn't kill him."

"Did you believe him?"

"Yes."

"Why?"

"It's hard to explain. His delivery, his tone of voice, the circumstances under which he said he didn't do it. All the ways in which we reveal ourselves when we're lying. I have some experience with people under pressure as a forensic financial analyst. He showed none of the signs a liar usually does. None."

"I see. Did Rus have any thoughts on who did kill him?"

"Yes."

"Who?"

"No one," I said. I softened my voice. She appeared so sharp and focused, I had no doubt she'd infer a reference to her illness if I wasn't careful. "He believes his brother died the way the police said he did. Accidentally."

"And you agree with him now? Did he change your mind?"

"Yes. He changed my mind."

"Why?"

"He made me realize I had my own agenda. That I had personal reasons for wanting to be in Hartford, and so I convinced myself my godfather was murdered. I believed what I wanted to believe."

"So you believe what Rus said. And yet he lied to you when you first met him in his house. He told you he didn't think his brother—your godfather—could have killed himself. You believed him then, and you believe him now. How can you be sure he hasn't fooled you this time? How can you be sure he isn't the murderer?"

I shrugged. "I can't be one hundred percent sure. But I trust my instincts. I said this was all about my godfather, but I lied. It was all about me. Rus was right about that. He knew me well enough from when he'd been my father-in-law to know I had an ulterior motive for my so-called investigation."

Mrs. Chimchak nodded for a moment, as though she were considering everything I'd said. "And what about me?" she said. "Why do you think I agreed with you? Why did I buy into your theory of murder so passionately and so thoroughly?"

Above all, she wanted me to be real and true. That much I knew from my first meeting with her in this same room. I could not disappoint her. I chose my words carefully.

"Perhaps it brought you joy to immerse yourself in something."

"Maybe. Or perhaps I'd lost control of my senses. Is that what you really think, Nadia?"

"No." The word escaped my lips so quickly it left no doubt that's exactly what I thought.

"You would be justified for thinking so," Mrs. Chimchak said. "You've heard, no doubt. By now someone's told you that I'm losing control of my mind."

I didn't know what to say. I wanted to comfort her, but I didn't know how. In a similar situation, a woman in my place might have stood up, walked over to her, and held her. Or at least touched her. If I had done something like that, however, it would have felt disrespectful. It would have felt like an insult. Mrs. Chimchak was, above all else, a warrior. She deserved to maintain her self-respect. Any display of sentimentality on my part might have diminished her pride.

"How is your health?" I said.

"I'm losing my memory, I find myself wandering around, at night and during the daytime. Yesterday I found myself barefoot in the park staring at the ducks, wondering how I'd gotten there. I was feeding them poker chips. And I'm forgetting how to do basic things. Yesterday I woke up and had no idea what I was supposed to do next."

"Have you seen a doctor?"

She waved her hand. "They'll put me in an institution. If there's one thing I'm certain, it's that I'm going to die in this house. Not in some asylum with a bunch of strangers. I will die here, with my memories." She cleared her throat. "Do me a favor, my love. Go over to my desk and bring me my tin of mints. It's in the top drawer. When a person doesn't feel well, a mint will always improve her spirits."

I walked over to her desk and opened the drawer. A box of Altoids rested atop a journal. It was black with a fleur-de-lis pattern around the edges. When I lifted the Altoids off the top of the notebook, a white square revealed itself. It was a place for the journal owner to print the title of his work, or, if it were a diary, his name. Two initials had been written in cursive in the white space: *PC*.

Mrs. Chimchak's first name was Roma. The "P" was the Ukrainian "R". This was probably her diary. It wasn't this observation that stopped me dead in my tracks. It was the way the "P" was written. The writer had made an extra loop after closing the semicircle around the "I" in the letter.

It was identical to the "P" I'd found in my godfather's calendar.

My mind reeled. I glanced at Mrs. Chimchak. She gave me nothing. I stared at the journal again. I raced through a series of deductions. They led to a preposterous conclusion, an utterly impossible one, which in my heart I knew was true. I planted my eyes on Mrs. Chimchak.

"DP," I said. "You wrote the letters in my godfather's calendar."

She confirmed my conclusion by remaining mute.

"You did so for my benefit. You knew I was coming over to search his home with Roxy, and you wanted me to see those letters. You wanted me to see them because you wanted me to investigate. And you wanted me to investigate because you wanted to be revealed. You wanted to be revealed as my godfather's killer."

A look of contentment spread on her face. "May I have my mints please?"

That was as good a confirmation as any. As I walked toward her, tin of Altoids in hand, I stared into her eyes and searched for a motive. Why had she killed him? Was it a function of her illness? Had she pushed him down the stairs accidentally? No, I thought. She wouldn't have looked so contented when I'd accused her of being the killer. Mrs. Chimchak had sent him flying down those stairs to his death on purpose. It may have been an act of passion, or a premeditated act. More like the latter, I thought. The woman I knew wasn't prone to acts of passion. But what could a ninety-year-old woman have cared so much about to have killed a lifelong friend?

I handed her the tin of mints, and then I saw it. The picture of her with her childhood love on the shelf beside her chair.

I sat back down and faced her. "Tell me about Stefan," I said.

She put the tin on her lap and folded her hands atop it. "He was dedicated to a free Ukraine at a time when that was only a dream. He was a leader of men at an impossibly young age. He was fierce and fearless. He was a commander in the Ukrainian Insurgent Army."

"Did you ever see him again once you returned to Europe for the second time? To a different DP camp?"

"No. I never saw him again."

"What happened to him?"

"He vanished. He was living in the camps under an assumed name. For his own protection. The NKVD's primary goal was to repatriate and kill all known leaders of Soviet resistance. They were constantly on the lookout for partisans. Once his true identity was revealed, the NKVD took him away. He was seen being hauled into a truck by four Russians. No one ever saw him again."

"Was Takarov among the men who took him?"

She shook her head. "I doubt it. He was an officer. He would have been the one who gave the order."

"And how did he know to give the order? Who revealed Stefan's true identity?"

Mrs. Chimchak's eyes turned to steel. "Please don't disappoint me. Not now. Not at this stage of my life. You know the answer already, don't you?"

"Yes," I said, my voice trembling a bit. I didn't want to hear myself saying it. "My godfather gave up Stefan to the NKVD. To Takarov."

Mrs. Chimchak looked away from me. Her hands kneaded the box of Altoids.

"Why did he do it? For money? Or was he himself blackmailed?" My mind raced to answer my own question. "If he had been blackmailed, I doubt you would have killed him. There would have been extenuating circumstances."

"The answer is he did it for money, but not the way you think."

"I don't understand."

"Your godfather didn't accept a bribe in exchange for revealing Stefan's identity. He accepted a paycheck."

Her words stunned me. I tried to think of an alternative conclusion but there was only one. "My godfather worked for the NKVD?"

"Your godfather *was* the NKVD. He was SMERSH. He was

the NKVD's ultimate weapon. An infiltrator. A Soviet agent assigned to assimilate in society. Was he Ukrainian? Of course he was. What, you thought there were no Ukrainians working against their own people? We didn't all know each other when we arrived at the DP camps. We were among strangers from day one. Your godfather, he became one of us. He *was* one of us."

"When did you find this out?"

"After the Crimean business started, I became suspicious. I pressed him on it over the course of several visits not knowing where it would lead. He became very talkative after a full bottle of wine. And I played him. Told him bygones were bygones, and that I just wanted to know the truth before I died. He knew my health was deteriorating, and bit by bit he told me everything."

"Did he stay in contact with Takarov all these years?"

"Lord no. Your godfather became an American. He found heaven in Connecticut. In his mind, he became a member of our community. He thought he was safe from his past. Until Takarov found him."

"And blackmailed him into being one of his distributors for stolen antiques. Which is why my godfather was so depressed initially. He was afraid he was going to be revealed as a former agent of the NKVD. Plus he was old and didn't want the aggravation. But then when the money started rolling in, he felt better about it. There was a reward for the risk he was taking."

"Yes, but the devil always takes back his gifts."

We sat quietly for a moment. I had to call the police. She knew it, and I knew it.

"Why didn't you turn yourself in?" I said. "I know how much you love this country. I know how much you appreciate America. I know you consider being a lawful citizen a moral obligation of the highest order."

"You are correct on all counts. But if I go to the police they will put me in prison where I will die in some infirmary. And that, as I told you, I can't allow to happen."

"But why did you leave a clue for me? How could you know I'd find it? Why . . . all this?"

"I knew you'd find it because you are the smartest girl I know. And if you hadn't found it, I would have created some other reason to lure you in."

I tried to understand her motive but my logical reasoning failed me. "Why?"

"A fractured family is the hardest break to mend. Sometimes . . . sometimes we need a little help from a stranger."

Visions of my meetings with my brother and mother flashed before me. Rus had said that I'd concocted a murder mystery to satisfy my subconscious need to return to my home. In fact, he was wrong on both counts. There had been a murder, and the killer had ensnared me in its solution for my own benefit.

"You and your brother must take care of one another," she said. "Some day soon, you will only have each other."

She opened the tin of mints and slipped one past her lips. I realized the typeface on the tin was printed in red, not blue. This struck me as odd because she'd always carried the blue tin. They contained mints. The red tin contained cinnamon drops. I also noticed that the tin was now empty. It had contained only one mint—

I suspected what she'd done and leapt to my feet. But by then it was too late.

Mrs. Chimchak died in my arms. I was later told she took something know as the "L-pill," a pea-shaped vial containing liquid potassium cyanide. After she bit down on it, her brain and heart ceased functioning in fifteen seconds.

She passed away in her home the way she told me she would. I held her in my arms the way I told myself I would not. She'd succeeded in her objective of luring me back to my family and community, just as she'd snuck into my camp during my childhood survival test to give me some aspirin.

In both cases, I never saw her coming, and she was gone before I knew it.

CHAPTER 37

Later that night I called Brasilia and asked to speak with my brother. A woman talked to him in his office and said he was unavailable. I told her to tell him a woman by the name of Chimchak had died in my arms that morning. Sixty seconds later he picked up the phone and agreed to meet me at the Thread City Diner in Willimantic.

We had Easter breakfast for dinner. It consisted of scrambled eggs and bacon. The traditional Ukrainian breads, meats, and condiments were missing. Marko bemoaned the absence of mashed beets laced with horseradish. It was his favorite growing up. He said he loved it with ham and *paska*, the Easter bread. The horseradish stung the nose and brought tears to one's eyes. In retrospect I suspected he might have loved it because it was the only time he ever permitted himself a good cry.

He listened intently as I recounted my conversation with Mrs. Chimchak in detail, and described how she'd ended her own life. How I called for an ambulance and told the police everything that had transpired. Mrs. Chimchak had avenged her lover's death by killing my godfather. By my reckoning, there was no justice due any living or deceased person. But I told the police what I knew because that's what she would have wanted. She was, above all else, a proud American. She would not have wanted American law circumvented on her behalf. Of that I was certain.

I kept my voice low lest someone overhear talk of L-pills, stolen art, or murder. When I was done, I told him her motive for writing DP in my godfather's calendar.

He sighed and shook his head. "At least she was right about one thing."

My heart soared. "That we have to take care of each other?"

"No. The devil always takes back his gifts."

After our food arrived, he asked if I was in any legal trouble for admitting to taking a gun from Donnie Angel's man in the vineyard and walking around with it.

"I'm not sure," I said. "I found a lawyer just in case. I don't have enough money for anyone high-powered. But I found a guy in New Jersey through a friend of mine who's willing to work cheap. He's licensed to practice in Connecticut, too. His name is Johnny Tanner."

Marko raised his eyebrows. "He's a lawyer and he calls himself Johnny? Not John?"

I shrugged. "He can call himself whatever he wants as long as he's competent and cheap. Speaking of competent and cheap, I talked to Paul Obon on the phone today. I told him I want to look into our father's past." I recounted my mother's surprising comment in the car that I shouldn't do so. "He said he knows some guy who knew him in Ukraine. Some guy named Max Milan. Obon is going to set up a meeting. Any interest—"

Marko raised his hand to stop me. "No. You do what you need to do but count me out. I have no interest. None whatsoever."

My eyes went to his mangled finger, as they always did. This time I didn't stop myself. I allowed my gaze to linger on the twisted knuckle and misshapen digit. I remembered my father's voice in the driveway the day he'd discovered Marko had used a typewriter to change an F into an A on his report card. My father opened the door to our Ford, pointed to the doorjamb and said:

"Put your fingers in there."

I didn't remember what happened next. In fact, I'm not even sure I was actually in the driveway. Marko or my mother may have told me the story years later about what happened to him. For whatever psychological reason, my brain had erased the memory. It had not, however, erased the image of a subsequent incident. My father had banished my brother for some other transgression and told him to walk laps around the neighborhood in the dark. When he rang the doorbell to return to the house, my father told me to open it and say:

"You're not welcome in this house."

Before I could shut the door in his face, per my father's instructions, Marko put on a brave exterior for my benefit.

"It's okay, Nancy Drew. It's not your fault. Don't you worry about it."

We sat in the diner and ate the rest of our breakfast quietly. When we were finished, we ordered fresh cups of coffee and savored a silence only people with an indestructible bond can enjoy. The truth was we didn't have many interests in common. There wasn't much to discuss. Fortunately, we didn't need to say a word to each other. We didn't need to speak.

Except I did.

In the diner, I had told myself I didn't want to ruin the moment. Nothing ruined the moment more than sentimentality, which we'd been raised to consider to be emotional self-indulgence. I told myself to wait until we were outside and ready to leave. That would have been a more appropriate time for me to say what I needed to say.

But after we paid the bill and walked to the parking lot, I began to fear I was lying to myself. Once again, I didn't know if I could form the words. Maybe I wasn't wired to speak them. Perhaps my brother wasn't built to hear them.

Marko had parked his Harley near the entrance to the diner. We stopped beside it. He held his helmet in his hands. Originally gold, it was shot with scrapes and scratches, like a gladiator's armor. Still functioning, though. Despite its obvious mileage, it was still battle-worthy.

As he fiddled with the padding inside, I felt opportunity slipping from my grasp. I pictured him prying jewels loose from my mother's box, heard the thud of my hand against his head, remembered him tumbling to the floor like a drunken, helpless child. And then I saw Mrs. Chimchak sitting in her chair, heard the words of advice coming from her lips, saw the vial snap between her teeth, and watched life leave her body.

"I'm sorry I hit you," I said.

Marko locked eyes on me. He didn't change his expression or say a word. Instead, he kept his eyes on mine for a moment, and then nodded.

I headed for my car, my body so light I could have raced the Porsche to the next stoplight. I managed six steps before I heard his voice behind me.

"Hey little sister, what's your name?"

I acknowledged his question with a quick turn and a smile. Three steps later he gave me the customary follow-up. He hadn't spoken it for decades, but it sounded as though I'd heard it yesterday.

"What does it mean?"

This time I simply extended my arm over my head and waved. I didn't turn around lest he see my face. Lest he spy the moisture in my eyes and I resembled a pathetic little girl, the kind of weakling I'd been before he'd made me strong, when I was a child and he was my hero.

As I fiddled with the door lock, he started his motorcycle, let it idle for a few seconds, and revved the engine to the red line twice, pausing for emphasis. Each roar felt like a kiss on the cheek.

I climbed in my car. Found some Kleenex in my purse and checked my face in the rearview mirror. Took a good look at myself.

Your name is Nadia.

My name is Nadia.

It means hope.

ACKNOWLEDGMENTS

An author presentation at the Ukrainian Museum in New York on April 26, 2013 resulted in my meeting Professor Roman Voronka and Dr. George Saj. It was during a fabulous reception that these extraordinary men sparked my interest in Ukrainian Displaced Persons camps. Special thanks to Professor Voronka for sharing authentic historical details that significantly enhanced the manuscript. Mark Wyman's excellent treatise, *DPs: Europe's Displaced Persons, 1945-1951*, served as reference, as did the essays included in *The Refugee Experience: Ukrainian Displaced Persons after World War II*, published by the Canadian Institute of Ukrainian Studies Press at the University of Alberta. Thanks also to Mrs. Zirka Rudyk, former Ukrainian schoolteacher and friend, for reading the final draft and sharing her expertise on all matters Ukrainian.

Finally, I am indebted to Alison Dasho at Thomas & Mercer for championing Nadia Tesla's cause.

ABOUT THE AUTHOR

Photo © 2011 Robin Stelmach

Born in America to Ukrainian immigrants, Orest Stelmach spoke no English when he started his education. He went on to earn degrees from Dartmouth College and the University of Chicago. He has held a variety of jobs, including dishwasher, shelf stocker, English teacher in Japan, and international investment portfolio manager. *The Altar Girl* is his fourth novel in the Nadia Tesla series, following *The Boy From Reactor 4*, *The Boy Who Stole From the Dead*, and *The Boy Who Glowed in the Dark*. He resides in Simsbury, Connecticut.